8-88

BYRD, MAX
   TARGET OF OPPORTUNITY.
c1988.

MAR 30
FEB 08

ILL JAN '97

DEMCO

TARGET OF OPPORTUNITY

TARGET OF OPPORTUNITY

Max Byrd

BANTAM BOOKS
TORONTO · NEW YORK · LONDON · SYDNEY · AUCKLAND

8-88 BA 1500

TARGET OF OPPORTUNITY

A Bantam Book / September 1988

Library of Congress Cataloging-in-Publication Data

Byrd, Max.
  Target of opportunity.

  I. Title
PS3552.Y675T37 1988   813' 54   88-6257
ISBN 0-553-05295-0

Published simultaneously in the United States and Canada

---

*Bantam Books are published by Bantam Books, a division of Bantam
Doubleday Dell Publishing Group, Inc. Its trademark, consisting of the
words "Bantam Books" and the portrayal of a rooster, is Registered in
U.S. Patent and Trademark Office and in other countries. Marca Regis-
trada. Bantam Books, 666 Fifth Avenue, New York, New York 10103.*

PRINTED IN THE UNITED STATES OF AMERICA

WAK   0 9 8 7 6 5 4 3 2 1

For my wife Brookes, *à cause de l'amour*

PRELUDE

January 1944
INVERNESS, SCOTLAND

"Hey, *Harvard*."

Spurling lowered his head quickly and concentrated on refastening his belt.

"Fairy Harvard," the voice on the other side of the basket hissed. "Spell chickenshit."

Spurling jerked at the belt and tried to keep his eyes away from the rectangular jumphole in the center of the floor. *Look away when the balloon goes up,* the British sergeant had barked. *Stare at the floor or the sky.* In the corner of Spurling's eye mottled brown and white fields swayed and sank, like an accusing face withdrawing. That morning in each of the first two balloons a man had already refused to jump and been brought down in disgrace.

He fumbled again, his fingers like sticks of dough. They said that at Fort Benning, five thousand miles away in Georgia, basic parachute training required six weeks, and recruits took their first jump only after two weeks of preparation, securely harnessed to an overhead cable that slanted a few hundred feet and ended in a pile of sand. But when Spurling's detachment had stumbled out of the buses at Inverness, web-eyed and yawning in the darkness, the British instructors had announced that everyone would take his first jump after breakfast, total training would last three days.

"Harvard cocksucker," Gianelli began again from his side of the basket.

"Save it for Jerry, boys," the British sergeant said mildly. He knelt beside Spurling, dangling one boot over the jumphole, took the buckles in both hands, and snapped the belt back another notch. "You want it loose," he told Spurling. "No need to cut off your legs when the chute pops open. Keep it one place past your usual."

In the next instant the balloon bumped to a halt, and through the jumphole the landscape wobbled briefly and then held, a bleak platter of light and dark seven hundred feet below. *Look away: hard Scottish rock, not soft Georgia sand.* Spurling peered over the sergeant's helmet to netting wrapped loosely like a skirt around a taut gray belly. Just beyond the suspension lines he could see the outline of another balloon two hundred yards away, tilting slowly in a gust of cold air.

"Remember to keep your legs bent when you hit, lads," the sergeant said. "Legs bent, forearms over face, head down, shoulders hunched. Roll!"

His breath made thin white commas of condensation as he talked. He moved from man to man, shaking the basket with the change of his weight, checking the parachute straps at shoulders and groin. "Stick your hands out to break the fall and your bloody arms will pop like twigs," he said, inches from Spurling's ear. "Legs, shoulders, roll—keep saying that as you hit."

Across the jumphole Gianelli smirked. Gianelli had grown up in the slums of east Cambridge, waging guerrilla warfare on Harvard all his life, and he had been the first to discover Spurling losing his breakfast that morning outside the latrine.

"It won't seem natural," the sergeant said. Round eyes and clipped black mustache swam in Spurling's vision. "You'll want to stay upright as you hit, not keep on falling. But your mind has to take charge of your body. Legs, shoulders, roll." He stuck his face very close to Spurling's for a moment and then moved to the right.

"Numbers everybody? They're starting to jump next door."

Spurling swallowed, a click loud enough to be heard over the wind, and felt a sensation of sand in his throat. There were five men in each balloon, a "stick" in airborne jargon, and one instructor.

"All right, then. One."

The man to Spurling's left slid forward. It was Brissac, as he could have predicted, always first somehow, by accident or calculation. Spurling swallowed sour bile again. Brissac was Spurling's French "marriage" partner—every American had been paired with a French or Belgian volunteer to make a clandestine team—"till death do you part," their British commander had nervously joked. Short, powerfully muscled, with the neck of a young bull, Brissac sat, hands on the rim, exuding confidence. He dangled his legs over the edge of the jumphole into empty space.

"Go!"

The Frenchman wriggled once, as if he were making himself comfortable in a chair, slipped down, and disappeared. The green canvas static line that ran to the ripcord sprang taut, then flapped loosely against the side of the rocking basket.

"Two."

The man on Spurling's right slid forward, dangled, dropped. Spurling watched the static line extend and recoil like a snapped towel. The basket pitched far to one side, rolling with the change of weight; in his mind he saw them all suddenly picked up like pebbles in a child's cup and spilled into the air.

"Three."

Spurling dug his fingers into the thick knobs of wicker and sat, swallowing again.

"Three!"

The British sergeant was staring at him across the jumphole. Under his boots a corner of white silk billowed, everywhere else dark ground. Spurling swallowed and shook his head.

"Four."

The sergeant moved around the hole and squatted beside his knee.

"Five."

Gianelli sat and faced him, kicking his legs easily, as if he were perched on the edge of a swimming pool. The sergeant glanced over the top of the basket and Gianelli mouthed, "Fuck Harvard."

"Go!"

He vanished with a grunt and another snap of the static line.

"You're the other Yank?" the sergeant said. Without the ballast of four men, the basket swung in the clear sky. The four green static lines blew at full length like party streamers. Spurling nodded, sick of the careening balloon, sick of himself.

The sergeant bent to peer down, then straightened.

"Come on, old lad." He laid a big fatherly hand on Spurling's shoulder.

Spurling flung it away.

For an instant he saw himself through the sergeant's surprise: wide blond face, fair enough to be a girl's. Bee-stung poofter's lips; dark-blue wind-softened eyes. A sensitive, beautiful boy's face, a crazy thing to find in a war.

Slowly, trembling, he extended his legs and stopped. At his feet the whole earth was falling away—brown fields, blue-tinged hills: a departing planet.

There was nothing to count on, nothing to hold you up. The more imagination you had, they told him, the braver you had to be.

The sergeant opened his mouth to speak, shut it. Spurling visibly forced himself forward another six inches. To the sergeant he lifted cold eyes, empty of everything but will.

And then he was falling through fields of light, hearing only the tom-tom of blood in his ears, the fiery ruffle of cloth as he fell free. At three hundred and forty feet, the parachute whispered open and bounced him upwards, twisting the harness into his armpits and thighs, and he floated soundlessly down, while the earth turned slowly back and forth under his feet.

Something amazing. A boy falling out of the sky.

PART 1
California and Boston, 1982
GILMAN

1 ──────

"There it is," Gilman said.

Donald Kerwin hit his brakes and downshifted gears at the same instant, making the tires squeal as the car turned off the highway. He bounced over a pothole, braked again, and pulled into a row of parking spaces.

"You want your book back, speedo?" Gilman asked. He held up a battered green and white paperback that had fallen from the dashboard onto the floor.

"I was thinking about something else," Kerwin said half apologetically, and switched off the engine. He glanced at the book. "That's actually my old maltreated Shakespeare. I found it last week in a closet. Believe it or not, I had a college English teacher who made us memorize a poem a month out of there. She said when we all got to law school it would be a momentary stay against materialism."

Gilman laughed and pushed the car door open on the side. His brother-in-law's precise, ironic diction always amused him. "Yeah, but did you remember to put Moosehead on your shopping list?"

"I distrust a cop who drinks only foreign beer," Kerwin said, opening his own door slowly. On the other side of the parking lot a red and green 7-Eleven sign blinked on and off. Kerwin stamped his feet in the chilly night air and blew into his palms.

"And the girls want the big fluffy sugar donuts," Gilman said over the roof of the car. "The kind recommended by dentists."

"I know what the hell kind of donuts they want," Kerwin snapped, and Gilman stiffened at the sudden impatience in his voice, the abrupt, uncharacteristic tension that had been jumping in and out of Kerwin's conversation all afternoon. Before he could speak, Kerwin jerked his head toward a pickup truck in one corner of the lot, no driver in sight, its engine running loudly. "You think there's a code of the mountains at Lake Tahoe?" he said in the same tone of irritation. "I've never seen anybody up here that turns off his engine when he goes into a store, ever."

Gilman started to answer, then shrugged and walked on ahead, noting automatically that there were no other cars in the lot and only a clerk wearing an apron and a paper cap in the store. On the other side of the highway huge pine trees rose black and tall against the gray sky and the few pale strings of clouds.

"They never heard of the oil embargo up here," Kerwin said, catching up. "Ancient history. Listen." He gripped Gilman's arm hard for a moment. "I want to tell you a story. I've been thinking about it—did you ever hear of the famous Colonel Verlaine?"

"No." Gilman squinted at him in the fluorescent light of the porch. What he saw was a tall, lanky man, almost as tall as Gilman himself, but twelve years older, grayer, beginning to show a stoop at his shoulders. In the fluorescent light his face looked pinched and drained of life.

"Colonel Verlaine was a French Resistance hero, in the war."

"They all were," Gilman said sardonically, pulling his arm free. "Every Frenchman was a hero in the war." He opened the door to the 7-Eleven. His father was a veteran of the OSS, his earliest memories were of hearing stories about the war, he hated the thought of the goddam war.

"There's a wonderful book about Verlaine by a man named Martin Spurling," Kerwin insisted. "I'll give it to you when we get back to the city."

"I don't want to hear war stories, Donny. The war's been over for forty years."

"It's only California where history's disappeared," Kerwin said. Gilman sighed and stood still. He liked his brother-in-law enormously, but not his lawyerlike habit of making stories into speeches. "Everywhere else in the world," Kerwin said, "everywhere else except California the past and the present intersect. Do you know what I mean? They crisscross back and forth. The past is alive. Listen, I do want to tell you this story. I want your advice—" He broke off to stare at the row of newspapers under the clerk's counter.

"They should declare resorts newspaper-free zones," Gilman said, but Kerwin ignored him and stooped to his knees to pick up a copy of the San Francisco *Chronicle*. In his excitement he held it up to show Gilman the big front-page photo. The Polish dissident Stefan Anders was Kerwin's hero.

"History repeats itself, my friend," Kerwin said. "Don't ever doubt it."

But Gilman had raised his head and looked away, partly because he had heard Donald Kerwin many times before on the subject of Stefan Anders, partly because a man in a ski mask had entered the store, aiming the barrel of a shotgun at the clerk.

In the instant that followed, Gilman realized too late that he had no gun with him, not in his sweater, not in his parka, realized too late that Donald Kerwin was rising to his feet, newspaper in hand, between the clerk and the gun, and the gun was rising as well, the clerk diving and shouting. When the shot came he saw it in slow motion—flame, smoke, blood, Kerwin spinning backward and toward him with a chest spewing blood. Together they tumbled onto the floor. Cartons of candy, gum, cigarettes flew slowly through the air, boxes of donuts, rolls.

As the room exploded into sound, Gilman could see Kerwin's lips moving. Over the roar of the gunshot he could still hear Kerwin's voice. Above him the ski mask turned, the wooden butt of the shotgun came swinging down. Blood was coming in bubbles from Kerwin's mouth, more words, louder—

Then Gilman heard nothing at all.

2

"If you turn the knob clockwise you'll get a rise in pitch," the doctor said. "If the battery starts to go you'll also get a rise in pitch, then a gradual weakening. Can you hear it now?"

Gilman closed his eyes and rested his head against the pad. He could always hear it. He had heard it for three continuous, unbroken weeks, since thirty seconds after the gunshot, an importunate whine that rang through the center of his head like an unstopped alarm. Sometimes the pitch changed suddenly on its own, as if the source of the sound were coming nearer, taking steps across the inside of his skull toward his ears and the open air. Sometimes the whole noise changed without warning to a buzz, like a hive of demented, microscopic insects loosed in the hollow spaces along his cheekbones and temples. Lately he had come to picture the sound as a white line on an electronic screen, pulsing faintly with malevolence. He could look away from the screen if he wanted, by an act of will, but after a few moments his consciousness always came back to it, swiveling like the needle of a compass.

"You may want to adjust it a little bit after you get used to it," the doctor said. "Fine tune it." He held up the battery pouch for Gilman to see and pointed to the thumb-sized dial on its top.

This one talks louder, Gilman thought, as if I were deaf too. For no reason at all he thought of his father years ago—if you don't know how to pronounce a word, son, say it *loud*! Then he spooned himself out of the bright orange plastic chair and stood up, squeezing his shoulders together in reaction to the closeness of the white walls, the stainless steel clutter of the examination room. His balance had not really been affected, he decided, not yet.

"Tinnitus can seem to go on even if the organic cause is mended," the doctor said in a preoccupied way. "It can also just disappear on its own, especially if it's associated with a psychosomatic stress like the death of your brother-in-law." He was reading the medical history folder as he talked, flipping the pages with the end of a gold Cross pen. Doctor Connelly—young, fresh faced, skin as smooth and taut as an egg. Gilman's regular doctor was an older man named Rodino, away at an ear, nose, and throat convention in Palm Springs, and the substitute, Doctor Connelly, had turned out to be unexpectedly sociable and chatty. "I like cops, by the way," he said, smiling, as he sat down. "I just did a year's residence in the Cook County emergency room. I saw every kind of cop in the world. I was practically a cop groupie." He flipped more pages as if he were thumbing through a calendar.

"So you were born in Boston," he said, tapping a box on the page. "I was born in Chicago." He ran the pen like a pointer down a line of numbers that Gilman couldn't read upside down. "I couldn't wait to get out of there, and I don't even think about going back. The weather, for one thing," he said. "Of course. But also, in California people are more comfortable with their bodies, you know? More natural, more Latin maybe. You think that doesn't matter to a doctor?" Gilman grunted and pulled at his ear.

The pen resumed its progress through the folder. "Started as a patrolman in 1973," the doctor read. "And made inspector in six years. That's very fast, isn't it?" When Gilman said nothing, he answered his own question. "Damn fast," he said.

Then he paused at the last page and squinted in concentration. That would be the page about the shooting, Gilman thought. The "etiology" of the tinnitus. Medical word of the day: the cause of an illness, reduced to Latinate sounds, light shattering, a bad shadow.

Gilman snapped the memory away, out of sight, like a blade folding into a knife. Then he picked up his suit jacket from the chair, dropped the battery pouch into his left pocket and tugged the two wires running from each ear until they hung loosely in front of his chest. For a cop he was known as a slovenly dresser, an easterner who wore baggy trousers and mismatched coats, or a shapeless gray sharkskin suit from the 1960s and no tie at all, while the other men on Bryant Street favored the retired-colonel look of plainclothes policemen everywhere: business suits, conservative ties, spit-and-polish from crewcut to brogues.

Doctor Connelly closed the folder and slid it onto the stainless steel tray. "People will just think you're listening to a Walkperson," he said, adjusting the wires into a neater V and straightening the jacket flap like a clothes salesman seeing a customer to the door. Gilman made a disgusted face into the mirror. Walkperson, for Christ's sake.

"The mind takes a while to adjust to things," Doctor Connelly said, "especially when people get older. So don't expect miracles."

Gilman was forty-two years old.

"You gave me kind of a start, you know, when you took off that jacket," Doctor Connelly said and patted Gilman's shoulder holster strap with the palm of his hand. "I didn't know you could still carry a gun like that when you were on medical leave."

"In case I arrest my disease," Gilman said, and while Connelly laughed he ran one hand across his forehead, brushing back hair. If he had been carrying the gun at Lake Tahoe, if he had had it ready to fire . . . . In fact, the last time he had actually fired his gun to arrest anybody, Gilman thought, had been in 1976, when he was thirty-six years old and still expected miracles, and he had emptied his gun at a fleeing rapist and one of the bullets had ricocheted off a brick wall and knocked the gun out of the rapist's hand. At the arraignment the rapist had still been furious, not because he had been caught but because the papers said he had been outgunned by police sharp-shooters. According to the diplomas on the wall, Doctor Connelly hadn't even finished college then.

"You'll have to call Janet later for your appointment," Connelly said as he opened the door into the hall and frowned at the receptionist's empty desk. "As usual." Janet was the briskly inefficient nurse who was supposed to administer Gilman's audio scan before a doctor saw him.

"Very unprofessional," Connelly said, clicking his fingers at his side.

Gilman nodded neutrally. He understood tedious jobs that you ducked out on when you could, or simply let die in the center of your life. The summer after he had left Boston he had worked as a bus-boy in the kitchen of a Los Angeles Holiday Inn. And after that he had been an apricot picker in the humpbacked fields around Los Al-tos and Portola Valley, a security guard for the Giants at Candlestick Park, a welfare counselor in Oakland, a bartender, a bouncer. Tinker, tailor, soldier. He noosed the wires to the center of his collar. Not soldier, he thought.

Connelly bent and made one last fussy adjustment and stood back. "Okay, let's give it a month at least. I don't know if it will do the trick, but if it broadcasts at approximately the same frequency as the noise you're hearing, the theory is that the ear muscles—that's not right, but call them muscles—will gradually relax and stop the ringing. If it had been a virus, the theory would probably work a little better, of course, but a gunshot so close to the ear drums . . . the trauma." He looked at Gilman's face again carefully, noticing the tension marks raked out at the corner of each eye. "Still pretty bad?" he asked. "Still pretty distracting?"

Gilman shrugged and looked down the hall.

"Well," Doctor Connelly said, smiling professionally, "be a hero."

3 ▬▬▬▬▬▬▬▬▬▬▬▬▬▬▬▬

Two hours later Gilman thought of the advice and returned the smile, grimly, to an empty room.

Four o'clock. He shook his wristwatch and checked it against the brass ship-captain's clock on the bookshelf, then stepped around the half-empty carton of "bargain" books at his feet that Cassie had lugged upstairs to his study last week and never finished setting out. At four o'clock Cassie would be unpacking new books for the store or wrapping sales at the cash register. He could see her turning the book this way and that, opening it at random and talking about it with the customer, her teeth that she always thought were too big showing in a smile, the reddish-brown pageboy haircut nodding. He touched the ice in his glass with the tip of his tongue and grimaced. Who was he trying to kid? At four o'clock today she would be holding her breath, picturing him standing there at the front window of the study, waiting for his sister-in-law, Nina Kerwin. Picturing Nina's face when Gilman began to tell her.

"They let him go, Nina."

Nina sat in the chair in his study without moving. Her face was just as it had been for almost the past month: brittle, drawn, an unhealthy starchy color scored with deep lines running from her eyes and nostrils to the corners of her mouth. Her face looks like a shattered windshield, Cassie had said one night. Gilman stood in front of her, watching for reaction, alert, professional, miserable, but she continued to sit tense and explosive—all of it, everything, an outrage too unthinkable to absorb.

And then she was up, as if her voice were being torn from her throat, and Gilman was following her from corner to corner across the little room, her voice ripping into his ears, whipcracks of sound.

"Who told you?"

He came closer, waving his hands—you try to make contact, you try to touch.

She backed away, shouting, into a corner between shelves, her fists pounding back against the wood, shaking books.

"An assistant DA, somebody official. I wrote the name down."

"Turned loose!" She spun away from his outstretched hand. "Two weeks, he serves two weeks for *murder!*"

She grabbed the drink he offered—had put ready by the hall phone twenty minutes ago—and sloshed it to her mouth, never taking her eyes from Gilman's face.

"How could they let him go?" she demanded. She swallowed half the drink in one gulp, then jerked the glass toward him, gesturing for more. "A punk like that, who did what he did?" Her voice was thickening, the choking sound rising again in her throat.

Gilman concentrated on his hands pouring scotch into the glass: touch, keep busy, let the pressure whistle out. From the corner of his eye he watched his sister-in-law pace madly to the other end of the room, grind her heel into the carpet, wheel. Under the blonde hair her face was pale and patchy with running mascara, crumpled in anger.

"How could they let him go?" She reappeared in front of him, screaming.

"I told you what the guy on the phone said, Nina. They had no choice. The judge signed the order, the kid walked. The case is gone."

"Gone," she said, trembling. "Over."

He nodded. Up close the skin under her eyes was stained the

color of coffee. What could he explain? You grow hardened to the courts, to the streets, to the lawyers and judges, the whole stinking system. Every day somewhere a cop who started out high-minded and idealistic is sitting down in a bar like a collapsing house, and the slimeball he arrested two hours ago is swaggering out a courthouse door with his thumbs in his belt and his shit-eating grin back in place. What could he explain? The day they required classes in law school on justice instead of accounting would be the day something changed. You grow hardened, even when the victim is your own brother-in-law and you were there when it happened.

"Can't you do something?" she hissed suddenly, "the famous cop?" and it was his turn to shake his head, letting the anger show, and walk away and glare at the walls. When the Placer County DA's office had called to say they were letting Victor Turelli go, he had done everything he could do, he had called the San Francisco DA's office, two prosecutors he knew, he had smashed his fist through the plasterboard wall of his little study. Dead-end justice. He and Cassie had stood toe-to-toe like boxers, arguing about who should tell Nina, who could, would tell her. I'll fall apart, Cassie had pleaded. Nina needs to hear it from a man, a cop who understands it. And you've done it before, you've walked up to complete strangers a hundred times and said: I have something very hard to tell you.

He reached toward one of the books Nina had pushed out of place and automatically straightened it. Boswell's *Life of Johnson*. He let his hand rest on the fat blue spine. Donald Kerwin's favorite book. He had brought a copy one Christmas for Gilman and insisted on reading passages aloud for him all afternoon: "Sir, patriotism is the last refuge of a scoundrel. Sir, no man is a hypocrite in his pleasures. Sir, all of life is but the keeping away of the thought of death." You needed the voice of a whale to do it right, Kerwin had said.

"I could kill him, Gilman," Nina's mad voice said, "the fucking son of a bitch." She had followed him to the bookshelves and stood at his elbow with her fingers gripping his arm like a circle of teeth.

He pried them away, shoved the book deeper into the shelf. It was impossible to recognize her this way, transformed. Nina Kerwin was sixteen years younger than Donald, four years younger than

Gilman, a woman of beautiful decorum, propriety. Once Donald had talked them all into skinny-dipping, like kids, at a cold, foggy nude beach near Santa Cruz, and Nina had hesitated and almost refused to take off her suit. So proper she shits ice cream, Cassie had told Gilman under her breath. Nina had attended private schools in the east and one of the Seven Sisters colleges, and she prided herself on her correctness of language, her elegance. In fifteen years he had never heard her say anything stronger than "damn."

"I could tear his goddam eyes out of his face," she cried behind him.

All of them were transformed, changed utterly. Nina was a fury now, a revelation. He was wired to his own ears, a freak with a Walkperson in his pocket that played the sound of his pain over and over. Cassie had lost her only brother. . . . And Donald Kerwin was a corpse.

"You were going to testify," she said, calmer for a moment, and he led her back to the one good chair in the room, the Boston rocker he had built three summers ago from a mail-order kit. Hands-on therapy. Cops who didn't drink their brains away were the biggest buyers of hobbies and crafts in the world.

He was going to testify, nothing could have stopped him. But what was he supposed to say? That Donald Kerwin was like a father to him? That he thought of him constantly, heard his voice morning and night? That when he drank he remembered the special mixture of two gins that Kerwin called his "bionic martini"? That when he stood up he remembered the habit Kerwin had developed of draping his arm around Gilman's shoulder and teasing him like a favorite pupil? Donald Kerwin would have been fifty-five the day after he was shot. And in fact he had lived three hours into his birthday, until a committee of doctors in Truckee had turned off the artificial lungs.

What was he supposed to testify?

No, he didn't see a face, not under the ski mask.

No, he didn't know if there were more than one of them.

No, he didn't understand why the guy hadn't shot at him too. Panic, maybe. A jammed gun. Another car swinging into the lot. No more than he knew why it was Donald Kerwin who had had his heart blown apart by a twelve gauge shotgun, and not the 7-Eleven clerk, not him.

Nina got up clumsily and walked to the desk where he had left the bottle of scotch, leaving the chair rocking gently behind her as if there were someone invisible in it.

"You could do something, Gilman," she said.

"What do you want, Nina?" He circled around behind the desk, putting distance between them, and steadied himself with his palms for a moment as the whistling noise changed direction suddenly and ricocheted off a tender place deep in his ears. "What do you want if I find him? There was a white line of pure sound moving across her face. "This isn't a Clint Eastwood movie. I can't walk into some coffee shop in Boston or Mattapan or wherever the DA thinks he went and tell him: Hey you, the punk over there on the third stool, you killed my brother-in-law and this is a .357 magnum. He got off." Nina swung her head around and walked four steps back toward the chair. "He got off, Nina," Gilman said to her back. "It's terrible. It's tragic. But he got off. The cops screwed up, the courts screwed up."

She stood looking at him, not speaking.

"I can't do anything, Nina." To escape her stare he glanced down and saw the morning's paper still on the desktop, folded to a story Cassie had marked as usual with her red pencil. His eyes stopped at phrases: "Pistol fired from the crowd. Polish Freedom Fighter Attacked."

"Not anything," he said.

She stood with the full glass held in both hands, and he saw the look rising black to the surface, heard the words before she said them: "You know people who could," she told him.

"Oh for godsake."

"You do."

He did.

"You know people on the street, the famous cop, it's your world. You tell me that, you tell Cassie. Your whole life is with low-life scum, killers, it's what you like. It's what you *love.*"

He made a gesture with his hand, a man waving away a smell.

"You could find somebody in Boston if you wanted to. It's your hometown. You could find him in an hour dialing the telephone. You know people there."

"I don't know anybody in Boston," Gilman said. The whistling in his ears was speeding like a rocket toward his right eardrum, as if it might hit it and explode.

"Christ," Nina said, and the tears came rolling down her face. "Christ, Christ."

"You don't mean this," Gilman said. "You can't be serious." Her hair was a blonde helmet, shaking. Far to the right he glimpsed the long whitewashed flanks of Russian Hill flashing out of the fog and into a cone of sunlight. "You've got to stop."

Nina stepped forward hard, wobbling on her heels, spilling a silver streak of scotch onto the black fabric of her dress. "Donny would have done it," she said. "He would have done it for you. He was loyal." She took a step sideways and her shoulder brushed one of the departmental citations that Cassie had framed and insisted on hanging in Gilman's study, five of them in a neat white row, next to the set of law books on criminal procedure. At Choisin Reservoir in Korea Donald Kerwin had been shot in both legs by a machine gun and had still dragged himself and his wounded foxhole mate to safety some two hundred yards away. Then he had come back and blown the machine gun nest to pieces with a grenade.

"I'll pay you a fee," Nina said, "whatever the going rate is. You're the expert. You're the goddam homicide cop. You don't have anything else in the world to do."

"Nina."

"You're a son of a bitch too," she said, and flung the glass at Gilman's face, batting the air with both hands as the ice and drink sprayed the desk. Gilman stood aside and she rushed toward him. She swept one arm across the little desktop and hurled the papers, the photographs, the clutter against the far wall. With the other arm she yanked the thick brown law books from the bookcase and kicked them over the floor, their white pages flapping in panic.

Then she spun and ran out, swallowing a cry that began far down in her throat as she slammed the door, cursing, gone.

*   *   *

Gilman stooped and retrieved a book at random, placing it on the window ledge beside the desk. It was the only window in the room, but it had a view of the water, a wide two fingers of blue-green bay running between the southern tower of the Golden Gate Bridge and the hulking shoulders of Mount Tamalpais, in Marin County. Stretching, he could just make out the milky cliffs of Alcatraz Island rocking in the water, and far past them the jigsaw puzzle of green and brown that was the Berkeley Hills. If Nina went straight to her car he would be able to watch her pass the building entrance. But as he stood waiting he could see only the empty street and the sidewalk on the other side and a Chinese woman in a quilted jacket, arms folded into her sleeves, walking carefully uphill, followed by a line of waddling children. Overhead the pigeon who lived in the traffic light peered down at the children and tilted his head curiously.

After a moment the woman turned and looked back, counting, as if someone were missing.

4 ▬▬▬▬▬▬▬▬▬▬▬▬

"Here," Cassie said, handing him a paper bag as she stood over his chair. "Early Christmas. For thirty-five cents I couldn't resist."

Gilman tilted the bag and let the book slide into his palm, a small faded red hardback, not much bigger than a pack of cigarettes, no dust jacket, the title embossed in shaky gold letters over an indecipherable logo: *Spinoza's Philosophy.*

"Benny was going to put it on the shelves," she said. "Only in California! He's starting a section called Used Metaphysics."

Gilman opened the book at random, read a sentence, closed it. He was not an intellectual, not even much of a reader anymore, but Cassie brought books home for him anyway whether he read them or not, as she had for her brother and soon would for her nieces.

"Is that thing working?" she asked, stopping for a moment in her cushion-straightening ritual to gesture tentatively at the two plastic buttons in his ears and the wires curling down the front of his shirt. "Does it actually get rid of the noise?"

"It actually makes more noise," Gilman said. "The doctor said it's supposed to mask the tinnitus with its own stuff." In fact, he could hear nothing at all from the buttons, and he had already checked the batteries twice to be sure they were in position. Mean-

while the whistling had gathered in one part of his head, a white line
of sound suddenly folded into a hot ball. He opened the book again
and flipped a page. In Boston a succession of dour, unsmiling prep
school teachers had done their best to give him a classical education,
as mapped out and paid for by his dour, unsmiling father. He had
gone without apparent difficulty or interest through three years of
Latin before rebelling loudly and refusing to sign on for more. You
have a great future behind you, his father had said sardonically. It
was only years later that Gilman recognized the remark as a joke.

"You know Spinoza originally wrote it in Latin," he said, "so
everybody could read it."

She stuck out her tongue. "Macho cop reads only dead lan-
guages," she said and pushed through the cut-off swinging doors into
the kitchen.

When she reappeared she was carrying a plastic tray of drinks
and her smile was clenched in place to keep the annoyance out of her
voice. "You didn't remember to put the casserole in," she said. "It's
going to take an hour at least to cook now."

Gilman shrugged and muttered an apology and watched her
bend to place his glass on the small table to the right of the chair.
Without stopping she kissed him on the lips, a wet, exaggerated kiss,
more cheerful than sexy. Hands-on therapy. He reached up automatically and she moved away with a matador's flourish, irritation disguised as flirtation. Full breasted, long faced, still trim at forty: her
body, Gilman realized with surprise, was noticeably younger now
than her face. Children bring lines to a woman's skin, people had
told them, worry lines, Eve's curse. But not to have children dries
out a woman too, others said, and then frustration digs lines just as
deep.

Gilman swallowed half the glass of scotch at once. Six years
into their marriage, after rearranging the apartment a dozen times in
a month, Cassie had gone to a toy store and bought an enormous
wooden Victorian dollhouse, which she had painted inside and out
and started to furnish with miniature rugs, wallpaper, commodes,
tiny hand-painted dolls. "Everything except a diaper service,"
Gilman had said, the joke turning to a look of horror on both their

faces. A week later she had given the dollhouse to Children's Hospital and taken a job at a bookstore on Powell Street.

"Benny told me he's refined his theory," she said from the couch, where she was shuffling through the mail. "Now he says people are either 'coastal' or 'landed,' like right-handed or left-brained, and it all depends on their earliest memories. Midwesterners are happy. Coastal people have unresolved conflicts with their parents."

"There are no resolved conflicts with parents," Gilman said. "Benny should stop selling *People* magazine in that store. He's inflamed with pop psychology, like the rest of the country. It's mental acne."

"So, do you like your Spinoza?" she asked. "Or did you already read him in your class?"

Gilman swallowed the rest of his scotch and tried to remember. Two years ago the newest police commissioner had ordered all officers below the rank of captain to enroll in humanities courses at San Francisco State extension—to bring new sensitivity and perspective to the men and women who guard the streets, he'd told the whirring cameras—and Gilman had found himself herded every Tuesday evening for six months into a night school class on the history of philosophy, From Plato to Kant, taught by a squeaky-voiced graduate student who had no idea what to say to a room full of grumbling middle-aged cops. "Start with ethics," a missing persons sergeant named Strickland had called from the back of the room. "We're supposed to learn something new." And later: "Do I understand this right? This Descartes sits down and decides he's gotta doubt the what'd-you-call-it, the material world exists, things like his arms and legs? He's got no proof? Hey, there's junkies on Eddy Street should be in the great philosophers." And he had started to sing "I Ain't Got No Body" until Gilman had to twist around in his seat and shut him up. "Everybody is in some sense a missing person," the graduate student had said desperately, trying to trim philosophy to police work. Gilman still kept his notes and books in the little study upstairs.

He came back from the kitchen with the scotch bottle and poured them both new drinks. Then he stood beside the couch holding the bottle by the neck.

"It was edited by Professor John Wild of Harvard," Cassie said, turning pages of the Spinoza. "Wild is a wonderful name for a philosophy professor—Wild of Harvard. I couldn't resist it."

"I talked to her this afternoon," Gilman finally said. They had avoided the subject for half an hour, long enough, he thought. He cleared his throat. "While you were at work, the way we said." She replaced the book on the butler's tray table that had also come from a kit and picked up her glass between her palms, running her tongue along the fresh ice cubes. Women could do that, he thought, eat ice, eat raw lemons. It would shatter his teeth to pieces.

"She was damn near hysterical," he said, "crying, throwing things. She threw all my law books down on the floor, everything off my desk."

Cassie took a drink and kept her eyes fixed downward.

"I still think you would have done it better," Gilman said. When she didn't respond, he turned and walked back to his chair. "She said crazy, hysterical things. She said she wanted me to hire somebody to kill the kid—can you believe it? Go over to the Tenderloin or to Boston where he's supposed to be now and find somebody, hire a killer? She said she'd pay me, him, she'd do anything. Hysterical," he added after a moment.

Cassie traced one finger along the rim of the glass. Donald Kerwin had been the only person in the world who called her Cassandra. A teasing big brother, successful and cosmopolitan, never quite serious with her. She hated the name herself and had legally changed it to Cassie the day she graduated from high school, after trying on dozens of other names for a whole year, just as she might have tried on a box of hats.

"I miss him," she said finally. "My big brother. Every day I miss him. While you were doing that, you know how I spent my afternoon?" Gilman shook his head. She said, " 'I always have to shit when I go into a bookstore.' That's what this guy said when he came up and asked for the key to the men's room. Some high school teacher from Berkeley. Crazy. He brings the key back and stands at the counter and tells me he's twenty-six years old and teaches American history and he has to go to the john everytime he goes in a bookstore or the library. And all the time I'm thinking about Donny. I keep thinking how it must have been in that miserable little store, staring at a gun barrel, knowing and not really being able to imagine that this was the end of your life, at fifty-five, with a beautiful wife and three goofy, sweet daughters down the road in a rented vacation condominium, waiting for you to come home and barbeque dinner. And you're going to die on the floor of a 7-Eleven in the middle of beer cans and donut boxes if the clerk makes a wrong move or the guy in the ski mask gets any more nervous. You know what happens when you get shot in the chest like that?"

Gilman knew. He didn't answer.

"Your muscles in your abdomen and your intestines all relax at once," she said, "like a sack splitting open, and your bowels spill everything down your legs in one stinking mess. You shit, is what you do. When they hanged women in the nineteenth century they used to put special rubber underpants on them so they wouldn't lose their whole guts at the moment of shock." She picked up her glass and drank loudly. "And this neurotic jerk stands there twisting his fingers and telling me how he has to run to the potty whenever he sees stacks of books."

She stood abruptly and started for the kitchen. Nobody had gotten drunk in either family, he thought. Since Donald Kerwin died they had been drinking almost without a pause, all of them, till they were sweating alcohol and their pores were like pinpricks and their mouths were fuzzy with booze, and none of them was drunk yet.

"I almost wish you'd do it," Cassie said. She walked from the coffee table to his chair and poured soda water into each drink. "I fell in love with your sense of justice, you know that? Big strong clumsy guy who stuttered a little in public and took a fierce stand, took a *fierce* stand against what was wrong."

Gilman closed his eyes. They had met at an antiwar rally in Oakland in 1968, the year the French students went crazy in Paris and Nixon got elected, the year he had made a speech outside the Oakland Navy Yard. He pinched the bridge of his nose with thumb and finger. How the hell had he ended up being a cop?

"This isn't just a local thing," Cassie said vehemently. "Some local tragedy. This is what the whole world is becoming—violence to solve anything, terrorism, murder. Americans are such political sheep, so blind. Look at the Middle East, look at Poland—the whole world's coming apart!''

Eyes still closed, he nodded. There were liberals, his father said cuttingly, and goddam liberals. Cassie had remained a protester—a marcher, a joiner—long after police work had worn out Gilman's own anger. Just as her brother had been, she was obsessed with the cause of Stefan Anders in Poland, the radical freedom fighter whose every appearance set off bombs, guns, riots. Two months ago she had marched to the Soviet consulate in Pacific Heights, protesting. In the squad room his fellow cops used to joke about locking her up and giving Gilman a break.

Maybe it was from not having kids, he thought, so now she loves the whole world. Maybe it was because the two of them were such different people now. Maybe it was just in the genes. "But if you saw for one day what I see every day of my life, out on the street": every cop in the world thought that. No cop in the world thought people would ever change. No cop in the world had heroes like Stefan Anders. What had he expected her to be? Like Nina before the murder? Nina the elegantly dressed suburban housewife, decorative and undemanding.

"This is rotten," Cassie said through her tears.

When the telephone rang, Gilman was suspended, floating in blackness. Water or sky, he could never tell. As he turned effortlessly from one side to the other, an old man's face appeared beside him in the darkness, and together they spun slowly, sinking. The old man's arm was curved tight around his neck. Gilman's nose pressed against thin white hair, flakes of scalp. Hot tears sprang from his eyes and flowed into his mouth, and as always the old man fell away, two hands touching and sliding apart.

At the second ring, before he could raise his head from the pillow, Cassie had rolled over and reached for the phone, frowning sleepily. As he lay waking, his sounds came hurriedly back, a hiss like static in his ears or the friction of air rushing through metal pipes.

She murmured into the speaker something he missed. Then she

said "Daisy," the name of her niece, Donald Kerwin's oldest daughter, and Gilman sat up straight.

"Did you call her friend Joanne?" she asked. "Don't cry."

She flung her legs from under the comforter and perched on the edge of the bed. Outside, through the thin fabric of the curtains Gilman could see the lights on the next hill, shaking gently in the blackness like candles in a huge tree.

"No, she wouldn't joke," she said and paused to listen to a high-pitched voice scratch inside the receiver. "I know she has," she said after a moment, "a lot of strain." She looked over the phone to Gilman, her eyes wide, and his heart went out to his wife.

"It's me, Daisy," he said as she handed him the receiver. "You take it easy now, OK? Just tell me what happened."

Her voice was hurried, feathery, trying hard to be good. She was the girl who most resembled her father, with her rangy build and fair hair and natural athletic ability, a tennis player and swimmer like him. One reason they had moved to California, Donald Kerwin had said, was to give Daisy a chance to grow up playing sports all year long, in a place where women's sports were appreciated. When Daisy had been born twelve years ago Cassie and Gilman had flown east to visit Nina in the hospital and had found Don Kerwin holding the baby in a chair beside her bed. He never got up, never let go of the baby for an instant, the picture of a father. I never saw a man who loved a baby so much, Nina's mother had marveled.

"No, don't call the sheriff," he told Daisy. "You girls just wait. Cassie and I are coming right over. This time of night it'll take twenty minutes at the most."

By the time he hung up Cassie was already dressed, waiting beside the door. "Gone," she said. "Nothing but a note on the mirror that said to call you."

By the time they reached Marin the three girls, terrified to be alone in the big house, had huddled in blankets on the front steps, under the porchlight, weeping. And two hours later, after a hissed and furtive conference with Cassie out of sight of the girls, Gilman had poured scalding coffee into a thermos, clumped out to his car, and pulled a map from the glove compartment. At six-fifteen, empty thermos rolling on the car seat beside him, he was driving eastward across the Sacramento Valley, on a half-deserted Interstate 80, heading toward the Sierra Nevada.

Call your uncle, Nina's note said, *tell him I'll do it myself.* The phone book in her bedroom had been open to yellow page ads for airlines.

At Donner Pass he began to descend the other side of the summit, through great empty halls of blue air, down toward the lakeside town of Tahoe City, where Donald Kerwin had been murdered.

5

"I prosecuted a San Francisco cop once," the Placer County DA said.

Gilman drummed his fingers on his knees and forced himself to sit still as the DA slowly, insolently inspected the black leather flip-case with the badge and photo-identification and then tossed it across the desk.

"This was a Chicano named Cruz," the DA said. He tilted the swivel chair back until he could cross his ankles on the corner of his desk and admire his new ski boots. "He was my first prosecution when I was assistant DA in Oakland. You probably heard of him— missing persons cop that turned out to be pimping teenyboppers on the side?"

Gilman grunted. He had sent in his name thirty-five minutes earlier, as soon as he had come off the road in Tahoe City, and cooled his heels in a chair outside the open door of the office while the DA called his broker in Reno, then his daughter in Meeks Bay. Nina would stay away a day or two, crying herself into exhaustion in a blank motel room somewhere, and then come back, contrite, to the girls, the big house in Marin, widowhood. That was what Cassie thought. Gilman thought Cassie was dreaming.

"I got Cruz room and board for five-to-eight in Soledad," the DA said. "He's probably pimping inmates now."

"I try to limit myself to swiping apples and running guns to Syria," Gilman said.

"Yeah." The DA dropped his feet from the desk and swiveled his chair in the same motion. "I'm not so diplomatic, huh? I got maybe a little hostility for Bay Area people." He picked up a folded newspaper from the top of his out-basket and held it at arm's length for a moment. Yet another photograph of Cassie's hero. Stefan Anders and his supporters were storming a Polish government building in protest: Free the People, Free the Workers. Gilman had had time to read the whole story twice while he waited in the DA's anteroom: Cassie was right about that, the world was about to blow up.

"I think San Francisco is a goddam freak hole, a swamp," the DA said, still apparently reading. "The Gay Area, right? Everybody's favorite sewer. I lasted five years and then I had to get out and come up here to breathe." He let the newspaper fall and pointed the index fingers of both hands at Gilman's ears. "Is that some kind of hearing aid?" Gilman nodded. "You look like you're wired," the DA said. "Every dope runner in Tahoe is going to spit in your face."

"I'm on medical disability leave," Gilman said. "I told your secretary. I drove up here on private business."

"I got private business too," the DA said. "In about half an hour I got private business over at Squaw. That was the first good snow of the season yesterday, and I want to be out on it before the Yuppies come up in their Nancy Drew roadsters and turn the place into a goddam parking lot. So tell me, who do you want dead, Gilman?"

Gilman pinched the bridge of his nose with two fingers as if he were about to drop off the edge of a diving board, a characteristic, unconscious gesture since high school days: Here I go. The macho epidemic was still spreading, he thought, quiche busters. Attila the Hun as DA. One more hard-talking, cop-baiting hack with a diploma on the wall.

The plastic sign on the desk said Whitney A. Ferril, Jr., but the man behind it looked more like a Jim-Bob than a Whitney, a square-faced good old boy in his late thirties, with a chest the size of an oil drum and a crown of styled black hair going gray in fluffy patches. He wore a checked lumberjack's shirt and a sleeveless down vest and he smelled of dog, and from time to time his eyes strayed to the corner of the office where four skis had been propped against a blue and gold California flag.

"Fuck it," Gilman said and stood up and walked out the door.

On the sidewalk outside he shouldered between two men in fur caps and followed the steep incline of the street, stopping when he reached a tourist overlook spot and gripping the metal rail hard with both hands. Beneath him stretched the whole northern tip of the huge lake, placid and blue-green in the sunshine. Around the shore tall pines and cedars, wearing toupees of snow, bowed and swayed as the wind moved across them.

There were DAs like Ferril in the city too, he thought, only they tended to strap themselves into three-piece herringbone suits, hang their Stanford diplomas around their necks, and sight down their noses at the poor cop in the chair twirling his hat in his hand. Fuck them all. He pivoted and began to walk again, slipping angrily on the thin snow and feeling the cold moisture seep into his shoes. There had been no snow three weeks ago, only the bitter late autumn chill that Donald Kerwin had liked because it reminded him of the east. The best time at Tahoe, he had said when he'd rented the condominium: too soon for skiers, too late for tourists.

At the top of the hill, underneath an enormous jeffrey pine that grew out of the center of the pavement, Gilman stopped and looked back. There was plenty of money in the bank for Nina: Donald Kerwin had been a first-class lawyer, still so much in demand that for a while he had flown once a week back to Washington, consulting at his old stand. Nina would be fine, the girls would be fine. He walked another few steps on the slick pavement. Who was he trying to kid? He had been a cop long enough to know the three strongest human instincts: survival, sex, revenge. If she had gone to Boston she would find someone to help. With her looks, her figure. With the right kind of luck in the wrong kind of bar.

He crossed the street to take a closer look at the gigantic pine tree, which seemed to have been shot out of the sky and into the ground like an arrow.

If you really wanted to find a missing person, Gilman thought, you went about it by empathy. He had served six months on missing persons when he had started out, rotating through all the departments like every other cop; he knew the drill. You get in their skins, you drop your own. He had heard about a novelist who never planned his plots, but simply dressed up and pretended to be each major character in his book for a week. Walked around his house in costumes, back and forth through the streets.

Downhill, Ferril emerged from his office and squeezed past the fire truck, moving toward a parked car.

I can go back to the city, Gilman thought, and forget it. He pinched his nose again and swallowed. At an altitude of six thousand feet his eardrums were bubbling and popping like blisters. Back to his one wife, three nieces, four walls. The shotgun had been six feet from his chest when it went off, the coroner's report had said in dry, official prose. Gilman only knew that Kerwin had been close enough to see down the barrel, wide like a tunnel, bright gray on the outside where the fluorescent lights glinted on metal, dark at the base where all light stopped. Donald Kerwin would have seen the ski mask turn, the gloves on the shotgun go up to the trigger.

Ferril slammed down the trunk on his car and rattled the handle. Then he walked back into his office, blowing into cupped hands. When Gilman reached the car the DA had reemerged and was strapping skis onto the rooftop carrier.

"Donald Kerwin," Gilman said.

"Oh Christ," Ferril said and tugged a ski with both hands to straighten it on the car roof. "What are you, moonlighting, Gilman? Freelancing on the side? I rode down to Truckee behind the ambulance on that one. My wife got somebody to sit with the guy's kids for a couple of hours so that the wife could be in the hospital with him, before they pulled the plug. That case is as dead as he is, Gilman. You're not up here on official business, blow."

Gilman cleared his throat and rubbed his eyes. Anxiety definitely increased the level of tinnitus, Dr. Connelly had said. Probably some inhibitor neurons were damaged in the inner ear, killed at the nerve endings, so that stress pumps more blood through than you need and increases the pressure and the ringing. Hard to think, isn't it? he had said, smiling, that some part of you is dead and the rest of you is alive.

Ferril walked around to the other side of the car and slid the second pair of skis into their rack. "If the family wants to sue this office, Gilman," he said over the roof of the car, "*or* the Tahoe City PD *or* the Truckee hospital, they're going to do it without one ant turd of cooperation from up here. Let them sue the goddam 7-Eleven for selling coffee twenty-four hours a day. Let them sue Rose Bird and the Supremes for ruling on the law with their nine heads up their asses. You want to see my files, buddy, subpoena them."

"Shut up, Ferril. I was there when it happened," Gilman said. "I'm the guy who was with him and got slugged, the brother-in-law. I was taken to the same goddam hospital."

Ferril slowly let go of the skis.

"His wife disappeared last night," Gilman said, thinking: Here I go. "She came to see me yesterday and I told her about the kid being released and she took it very hard." He paused and selected his words. "She wanted me to trace him. She said she wanted to find him and talk to him. Just scream at him, get it out of her system. She was hysterical. I told her no, to forget it, and she left. She went back to her house in Marin and packed two suitcases full of winter clothes and left. Her oldest daughter called us at two in the morning, and I started up here about five."

"Brother-in-law." Ferril crossed his arms on the roof of the car and stared over them at Gilman. "You tell a story your own sweet way, don't you?" He rubbed his chin in the elbow of his checked shirt and stared uphill at the big pine in the center of the street, its lowest branches held out like white arms to bless a Quik-Stop gas station and a Rexall. "All right, get in."

"My car is parked at the coffee shop," Gilman said, folding into the passenger seat and holding the wires of his tinnitus masker away from the police radio mounted on the dash.

Ferril leaned across him and punched the radio on. "You can take the shuttle back from Squaw," he said. "I promised my daughter I'd have the skis to her there at one o'clock." He made a U-turn and drove slowly through the center of Tahoe City: a giant Lucky supermarket, its parking lot filled with pickup trucks and four-wheel-drive jeeps; a three-story motel painted a rancid green to blend in with the pines; in an intersection, a rusted statue of two great brown trout tangled together and arching into the air.

"Your wife works in a bookstore, right, Gilman?" Ferril drove with his left fingers curled easily over the top of the steering wheel, his right hand adjusting the police radio for volume. "I met her when they were all at the hospital. Tall woman, about forty-five?" It irritated Gilman that he had guessed her to be older than she was, older than he himself was, but he nodded and looked out the window as the Lucky market gave way to an Exxon station and then forest.

"My wife works at a greeting card shop in Stateline," Ferril said. "That's as near as we get to bookstores in the mountains."

"So what's the possibility the kid went back to Boston?" Gilman asked.

"Who knows where the fuck he went?" Ferril said. They were riding along a curving road overlooking the Truckee River on the left, a fat, wide river with wisps of steam rising from its surface like ghosts. It could be New England, Gilman thought, except for the scale of things, the huge trees. It could be Lake Sunapee, in the hard-boned New Hampshire countryside where his father had once taken him to practice snowshoeing and ice-fishing. The river narrowed and the forest crowded in, revealing that the snow lay in uneven white daubs through the underbrush, as if an enormous painter had splattered his brush at random. But far more beautiful than New England, Gilman thought. He had no desire at all to go home to Boston.

"You ski?" Ferril asked, watching Gilman's face.

"I think snow is unnatural," Gilman said, and Ferril snorted.

"I didn't handle it personally," Ferril said after a moment. "I had one of my people stay on the cops' asses for a while, but what can you do, you know?"

"The exclusionary evidence rule," Gilman said.

"The exclusionary evidence rule." Ferril turned up the radio for a moment to hear a dispatcher calling for a patrol car in Carnelian Bay, then turned it down again. "Two new patrolmen, less than three years' service each. They get to the 7-Eleven and it's mobbed, ambulances and black and whites stacked way out into the road, sirens, horns. We get two, maybe three honest-to-God murders a year up here, Gilman. The rest is skiers that try to straight-arm a tree and drunken hunters trying to shoot each other's caps off. You're unconscious. The high school girl that drove up two minutes later and found the bodies is no good, screaming her head off. All she can remember is seeing a tall, skinny guy wearing a ski mask going off in a pickup truck. So the patrolmen haul ass to the Tahoe Pines motel without calling in—we passed it back there, the three-story job painted puke green. See, there's a tall, skinny guy in town, kind of a weird kid, that they rousted out of a bar two days ago. No charges, just some barroom noise, but later the computer shows him on probation from Massachusetts."

"He's clear to travel?"

"He can go to the fucking North Pole as long as he sees his PO once a month. Is he busted for armed robbery? Is he busted for assault? No, the little prick's busted for possession with intent to sell in Dedham or Waltham, whatever." Ferril turned his face, flat like a shovel in the glare from the river. "You got any idea what goes on in these mountains in the summer, Gilman? I got horse stables that run drugs through the woods like the goddam pony express. I got casino workers that deal blackjack and coke; I got tourists with backpacks full of smack; I got every kind of half-educated ponytailed hippie gets tired of seeing nothing but bookstores in Berkeley comes up here to light up a joint in the great outdoors. You can throw a paperclip out my office window and hit somebody that's got a record on drugs."

"No probable cause," Gilman said.

"No probable fucking cause," Ferril said. "Mapp versus Ohio. 1961." He bounced his fist off the steering wheel horn and lurched around a station wagon. Children swam against its windows like fish in an aquarium. "It still makes me mad. They think, skinny long-haired guy with a ski mask; he's got a record—bring him in. So they go breaking down the motel door with their popguns out, doing John Wayne; they bounce the kid off the wall a few times, toss the room, and bingo! they find a ski mask in the closet. You're a cop, Gilman. You got some years under your belt." Gilman rubbed his ears and watched Ferril pass another car on a double yellow line. "What's the kid's lawyer going to do, just as automatic as zipping his fly?"

"No warrant, no probable cause," Gilman said, playing Ferril's game. "Move to suppress evidence and release without charges." He had heard the story before, from the assistant DA who first called him, but lawyers have to talk, he thought, the way junkies have to score. He twisted in the seat and braced one hand against the dashboard as Ferril began to turn left off the highway. A few yards beyond the crossroads, on a metal tripod in the snow, burned a natural-gas torch; underneath it a battered white sign said Squaw Valley—Winter Olympics 1956. Gilman tried to remember what he had been doing in 1956, how old he had been.

"You discipline the two cops, you let the kid go, and you hope to hell nobody sues," Ferril said.

"Did he do it?"

"Hell yes, he did it." Ferril slowed at a curve that was fronted on one side by brand new condominiums built with wood and plaster walls and imitation thatch roofs, in the style of Elizabethan cottages.

"Hell yes, he did it. We sent the ski mask through the lab and got powder burns and microscopic blood spatterings that match Kerwin's type. We don't know what he did with the shotgun, but if the cops had waited half an hour for a warrant—half an hour!" he pounded the rim of the steering wheel with his fist, "the kid would be in San Quentin right now, for life."

They had entered a narrow two-lane road. On three sides sugary mountains tilted over them, closing the sky. To the left of the road lay a snow-dusted meadow almost half a mile wide, stitched occasionally by cross-rail wooden fences. At the base of the farthest mountain, Gilman could see buildings and a red ski lift housing, its bright silver veins vanishing overhead into the backdrop of snow. Along the nearest slopes hundreds of tiny skiers were weaving back and forth, sliding down and climbing up again, like children on an enormous rumpled blanket.

"I'm parking over by the lift," Ferril said and aimed his two fingers like pistols over the wheel in the same gesture he had used to point to Gilman's ears. "That's my daughter's car by the gate, the blue Camaro." As he pointed the car door swung open and a teenage girl in green ski clothes waved both arms in a signal.

Gilman opened his own door and watched the girl run over the slushy pavement toward them. A good DA would still be looking for the shotgun. A good DA would be obsessed with finding a way to convict the kid.

"This is my daughter Lynn," Ferril said. "Inspector Gilman."

Gilman saw fringes of blonde hair curling from under a knit watch cap, a grid of shiny metal braces on her teeth.

"Inspector Gilman just came up from San Francisco."

Gilman stood up, resting one arm along the top of the open car door, and said, "I have a niece named Lynn," amazing himself with the lie. Once years ago chatting in the Chicago airport he had shown a stranger photographs of his three nieces and called them his daughters.

"Neat," Lynn said, aiming a smile past him as she turned away and grabbed a pair of skis from the rooftop rack. Ferril unstrapped his own skis from the rack and stood them on end beside his shoulder, like a fisherman posing with his catch.

"You can get the shuttle bus tickets up there," he said, watching Lynn hurry ahead to the lift. "They go every fifteen minutes— double-decker London buses that the ski people brought in for a gimmick. Or you can rent some skis and stuff at the lodge if you want to."

Gilman shifted his weight uncomfortably in the snow. Around him moved people in shiny pants and bright puffy jackets, waving mittens, their faces flushed with sun, their caps like gum drops of color. In his thin city raincoat and baggy clothes he felt out of place, offensive.

"I already know the kid's name," Gilman said. "Victor Turelli."

"A Boston wop."

Gilman let his face stay impassive. "From Boston. To start looking for him I need to know his parents' name and address, his parole officer in Boston if you've got it. I want to see his booking picture, the transcript of the arrest, his lawyer's name, whatever else you have in the files. This is standard procedure, Ferril, you know that. Except this time to find one missing person I've got to find another one first."

Ferril rubbed his mouth with the back of one hand and glanced at his daughter, now twenty yards away and joining a line for lift tickets.

"I want to get up the slopes, Gilman," he said.

"And I want to find my sister-in-law."

"You're telling me straight? She's not shacked up with some Studley in Carmel? She's really gone off to Boston to yell and scream at the kid?"

Gilman walked around the front of the car and stood blocking the path to the ski lift. Ferril shifted the skis to his left hand.

"She was out of control when she came to see me," Gilman said. His ears were howling in pain. He forced himself to speak deliberately. The helpless, incompetent woman would suit Ferril better than the vigilante. "She never saw the kid when Donald was in the hospital," he said. "None of us did, none of us could stand to. When the kid got loose it was too much strain. Maybe she wants somebody to blame so she can stop blaming herself. I don't know. Ask a psychiatrist."

"Kerwin was a Washington attorney, I heard. A pretty well-known guy back there?"

Gilman said nothing. Ferril had the kind of face that reveals every calculation. He was too self-interested a politician not to have already looked up Donald Kerwin's record: Rhodes scholar from a small liberal arts college in rural Virginia, *Harvard Law Review,* Distinguished Service Cross from Korea, special counsel to the Department of Defense. He wouldn't have known that Kerwin had pulled suddenly out and come to Marin County because, he said, he was tired of the faceless bureaucracy, tired of the humidity, and wanted the girls to live in the west and get to know his sister before they grew up. And their uncle the plainclothes cop, Kerwin liked to add affectionately, fingering the lapel of one of Gilman's shapeless jackets. When both of them had briefly taken up squash six months ago, Donald Kerwin in his three-piece lawyer's suit had gone to a Tenderloin pawn shop and bought the biggest, gaudiest loving cup he could find, christened it the "Heistman Trophy," and instituted an annual tournament between just the two of them, the loser to cook a banquet for the winner. After the funeral Gilman had put the trophy in the farthest corner of his study closet, unable to look at it without wincing.

Ferril drew a line in the snow with one ski, separating his white ski boots from Gilman's wet black shoes.

"The kid had a hell of an expensive attorney," Ferril said, his eyes on the line. "Big firm in San Francisco. That bugged me, a punk like that. I don't know where he got the money."

"Let me see your files," Gilman said, and Ferril looked up and slowly nodded.

"She was *not* hysterical." Cassie swung the knife through a short arc and slapped it into the pyramid of mushrooms piled on the kitchen worktable. For two days, ever since he had come back from Tahoe City, her speech had been explosive with anger, rapped out from behind clenched teeth. "I listened to the whole thing on the extension, don't forget. She had on her helpless-little-me voice, trying her best to charm the big strong man-ums out of the tree." Her right hand swept the chopped mushrooms off the cutting board with the knife, and she dropped a handful of them rattling into the pot.

"I don't want you to go to Boston," she said. "He was my brother and I can't stand the idea that he's dead, but I can't stand it either that she goes running off like Mata Hari."

Gilman pressed the tab into his beer can and studied the foam.

"She'll be all right," Cassie said. "She'll be fine. She's got plenty of money, I can take care of the girls. I can do fine with the girls. Let her storm around Boston for a week and get it out of her system and then come home when she's ready." She spread more mushrooms and started to chop again, shaking the wooden board with each stroke. "You don't have to do this, you know."

"Family is family," Gilman said.

"You don't even want to go. You've got your doctors, your ear appointments—you're not well. And you hate Boston."

"She's going to walk into some bar looking for this creep," Gilman said. "And she's going to walk right into trouble. With her looks—"

"I know how you feel about her looks," Cassie said.

"Cassie, do you want me to set the table?" the girl asked, opening the kitchen door halfway. She looked obliquely at her uncle on the stool in the corner and tilted her head toward her aunt.

Cassie wrung the air with her left hand and smiled. "Okay, honey. You and Daisy can do it. But watch your program first. We won't eat for another half hour."

Then, as the bass grumble of the television suddenly grew louder, her smile vanished. Over the hiss in his ears Gilman could hear the voice of the President denouncing the latest attempted assassination of Stefan Anders. Glancing significantly at him, Cassie went to the door and held it fully open, listening. In her strained attention Gilman felt a silent reproach of his own stolidity, his middle-aged accommodation to the world. He crumpled a paper napkin and closed his eyes. He wasn't indifferent; he wasn't oblivious. But you can't change people. You don't change the world. In Washington, the President compared Anders to heroes of the American Revolution. In Warsaw, before a thunderous crowd and a ring of tanks, the announcer said, Lech Walesa had called Anders a hero.

"I can't live through another assassination," Cassie said. "Kennedy, Sadat, Martin Luther King."

Somebody switched channels and global politics gave way to the contrived exuberance of a game show.

"Stefan Anders is a great man," Cassie said defiantly, as if he had disagreed. She swung the door shut. "A peacemaker. You want to talk about loyalty, look at his kind of patriotism: 'one life for millions,'" she quoted. "Look at the way he took up the workers' cause when the rotten party hoodlums murdered his son. No wonder they all want to kill him. The way of the goddam modern world. Every generation slaughters its heroes, doesn't it?"

She brushed past Gilman and pulled one of the white curtains aside to peer into the yard. What outrage could she see there? After a moment she took a deep breath and stepped around the worktable, stirring together cheese and beans and holding one hand on the open cookbook.

Gilman let his own breath out and watched her work. In a minute or two the girls laughed on the other side of the door. If he had married somebody like Nina instead, he thought, this was an instant fantasy of how it would be: polite children in front of the television, placid wife in front of the microwave hearth. No reproaches, no marches, no sermons on the international plague of violence. The only books in the house would be Julia Child. He sipped beer from the can and pinched his nose. Family was family. You were loyal to family. There was enough of New England still in him to believe that you made your decisions and took the consequences.

"If you're going to go," she asked finally, "have you seen everybody you're supposed to?" He watched her hands work the food, the gold ring going in and out of the crumbled cheese, and felt his mind slowly turning, lifting, an old stump pried loose. He had seen the two arresting officers in Tahoe City, now back on duty and instant constitutional experts, loudly contemptuous of the courts. He had copied everyone's notes and records, and he had studied the two booking photographs, profile and front, until he could have drawn Victor Turelli with his eyes shut.

He had even gone to the San Francisco department and spent most of a day talking with the missing persons sergeant, Strickland, reviewing the standard techniques. And Strickland had had plenty of spare time to teach him. Because paradoxically, although next to high-tech espionage, missing persons was the great new investigative wave of the eighties, police departments everywhere had dropped out of the business almost completely, leaving it to private detectives and tracers. It was not a crime simply to disappear, not unless you vanished in order to avoid payment of debts or prosecution for a felony. And while there would always be genuine rabbits for the police to chase—the bail jumpers, the embezzlers, the murderous drifters—who was supposed to chase the millions of runaway kids and runaway parents? And who chased the wives who got liberation and the husbands who didn't? And the fathers who kidnapped their own children? And the children with the new-time religion who joined congregations that lived in barracks and carried handguns under their sarongs? The whole country is AWOL from the middle class, Strickland said. Everybody's trying to find themselves by getting lost.

Cassie put down the two big spoons she was holding and walked around the table to him. Her eyes shone with tears, like a young girl's. She stood in front of him and linked her hands around the back of his neck, damp, thin-fingered hands. She had generous features, he thought, easily set in motion, laughing or crying. He felt the pressure of the ring against his head, and she waited until he had set the beer can aside and laid his face like a heavy carved stone against her breasts.

"I'm sorry," she said. He nodded and lowered his hands, sliding them down her hips, sculpting. She tugged gently at one of the wires from the tinnitus masker, as if she were straightening a ribbon. "Did you call your father?"

Gilman shook his head. He talked to his father in Boston twice a year on the telephone. Stiffly, formally. Across the Grand Canyon of the generation gap. His straight-spined autocratic Harvard-educated father couldn't decide whether he was more humiliated by having a policeman or a Californian for a son.

"You have to call him when you're there," Cassie said. "He'll be furious you're staying in a hotel instead of with him." Gilman stared past her hip toward the calendar she had bought mail-order from the Museum of Modern Art, a pointillist landscape by somebody whose name he couldn't read or remember. The message of art, he thought, is that thousands of tiny brushstrokes in a painting suddenly become a figure with shape and color, a composition, just as a thousand small decisions make a pattern, a life.

6 ▬▬▬▬▬▬▬▬▬▬▬▬

What Ferril hadn't liked about the kid's file was the lawyer.

Gilman liked it even less.

He looked out the black window at the world falling away from the airplane wing. Steven Keppleman, he thought. Senior partner in a top-ranking San Francisco society firm: Carlisle, Broadus, Murdock, Number One Embarcadero Center, a better address than the mint. He had hair the color of cigarette ash, an Italian silk suit that had cost twelve hundred dollars from Wilkes Bashford, and a set of Claremont and Stanford degrees smoothed on his office walls. A huge Shiraz rug led to a plate glass window that stretched the whole width of the office, as if it were a magic carpet lifting the desk, the bookcases and Keppleman himself high above the city. He had stood up politely when Gilman had come in, tugging the points of his vest, and smilingly refused to answer anything. Confidentiality, he'd said, smiling. He had spread his arms and held his soft palms up in a torch singer's pantomime gesture for sincerity. Nothing I can do to help, Inspector, bound as we both are by the ethical code of confidentiality between attorney and client. They should spray for lawyers, Gilman thought, the way they do for mosquitoes.

The plane banked slightly, and Gilman hooded his eyes with his hand. If he squinted he could detect dark shapes moving slowly across other dark shapes below the wing, different stages of blackness evolving. Clouds changing into mountains, mountains dissolving into smoke. He sketched a cartoon on the cocktail napkin of a magic carpet with wings and a tail and two jet engines. A psychology professor from Berkeley had lectured to the extension class one night and announced that the mind is a symbol-making device which cannot accept randomness. It turns every stimulus it receives, no matter how casual, into part of a meaningful message or picture. In fact, people can't generate a simple list of random numbers—they begin to repeat and make patterns—only computers can. We fit every change that we perceive into a pattern, even death. Had Donald Kerwin seen a meaning in the split second when the shotgun barrel had swung up and the cartridge had exploded toward him?

Gilman raised the olive in his plastic cup with the tip of his tongue. When they're not hog-tied with confidentiality, silk-suited lawyers like Keppleman charge two hundred dollars an hour. So how did a derelict kid like Victor Turelli pay his fees? How did a kid like that ever hear of Keppleman in the first place?

The shapes beyond the wing collapsed into the same shade of darkness. He felt giddy with drink and tension, and no matter how hard he tried to distract himself, his mind kept swinging back to Boston. Home was the place you left behind, slamming the door. Going home was climbing back down the mouth of the cannon. He had booked a room in a hotel because he couldn't face the idea anymore of staying in the same house, the same room, with his father.

He won't ask you about having children, Cassie had said, trying to change Gilman's mind. That's a closed subject now. Closed and wrapped with barbed wire, Gilman thought. But he won't have to ask; his tone of voice does all the asking. Once, when they were still consulting the fertility specialists, his father had called late at night and urged adoption. Cassie had shaken her head stubbornly, furious at interference. But you *need* to have children to carry on, his father had insisted; it's a *biological* need. Cassie had hung up.

Gilman chewed bits of ice and tasted the vodka. You come to terms with needs, he thought. You accept what you get used to. Cassie had found a quote somewhere, the king of Holland during the

German occupation: "It is not necessary to hope in order to undertake, or to succeed in order to persevere." He hated not having children. Not having children was a physical pain, like the pain in his ears. You got used to it. His father wanted a mirror, not a son.

Thinking of Boston, drinking more vodka, Gilman abruptly saw brown brick walls, Beacon Hill and Back Bay, gritty with age, the scruffy waterfront along Essex Street turning its face sullenly away from the Atlantic. He saw his father's jaw, weighted like an anvil with disapproval. And everywhere, from Park Street to Brookline, he saw the claustrophobic, mean-spirited, stiff-shouldered streets coiled into knots. When the first settlers reached California they must have roared downhill laughing in excitement, down the slopes of the Sierra Nevada, tumbling into the new life like babies out of a closet. The last time Gilman had seen Boston the gray rain was whipping the back of the old city in a frenzy until the gutters overflowed.

He turned away from the window and watched the stewardess walk up the aisle, her fingers lightly brushing the top of each seatback. Two rows ahead of him she bent to adjust a cushion, and her skirt flattened her buttocks into half moons.

I fall in love with girls on the bus, doctor. There's a divinity that shapes their ends.

He swallowed the olive and wedged the cup in the seatback ahead of him. The other thing he didn't like about the file was the kid's vocabulary. "Moribund." Where did an unorganized asshole punk learn "moribund"? He opened his briefcase and flipped through the interrogation transcript until he found it again.

> OFFICER. You don't feel sorry at all, do you, Victor? You don't have any regret that a man is dead.
>
> TURELLI. Hey, man, this whole society is moribund. You know? Dead on its feet. I'm supposed to gas myself because some dude is dead I never saw in my fuckin' life?

He lowered the transcript into his lap and pinched the bridge of his nose. Moribund. A solidly obscure old word that Gilman had learned thirty years ago when sour-breathed Mr. Quentin Rumble had given his weekly vocabulary quiz in second-year Latin: in a dying state; dying. Two facts distorting the pattern. Petty thieves don't hire society lawyers; petty thieves don't sprinkle their obscenities with classical English.

When they landed for a stopover in Chicago, Gilman woke up and watched sleepily as smaller planes nearby pushed their snouts through a light snow, circling the terminal, sharks nosing across shallow water. When they took off again he closed his eyes and dreamed that the sound in his ears was a fife, welcoming him home.

7 ———————

"I wish I was in San Francisco," the stewardess said, hurrying past him toward the terminal.

So do I, Gilman thought. He felt like dropping his bag and running the other way, back into the plane, but he tensed his shoulders and lowered his head and followed her along the tarmac runway.

He owed the trip to Donald Kerwin, he told himself, raising his collar against the cold and rain; he owed it to Nina. The wind gusted and spun the briefcase around in his hand. And Nina was a day and a half ahead of him, a day and a half into trouble, no matter what Cassie thought.

Cassie. He fought the briefcase back to his side—he hadn't been on a trip without Cassie in five years. She had driven him to the airport in clenched-teeth silence, sullen again at the whole idea, relenting and kissing him good-bye only when they reached the curbside check-in and the porter was swinging the bag out of the trunk and into his cart.

Boston, goddammit—cold drizzle rolled down his hair and his cheeks; wind pushed oily water over his shoes and into his socks. The stewardess was holding the door open for him with one arm, calling over her shoulder to somebody inside, near the counter. She had a Massachusetts accent, Gilman noticed, wrenching his mind away from Cassie. Did he still have one himself? Or had he scraped it off, the way you would scrape mud from a heel, and substituted the mucous civilities of a West Coast voice. The single phoniest sound I ever heard, his father had said contemptuously after his one trip to California. Everybody in California talks like radio announcers with adenoids. They want to sound "sincere." He had cleared his throat as if to spit. Sincerity is not a virtue, his father said.

The taxi driver was a smiling Puerto Rican boy who apparently spoke no English. Gilman wrote down the name of the hotel on his pad of paper and sank back into the seat cushion, squinting in pain as his ears filled with sound again, in protest against the cold and the cruel change of altitude.

When they plunged into the eerie, white-tiled Sumner Tunnel, on the way from the airport to the city, he held up his watch to the fluorescent lights: six-ten a.m. The red-eye special. The old man would have been up for half an hour at least, glowering over his coffee cup at the sodden, impertinent leaves on the lawn outside, the skeletal trees and bushes, the whole city shaking itself slowly awake and turning toward the pale New England sun.

"Why are you always so goddam depressed and negative?" Gilman had shouted during one of their last arguments. "Don't you get pleasure out of anything, dammit?"

"It's my nature," his father had said at the other end of the telephone, his voice sounding taken aback, almost prissy.

The cab stopped at Beacon Street and waited for a long traffic light, then for a trailer truck that had made the turn too wide and had to back up and start again. "It's my nature," Gilman thought. A new phrase. They mutate like viruses. Nobody knows where they come from. "Chief Executive Officer." "At this point in time." "Let me share a story with you." For six weeks half the country had walked around saying "It's my nature," and then some jargon antibody had set in and the thing had gone away like a summer cold. The trailer truck backed up for another try and the driver signaled the cab to go ahead first. The Puerto Rican boy crossed to Commonwealth Avenue and Gilman saw a red, white, and blue metal pedestrian sign for the Freedom Trail. Overhead, rising into the low clouds as the cab accelerated, he saw the shoulder of the John Hancock building, the Prudential Center, the rich brown spires of Trinity Church in Copley Square. "You sound like me talking to you," Cassie had said, "telling your father to cheer up."

"If I lived in Boston I'd be depressed too," he had said, storming away.

They were building condominiums in Copley Square. Not Alpine cottages like those in Squaw Valley, but big highrises with shiny steel skin stretched tight enough to reflect the arches and angles of Richardson's great church. It would drive the old man crazy, of course, like everything new they did to Boston. Gilman rubbed his eyes and watched as the cab crossed Dartmouth Street and cut in front of a bus to the curbside of the Lenox Hotel. The meter said eight-forty. Gilman gave him eleven dollars, overtipping as usual, and walked impatiently around to haul the suitcase out of the front seat himself.

"You come to Boston for pleasure?" the boy asked in shy, syrupy Hispanic English, standing awkwardly by, ready to take the bag if Gilman changed his mind and put it down again.

"I come to Boston for goddam anger," he said, suddenly releasing the bag and flinging it like a hammer halfway up the steps to the lobby.

How the hell could she just walk out and leave her children?

"You could go over there and show 'em your buzzer," Vico said.

Gilman nodded. Vico was the first homicide cop he had found in Boston that morning who had time enough on his hands to talk.

"It's a San Francisco badge," Gilman told him and rubbed his eyes. Jet lagged, head throbbing, he had drunk coffee at the Lenox, rented a car when the Hertz office opened at eight, and driven restlessly around the city for an hour, getting his bearings again, seeing Nina on every corner. When he'd finally clambered up to the second floor of the homicide bureau, Vico had been sitting there, a pair of worn rubber heels on the desk, a slender, good-natured doggy face with cautious black eyes, curious to see what would come through the door next, surprised to find it was only a visiting cop.

"A San Francisco badge might work with two, three managers.

This one"—Vico flattened one thumb across the Park Plaza ad in the Yellow Pages—"this one is going to tell you to come back with a Boston cop. This one"—the thumb slid to the Ritz, leaving a smear of ink—"this one is going to tell you that all guest records are confidential, you're going to have better luck breaking into Jimmy Carter's grits. Some of these others I don't know. That's why private cops charge by the day, Gilman. Check every one of these out, could take you a week. By then, this sister-in-law could have moved to another place, you got to start all over again."

Gilman pushed the swivel chair backwards and looked up at Vico's face: brown, buttery skin, rows of pointed teeth like a catfish. Vico nudged a stack of telephone directories over the desk blotter.

"You got Cambridge, Framingham, Waltham, Newton, West Newton, the North Shore," he said. "You got Milton, Dedham, Braintree, Plymouth all the way to the Cape. This is a big place. She could be in any of those, in a Holiday Inn, a Best Western. Is she a good-looking chick, Gilman?"

Gilman grunted and pushed the books aside, next to the road map of Boston he had bought in the Hertz office.

"This is a big place," Vico said, letting his coffee cup drift up toward his mouth, studying Gilman's red eyes, his white face.

It's not a big place at all, Gilman thought sardonically. Boston is just a small town surrounded by large suburbs. But Vico was right. There were half a dozen hotels in the city that wouldn't reveal a guest's name to a strange cop. And there were hundreds of motels within half a day's drive of Boston where she could be staying.

"How about you spare somebody to help me check?" Gilman said. "Maybe a patrolman and a car?"

"Oh, come on, Gilman. You're a visiting cop. I'll let you sit at the desk all day and dial the phone. I'll give you coffee and phone books. If you're really hurting I'll let you ride somewhere in a black and white. That's it."

Gilman wrapped one hand around the cup in front of the telephone, a strange green ceramic cup that transferred its color to the coffee and made him think he was drinking antifreeze.

"I got crime to fight, Gilman. Look at this." Vico lowered one skinny buttock onto the corner of the desk and extended a Polaroid photo. Gilman took it reluctantly and held it over the coffee cup, blinking to focus. In the hallway outside the shabby cubicle somebody shouted for Rosalia to get her ass to the phone before Hoskins left for Walpole. The photo was of a black-haired girl with Oriental features, lying on her back. The pupils of her eyes reflected the explosion of the flash bulb. She was wearing black pedal pushers and a ripped white blouse and had a dozen red streaks on her throat and breasts, slash marks that looked like places where somebody with bloody lips had kissed her in great passion.

"Vietnamese," Vico said.

Nina, Gilman thought. He saw Nina's small white breasts under the streaks of blood. He wanted to smash his fist through Vico's pointy teeth and ram the photo back down his scrawny throat. Instead, he slowly placed it on the desk, neutrally. Homicide cops everywhere love to show pictures to each other. A long time ago, when he had started in police work, he had wondered why. It dehumanizes death, the philosophy instructor at the extension course had told him when he raised the question after class one night; it distances death so people can deal with it. Vico looked at the photo one more time before he slipped it back into his jacket pocket. At thirty-five or thirty-six he was young to be a detective in the PD, but he had the right kind of Boston manners, rude and clever, and the snapping smile. Gilman thought pictures like that had to be erotic in some perverted way. He glanced at his watch. He had been glancing at his watch obsessively since the wheels had touched down in Boston.

"Pushed her out a third-floor window," Vico was saying. "And she landed in the bushes, and maybe broke her neck, maybe not, so they stabbed her to be sure. Drug deal probably. They're not as crazy as the Puerto Ricans," he said, making the coffee bubble under his breath and the cup tilt dangerously over Gilman's map. "And they're smarter than the niggers. Give 'em four, five more years they'll be organized; they'll be very good."

"Better than the goddam wop Italians," a man said from the door. "Vico, you gonna get your buns on the street today or you gonna talk fucking race relations?"

Vico grinned and got off the desk. Gilman folded the map without looking up. He liked most things about cops except the bigotry built into the street life and the macho banter. Cassie hated it and told them so.

"I'm Vern Kessler," the man said, coming into the cubicle and handing Vico a metal clipboard stuffed with green-inked forms. "You the guy from California?"

"From San Francisco. Gilman, homicide."

"Gilman's looking for his sister-in-law," Vico said and dropped the clipboard on the desk. "She skipped out last week and came east to find some punk kid that killed her old man in an AR and the DA let him go. Gilman don't know what she's gonna do, bash his head in with her purse, hire a hit man in the Ritz bar."

Kessler pumped Gilman's hand once and stood with his feet apart, back stiff, taking in Gilman's size, his unkempt clothes, the expression of anger spiked into his face.

"You're big enough to hunt," Kessler said. "You know a guy named Marty Samuelson in Oakland homicide?"

Gilman nodded and ran one hand through his hair, then looked at his watch: time, time, time. Cops sniff each other like dogs. Kessler had the pale, weary face of a man who had been indoors too long, under bad lights, drinking weak coffee and picking at his face. Unlike Vico he wore his gold badge on the pocket of his white shirt, and he let his left hand drop and massage the butt of the service revolver on his belt while he talked.

"Sure, I know him," Gilman said. Nina was somewhere outside, uptown, downtown, walking back and forth in front of trouble while he played who-do-you-know? "He's a smart cop. We go to ball games together in Oakland sometimes, to see the Red Sox. He transferred from homicide to internal affairs last year."

"I met him at a convention," Kessler said. "He was dumb as a box of rocks."

Gilman lowered his hand slowly from his hair and twisted his mouth. Boston. If you can't say anything good about somebody, welcome to Boston. It was ten o'clock in the morning; he was out of time, out of time for stuffy plasterboard cubicles full of swaggering Boston cops.

Vico handed Kessler the photo from his jacket and he looked at it without expression. "Don't give me this shit you're too busy with the Vietnamese Mafia, Vico," Kessler said. "I want those reports before you go home. I come back from Walpole tonight and go right to court tomorrow morning. Judge Francis X. fucking Heaney." He gave the photo back and half turned and started for the door. "This guy," he said, jerking a thumb toward Vico.

"Gilman's asking for somebody to check hotels with him," Vico said. "Like hands across the sea, he says."

Kessler stopped and posed at the doorjamb, right hand splayed across the revolver butt. "Fahey," he said. "Give him to Fahey. The old bastard's just sitting in the Blue Grill all day reading his pension check and getting mushed." Kessler studied the masker wires and then adjusted his belt and sighted over his glasses at Gilman like a solemn teacher. "What you want to do, Gilman, look for the kid she's after," he said. "Instead of horsing around hotels all over Boston go find the kid and figure your sister, sister-in-law, she's going to find him too. You ever think of that, Gilman?"

Did he ever think of that?

Gilman braced an arm against the lamppost and leaned over on one leg to shake a pebble from his shoe. A south wind had blown the gray clouds flat and long like flags, and the sky seemed full of silt. He lowered his foot to the sidewalk and while he tested the shoe he watched the traffic roll fitfully up and down Dorchester Avenue, a few cars still with lights and wipers on after the latest drizzle, the slow-speed wipers flicking occasionally like fingers brushing across a brow. Cars fell apart in the east, he remembered. They rusted from rain and snow and the salt on the highways, and shook their joints loose on the potholes and the bulging, uneven streets. Nobody bothered to wash their cars here the way they did in California. Nobody painted palm trees on their fenders and sunsets and Sierra vistas on their doors and panels. They just jolted them from place to place until the carburetors strangled on salt and sand and the transmission spat out in bits on the road, like teeth falling out of a bloody mouth. In San Francisco, in the sixties, there had actually been a topless carwash three blocks from the central precinct station in North Beach, a bunch of giggling girls in red short-shorts with yellow chamois mittens on their hands who pressed against the soapy windows and tickled the car's body as if it were a man. Like riding through a brothel on a conveyor belt. In South Boston, where the homicide bureau kept its offices, all he could see from the main entrance were rows of tired, weak-kneed wooden duplexes and a cyclone fence around a junkyard.

Did he ever think of that? Condescending son of a bitch. There was a book on finding missing persons in a strange town. There was accepted procedure that a good cop could follow with half his brain shot out. Of course he had thought of it. Of course he could drive his midsized discounted Hertzmobile across the river to the Suffolk County courthouse and lean on the kid's probation officer until he came up with a good address, or else he could track down the cop who arrested him and find out where the kid hung out now, what shopping mall in Medford or Braintree he favored these days when he sold dope. He could show a few photographs too, pass out some twenty dollar bills torn in half—you get the other half when you point out Victor Turelli to me, kid—and then when Nina Kerwin showed up one day he could step out of the car and raise his hand and hustle her back on the plane to Cassie and California.

The problem was time. The problem was what Victor Turelli would do if Nina found him first. If he looked around, grinning, from whatever barstool, whatever dive, and found himself face to face with a tear-streaked blonde whose friends had no way to reach her, protect her, stop her. Gilman pinched his nose hard enough to make his eyes water. He thought he knew pretty well what Turelli would do.

He started down the sidewalk toward the vacant lot where half a dozen parked cars sat tilted on banks of rubbish and fill dirt, straddling puddles of oily water. "You don't walk around this part of Southie after dark," Vico had said while he was writing down directions for finding retired police lieutenant Fahey. "Even somebody your size. This is Irish Estates, Gilman. You been away too long to remember. Somebody's gonna peek out of one of those white lace curtains and say this bozo ain't married to my wife's cousin's aunt Kathleen and he ain't Irish and next thing you know three or four kind of overweight, kind of beer-breathed, kind of mother-fucking savage Micks are gonna be waiting at the next corner to play patty-whack your bone with a Louisville Slugger. Take my advice, you find Fahey and then go down to Hanover Street in the North End where the *paesani* can keep you well fed and all in one piece."

He stepped over half a bedspring sunk in the mud like a fossil and unlocked his car door. "It's worth your life," Vico had said.

Your life. My life. Possessive case. From behind the wheel, through the windshield, he saw the tall, narrow windows of a brick schoolhouse across the street. Our Lady of Something. A white cross worked into every window frame by pious Irish masons. The newspaper box twenty feet to his left was double-chained to a lamppost and broken open like a bent jaw. The headline on the Boston Globe that day screamed "Stefan Anders to Speak at Harvard!" Gilman thought of Cassie, then Donald—Donald rising with Stefan Anders' picture in his hand, then falling. Gone."

He thumbed the key and listened to the car engine drown out the hiss in his ears. Overhead, gleaming against the gray background, a white Pan American 747 slowly banked and climbed, alone in the sky, free of the earth. For a moment Gilman thought it was turning west, toward California. But the climb continued, a solitary, unhurried semicircle, and when the wings leveled at last into the woolen obscurity of the clouds it was turning toward Europe.

PART 2 ■■■■■■

England and France, March-June 1944

■■■■■ **SPURLING**

8 ━━━━━━━━━━━━━━━

"Now the original idea for these came from a Yank," the British lecturer said. He paused with a comedian's timing and tugged at the lanyard on his starched RAF uniform while he surveyed his audience. Then he let go of the lanyard, held up a handful of dark brown animal droppings, and made a face. "Naturally."

Most of the lecture room burst into laughter.

"The originals in fact were devised by an OSS chap who was formerly a professor at Harvard University. A Major Carlton Coon." More laughter.

Martin Spurling twisted in his seat toward Brissac, indignant. Carlton Coon was a real person, a real professor of anthropology at Harvard. Spurling had actually seen him and admired him. Brissac shrugged.

"Major Coon," the lecturer said. Some of the Englishmen laughed again and, encouraged, he repeated the name with precise, mocking articulation. "Coon. Major Coon is with the American OSS in North Africa, our sister service, and he devised a kind of ingenious camouflaged road mine for conditions down there." He placed the animal droppings carefully on a folding table and reached inside a black metal armory box. One or two men in the back of the room stood up to see better. Major Sherburn was known for his dramatic flair in the weapons lectures—last week he had shot out an overhead light with a miniature "mitt" pistol the size of a pocket watch—as well as for his sardonic anti-Americanism.

"The professorial mind," he said, "addressed the problem of Rommel's tanks and half-tracks in that direct and droll American fashion. Working behind the lines with partisans, as you will be, Major Coon was directed to send back samples of North African stones, so that the boffins could make up some authentic-looking plaster of Paris tire busters. But there are in fact very few stones along the main roads in Tunisia, and so, following the first principle of sabotage—make it look natural to the place, gentlemen—he looked around for the next most common and natural thing in all of North Africa. Major Coon thereupon invented"—here he held aloft in a white handkerchief a slightly larger piece of brown material— "what he elegantly described in an official document, forwarded with samples to MI-6 in London, as 'The Coon Plastic Exploding Mule Turd.' "

Smiling, the major paced back and forth on the small wooden lecture platform until the laughter died down. Their black cylindrical Nissen hut, half a barrel of corrugated iron on a concrete floor, stood a quarter of a mile from the main buildings at Milton Hall, as if it had been rolled downhill and tucked under the skirts of the New Forest. Overhead a painted silk canopy shielded it from the occasional German reconnaissance planes circling out of the Channel on their way to Dover. Sixty men, mud-colored soldiers, jammed closer to the major's platform. Spurling turned his head and through the open door heard the sound of drizzle in the forest.

Major Sherburn lowered the white handkerchief to eye level and pretended to inspect the mule turd, his nostrils flared in distaste, his right eyebrow arched into an inverted V.

"Smaller than you expected, yes? You probably thought a mule lets drop a whacking great thing, the size of a cannon ball." He held one at arm's length, delicately pinched between thumb and forefinger, and squinted. "About the size of a snooker ball, in fact. Drop it on the games-room table one day for a laugh." He tossed it a few inches into the air as if it were a coin and murmured in theatrical sotto voce, "What's in a name? Major Coon indeed." Then louder: "It feels like the texture of warm butter, but I am no judge of its realism, gentlemen, not having seen the North Africa campaign or"—Spurling imagined his eyes sought him out—"attended the Harvard University."

With a sudden sweep of his hand the major hurled the bit of plastic to the far end of the platform, and the room rocked with the crack of the explosion, filling instantaneously with an acrid sulfurous smell and fine, powdery smoke.

Major Sherburn poked the toe of his shoe at a hole in the platform the size of a hand.

"That was quarter strength Coon Turd, gentlemen, and you can see that it has pulverized the wood into splinters and badly twisted the metal plate we had attached under the wood."

The first rows crowded closer and knelt. Beyond them Major Sherburn was holding up again the original set of animal droppings.

"Cyclonite plastic, gentlemen," he said. "And I cheated a bit. It won't explode until you insert a pressure detonator cap in the center, as I had done beforehand. Without a detonator you can punch it or stretch it all you like, harmlessly. Roll it into a ball and play cricket. The OSS staff in Washington have actually made cyclonite pancake flour—code name Aunt Jemima—and cooked it for volunteers, who have eaten it with no apparent damage. But once you embed the detonator cap in the center, it works. It works extremely well. Scattered on roadways, a few mule patties will blast the treads off a panzer half-track. A dozen or so will bring a bridge down very nicely."

He placed the animal droppings on the folding table and picked up his swagger stick. Spurling had yet to encounter a British officer who could speak in public without a prop—swagger stick, teacup, even in one case a genuine monocle, worn by a Colonel Blimp type from signals who had almost been laughed out of class by the growing contingent of Americans. One American sergeant, a radio operator named Poole, had so far gotten away with addressing every British officer except the colonel as "Sugar."

"When you drop into France," Sherburn said, "you will not be carrying Tunisian mule turds." The laughter was lighter, nervous.

Most of those in the room had completed two to three weeks of their four-week course; some early volunteers had already departed unseen in the bleak January mornings, clearing out their rooms secretly, leaving only notes and sealed envelopes for next of kin. Others had moved into their rooms while the beds were still warm, like patients in a desperate and efficient hospital.

"But you will be supplied later on with these animal droppings, which are appropriate to French roads, resembling as nearly as possible the droppings of pigs and cattle. A more advanced formula than Major Coon's, and refined, you may care to know, by biologists at the University of Oxford, not Harvard. 'Hands across the sea' hardly seems the right expression, however." He paused for his laugh, frowned at the silence, and after a moment reached into his box again. Like a magician at a child's party, Spurling thought scornfully, pulling out trick after trick. When we're over there, our pockets stuffed with exploding pig turds, he'll still be here in England, preening and strutting.

"Now military science has forged past Major Coon and built an even better mousetrap," Major Sherburn said and, as the soldiers began to groan, he held up a limp black rat and waved it back and forth by the tail. "A fake, also, made of dyed cyclonite and hair and tested successfully, I'm happy to say, gentlemen, just two weeks ago at a German railway yard in Besançon."

Spurling turned away again and stared at the drizzle. Jokes and schoolboy stunts. A professional conjuror had actually come down from London one day to teach them principles of camouflage. "The German coal tender will find one of these buried in the coal stack," the major said, "and think it just an ordinary dead rat, which he will then proceed to shovel into the boiler of the locomotive, according to railroad custom. The heat and the chemical detonator do the rest—kaboom!"

He grinned at the patter of applause. Brissac laughed out loud. Those volunteers who had survived parachute school at Inverness, and another week of commando training in the black, treeless hills to the west, had been brought here, to the southern edge of Hampshire, across the length of England, for a final course of preparation. They had traveled by night, with blinkered headlights, long distances between each vehicle, and frequent, unexplained stops in the middle of empty roads, and they had driven through the stone gates and lovely rolling parkland of the estate like an invading army out of a time machine, bus windows bristling with rifles and helmets while grazing deer looked up, wide-eyed and pale.

Spurling's hands were trembling, but he raised his head in pride and looked disdainfully at the rest of the class. There was no one in the room, he thought, chosen as he had been.

9 ▬▬▬▬▬▬▬▬▬▬

"American," the Group Captain said, scorn on the blade edge of his voice. He held up a book of paper matches.

"American matches, common as salt to some of you. They carry the names of restaurants or bars on their covers; they are virtually unknown in Europe. The last inter-Allied team to drop into Brittany disappeared when the American member sat down in a cafe and casually pulled out a book of matches he had shoved in a pocket his last night here. Now we vet everyone before you climb on the aircraft."

He lifted a white mug of tea to his lips, and Spurling could see the fingers of his right hand shake, the brown worms of tea run down the sides of the mug.

"We give you European eyeglass frames and haircuts," the Group Captain said. "We buy European clothes from refugees in New York and issue them to you, with local laundry marks still intact. We have a team of counterfeiters in MI-6 printing out German identity cards, French money, travel permits, personal letters. We have one station in Paris that does nothing but mail letters and receive them, so that when the SS guard pulls you to one side and empties your pockets, there are personal letters with French postmarks and German censor stamps. But we make mistakes too, and every moment that you are pretending to be someone else in France you will be aware that we might have ballsed up in ways you could never check or prevent. Two agents last month went out with beautiful documents, perfect clothing, good French accents. SS stops them both in a routine train inspection north of Limoges. Papers in order, good. Exempt from military service in order to work in vital industry, sheet metal foundry, good. *Ausweiss*, travel permission to come to Limoges from two different French cities, good. But both permissions were signed with the same name! In the same bloody handwriting!"

Spurling closed his eyes, hearing the train rattle, the papers drop to the floor, the German words.

"The greatest psychological difficulty for a normal, decent person," the Group Captain said, "is having to live a lie."

He glanced mechanically up from his notes to the row of faces. "Jean Moulin," he said, naming the first authentic hero of the French Resistance, betrayed by someone to the notorious Colonel Klaus Barbie in Lyons in 1943 and known by reputation to every man in the room. "Jean Moulin was followed down the street in all strange towns by a reliable friend who carried a wallet with a completely different set of identification papers, which she could slip to him in case of need. Think of it: already traveling under one false identity, he had to be able to change instantly to another, shift mental gears, and remember a whole new set of information for the routine German questions—mother's maiden name, school attended, year graduated. For citizens of free societies, accustomed to life as straightforward, direct in nature, this will be the hardest thing: to deceive everyone, to trust no one. But a clandestine network is not a fraternity. Once the reception party has hidden your parachutes and hurried you to a safe house, they will scatter. Much of the time you will be alone except for your two partners—who may soon be moved—and the wireless. At other times you will organize meetings of resistants, virtually certain that someone in the room is an informer. You must lie to everyone. If it helps you to survive you must lie to yourself."

It was said that the Group Captain had bailed out of his Lysander in late 1942, over the Loire, and had broken both legs when his parachute was blown in the darkness against the abutment of a bridge. He had crawled out of the water somehow and into the woods alongside the river. Three days later a poacher had found him and brought a priest to give him last rites. Instead the priest had concealed him in the supply closet of a village church, where he lived for almost six months, beneath an overturned old desk and a stack of tables, while German troops set up a district headquarters in the church itself. A doctor came to see him once, at midnight, setting his legs crudely, in the dark, with four broomsticks and a torn sheet. When he could hobble, he had been passed along a Resistance network from one safe house to another like a cumbersome sack, a ticking bomb—left on park benches by a man whose name he would never learn, picked up hours later by another, who only signaled from the opposite side of the street and walked on ahead. He had come out through Lisbon after three months in transit, and those who had seen him in the officer's shower or in the infirmary said that both legs were zippered with leathery black scars and knobbed with balls of tissue like rotten oak.

"You will be like missing persons hunted down by the police," he said. "On the run, disguised, pursued unceasingly by the Gestapo—subject to betrayal at any point."

He folded his notes and began to rise slowly from behind the table where he sat.

"The war changes everyone and everything," he said. "Just as this building is changed, Milton Hall, just as the cities and maps are changed. Some of you will discover virtues you never imagined you possessed. Some of you will unearth sides of your character that, with luck, you can later rebury. Some of you will lose your self-respect eternally, your humanity, your souls." He paused and looked at the ornate ceiling, a baroque whirl of gold and white ferns arching into a crystal chandelier. The Group Captain's pauses were massive, legendary, as vast as canyons. Spurling worshiped him.

"Some of you will even survive," the Group Captain said. His face was a stiff white kite, rising.

* * *

"Harvard is the best, the Group Captain is the best," Brissac mocked in his excellent English. He lit a Gauloise and exhaled foul blue smoke. "You pick a strange, cold man for a hero, Harvard."

Spurling felt his face redden against his will, as if he had been slapped. It was his strongest trait, loyalty. He was loyal to Harvard because it had made him what he was, out of nothing. He was loyal to the Group Captain, first because he was always loyal to his teachers, second because the two of them shared a great secret.

Brissac himself he did not admire. In one of its clumsier assertions of Anglo-Saxon priority, the army had consistently named an American or an Englishman as commander of a clandestine team, but Brissac had pointedly ignored Spurling's rank. It existed, he made clear with every scowl, as no more than a military fiction. At meals they sat down together in a corner of the great transformed ballroom, permanently wary and uneasy. And in four more days they would parachute, at night, deep, deep into the occupied territory of southern France and join the Resistance maquis of the famous Colonel Verlaine. Spurling woke up before dawn drenched in sweat, dreaming aloud. He marked each day off on a pocket calendar hidden under his pillow and had no idea in the world what he dreamed about.

"Sabotage," Brissac said to their new radioman, Poole. He poked his fork at a slice of dubious meat. "We put the *sabot* in every train we could." To Spurling: "You know the word?"

Spurling nodded impatiently. His French was ten points over "fluent" in the Army language school exam, six points under perfect. *Sabot* meant wooden shoe; in the early nineteenth century French workers threatened with loss of jobs would drop them into complex factory machinery and bring it to a splintering halt.

"We made special grease to lubricate the locomotives," Brissac told Poole, "real looking but full of sand and so abrasive that it wore down engine parts in a matter of days. We shoved it in the hotboxes when the Boches weren't looking."

"Is that how . . . ?" Poole dipped his own cigarette toward Brissac's food tray. Brissac had no index and middle fingers on his right hand.

"A Frenchman did it," Brissac said, dramatic, indignant. "The Milice are French, you know—they're the Vichy police, they work for the Germans. And one day they see me coming out of the Bordeaux freightyard, no papers, and even though it's the Free Zone they let a German officer sit in on the interrogation." Brissac twisted his lips as if he were about to spit into the tray of food. In unarmed combat training the instructors always treated Brissac with cautious respect. When a sergeant one day had asked for comments, he had leapt from the mat and shown them how to kill a man by stabbing a rolled-up newspaper into the soft white part of the throat, just below the chin.

Four short days. One short jump.

"The Nazi winks and leaves the room," Brissac said, "and the Milice captain hacks the fingers off with a carpenter's filthy handsaw, and he tells me, 'Maquis or not, now you have nothing left to pull a trigger with against the Reich.' Frenchman against Frenchman—that much the Ice Captain knows. Communist against Gaullist, monarchist against Jew. You see this?" He raised his upper lip with one finger to show Poole a bridge of false teeth, clearly new. "He knocks out my teeth with the butt of his pistol. The Milice say it happens when I resist arrest. The dentists in London fix the new teeth so I'm not like Moulin."

Poole began a question.

"Moulin cut his throat in May nineteen-forty with a piece of glass," Brissac interrupted. "In Chartres. To commit suicide. The Germans had beaten him and locked him in a stone hut with the corpse of a woman, to scare him, until he would confess to whatever they said. Someone found him in the morning bleeding to death. But always there was the big jagged scar under his chin, and in all his disguises he had to wear a scarf or a high collar."

Behind him, facing the long table, was the fireplace for the great hall, a huge stone mouth large enough to stand in. Above it Spurling could see a series of portraits of long-forgotten viscounts and famous dead horses, and to one side of the mantlepiece a trio of sandy-haired British officers, their heads bobbing up and down in after-dinner conversation.

"When the Germans killed Jean Moulin—" Brissac said, grind-

ing out his cigarette in the tin tray. "When he died the first thing that
happened was that the Resistance networks all scattered and ran
away—nobody knew who betrayed him. Then they got angry, because it had to have been a Frenchman, and they came back stronger
than ever. You survive if you want to," he said, "if you get angry
enough."

Spurling watched the bubbles rise in his coffee mug, float, and
vanish. He had a memory for tastes, smells. He had drunk his first
cup of coffee when he was sixteen years old, a precocious scholarship student arriving at Harvard before he had graduated from high
school, slipping diffidently into his chair at breakfast in the Freshman Union beneath the head of a buffalo that Teddy Roosevelt had
shot and donated to higher education. He had finished Harvard in an
astonishingly fast two years, graduating summa cum laude in Greek
and Latin, and when the war had come he was already three years
into his Ph.D. in classics. His Army scores in math and French had
been the highest in New England, and the OSS, the "Ivy League of
the Army," had snatched him before any other corps had even seen
them.

"I had a younger brother like you, Harvard," Brissac said gently, in a sudden change of mood. He studied Spurling's face thought-
fully for a moment, and his hand moved to Spurling's wrist. "Very
brilliant like you. Another hero worshiper. He studied at the lycée
while I went in the army. He taught school in Tours, a very beautiful
old town. In December 1941 the Boches carried him to Mauthausen,
because they found him after curfew with a Jewish girl." Brissac
closed his face into a fist. "At that camp there was a rock quarry
where the inmates worked, in a nightmare. No food, no medicine.
You worked till you died. Many of the Jews would go to the top of the
quarry when they couldn't stand it any longer, and jump. The SS
guards would stand at the top and laugh, clap them on. The bombers
have closed that camp, but one of the Jews escaped and I met him in
Spain. He knew my brother." Spurling looked up, everywhere. Brissac's huge hand circled Spurling's wrist and pinned it to the table.
"My brother struggled to the top of the quarry and waited swaying
over the rocks, and one of the SS guards came to see him jump. My
brother turned to give him his hand, to shake his hand in farewell,

and the guard smiled and took it and my brother stepped backward into space never letting go.

"I'm not afraid to die," Brissac said. "Every beat of your heart carries you closer to death."

10 ███████████████████

"Lieutenant Martin goddam Spurling," Poole said drunkenly. "Lemme tell you something, Lieutenant. They don't expect us to come back. Did you know that? Did you know the Office of Strategic fucking Services is sending us off on a suicide mission?"

"Bullshit," Spurling said. The OSS were great men. General Donovan was a great man. The taxicab rocked around a corner and sped into utter darkness while Spurling clutched the handstrap drunkenly and watched the city reeling past in a kaleidoscope of shadows. Toward them, on the wrong side of the road, other taxis approached at high speeds, their headlights hooded except for narrow white slits in the center. London was a darkened room full of black cats springing at random. The Luftwaffe hadn't bombed the city in five days, and rumors had already begun: the Germans had retreated to Paris, the long-awaited European landing was at hand and the Germans were saving firepower in preparation for it, the Germans were developing a terrible new long-range bomb that they could launch from Berlin. In the daylight, Spurling had seen bomb craters two blocks from the British Museum and the brick shell of an apartment building in Gordon Square, divided in half by a blackened staircase that led three flights up into empty space where a charred bed frame tilted and hung over the street. Sandbags lay everywhere, in every public doorway and tube stop, piled as high as a man's shoulders in order to absorb the blast waves of the bombs. On the sidewalks and in the gutters he had seen thousands of shards of broken glass from bombed-out windows.

"I can *tell* you why," Poole said.

Spurling closed his eyes and felt happier than he had ever felt before. Poole was a great man, Poole was his best friend. And Brissac, too, who had disappeared somehow from the pub where they had started, then reappeared in the front seat of the cab. Great men, teachers. Spurling had always admired his teachers. Poole was taking him to a brothel.

"I checked out my goddam equipment," Poole said. They would jump in forty-eight hours, at night, out of the belly of a Halifax bomber over a blur of landscape no longer than a football field.

"You know how the goddam army is about equipment?" Poole asked. "You sign for everything, every goddam bullet—am I right?" Spurling nodded and smiled, his eyes still closed. Fact: the rarest signature in American history was that of Button Gwinnett. Why on earth did he know that? How did the taxi drivers find their way in the blackout?

"I get the Colt, I get the 3 Mark II," Poole said. Spurling tightened his eyelids and remembered. The 3 Mark II transceiver, a suitcase-sized radio transmitter and receiver, standard issue for agents dropping into France. Two hundred and fifty volts from house current, usually lamp-socket outlet or six-volt auto battery. If he lost the main power in a building, the radio operator could reverse his fittings and switch to the battery within two seconds. Spurling had taken one apart with a flirtatious trainer named Doris and put it back together in half an hour. Too slow.

"The Biscuit," Poole said, the short-range transceiver for communications within France. "Clothes, shoes, everything. I start to sign the sheet and the quartermaster sergeant pulls it out of the clipboard and says forget it. Can you believe that? I didn't sign for one goddam thing. They *know* we're not coming back."

"Nos morituri," Spurling said, and the cab bounced to a halt in front of a row of buildings blacked out except for the wormlike beams of light from passing cars that crawled up their sides, and occasional pencils of yellow glow that marked an upstairs window. Button Gwinnett had died when he was forty; that was why his signature was so rare.

"Fuckin' Latin," Poole said. "We're going to be classic corpses in fuckin' France."

"It's what gladiators said," Spurling told him as they staggered up steps and Poole leaned one big fist into an electric door bell. *"Nos morituri te salutamus.* It means, 'We who are about to die salute you.'"

The door swung open two feet, letting a corridor of light down the stone steps, catching Poole's dirty brown hair and making it flare. A heavyset woman wearing tortoiseshell eyeglasses and a navy blue housecoat peered at him, her left hand clutching a policeman's wooden truncheon.

"We who are about to get laid," Poole said, "salute you."

The woman slammed the door with a thunderous bang, and Poole slipped abruptly out of sight, landing on the first step in a sitting position and then toppling sideways until he leaned against the iron railing. "Wrong house," he said, giggling, and Spurling reached a hand toward him and fell down the steps too, giggling.

Ten minutes later, half a block farther away, they squeezed around sandbags and through the semicircle of blackout curtain inside a doorway, past a thin middle-aged woman with surprising breasts as big as pillows. In front of them stretched a long hall of closed doors. To their left, double doors opened into a brightly lit room facing the street. Some of the girls who came tumbling toward them called, "Sergeant Poole! Sergeant Poole!" and others grasped Spurling's elbows and waist and spun him from one red smiling mouth to another, down a gauntlet of bosoms and teeth. When he sank backward into a chair, two girls jumped sidesaddle onto its arms and set their hands free in Spurling's hair, on his chest; another hand thrust a tumbler of warm scotch toward him, and he heard wild shouts in French from men standing at a bar beside the doors. Between waving arms he glimpsed Brissac hanging on to the bar and scowling.

"This is Doris, and Doris," Poole shouted over the other shouts, his big hand gripping Spurling's chin and wrenching him from one smiling face to the other. "And Doris number three—he wants you all to be Doris," and the girls cooed and dove toward him again as Poole sang toward the ceiling:

"The soldiers all died
Of a broken heart,
A broken heart."

Poole's scotch glass tilted and spilled into Spurling's lap, and while the girls laughed Poole fumbled his hand between his legs and grabbed Spurling hard, tugging his cock from side to side.

"This equipment has not been signed out," Poole announced with a roar. He released Spurling and straightened to drunken attention. "Ladies, this man has not signed out his equipment." One of the girls walked her fingers from Spurling's belt to his crotch. "Will you please check it out?" Poole said, and executed an about-face, buckling at the knees.

The room fell into fragments, great dazzling triangles of white and gold, then steadied and focused again, and Spurling found himself at the door, right arm around a woman's bare shoulders, a new glass in hand, watching Poole shove blue five-pound notes one by one at the woman with the huge breasts.

"How the hell old are you, anyway, Lieutenant?" he said as he counted.

"Twenty-two," Spurling said.

"Jesus Christ," Poole muttered. "This is the youngest man in the goddam army," he told the woman, raising his voice to a confidential boom. "Every day he goes off by himself at four o'clock, for a secret pow-wow with the captain. We're not supposed to notice. What are you, a secret agent, Lieutenant? Hey, we're *all* secret agents. Look at us. Come to London for a party before we go off to get ourselves goddam killed, right?" Poole staggered out of Spurling's focus, staggered back. "So this secret agent goes to see a *play*

first, a goddam matinee when he comes to London." Suddenly
Poole's face was inches from Spurling's, huge and distended, as if
seen through a magnifying glass, a vast balloon of sweating flesh and
black whisker ends. "What goddam play did you see, Lieutenant?
Tell the girls."

"Love for Love," Spurling said seriously, "with John Gielgud."
Then he thought of where he was and began to giggle again while
Poole smiled and roared insults in French toward the bar. Spurling
tried to speak into the gale of masculine voices, tried to halt his gig-
gles and round his own voice into urbane tones, as if at a garden
party, and remark casually how amazing it was that in the middle of a
war, a bombardment, London should go on as usual with plays, con-
certs; how even the British Museum was open and if he weren't
about to jump out of a plane to certain death he would come back and
see the Elgin Marbles and the Magna Carta, but Poole was turning
away, toward the brightly lit room, his arms stretched out and draped
limply across the shoulders of two women, singing loudly, "Mother,
make my bed soon." He staggered between the women and bowed
his head.

When the door closed, Spurling found himself standing unsteadily in a tiny bedroom illuminated only by a dim table lamp in
one corner. In front of him a woman about his own age was undoing
the knot of his tie. The noise from the front room had grown muffled
and faint.

"You're a fair one, aren't you, love?" she said. "Got a girl's
eyes and mouth. Tell us your name."

"Martin," he said. He was lightheaded with beer and scotch.
He would listen to her accent; he would guess what part of England
she came from, amaze her with his brilliance. He would tell her his
secret. Her hands sawed the loosened tie back and forth and dropped
to his shirt buttons. She wore her hair in a permanent, light-brown
English mouse hair that frizzed to each side of her head. Her eye-
brows were plucked, her face was long and boneless. Somebody's
sister, Spurling thought as she pulled the shirt up and out of his trousers and he saw her breasts buoy and then vanish down her blouse
again, great fleshy bubbles.

"Brought a Durex with you then, Martin?" she said. At Harvard he had gone to the whorehouses once in Scollay Square, drunk and overanxious. Her hands stopped, poised on his belt buckle. He shook his head and placed his own hands tentatively at her waist, feeling her hipbones hard beneath a slick fabric. Durex was the British name for rubber. They sold them in barbershops and chemists, and Spurling had left his packet of six tucked away in his shoes at Milton Hall.

"That's all right then," she said. "We'll put it on your friend's bill."

From the narrow bed he asked her name and she smiled, showing wide strong teeth, and told him she was Felicia.

"That's a pretty name," he said, raising his head from the pillow for a moment and seeing the room spin away into outer space, as if someone had hurled it like a plate into the black air. He felt that he had said something foolish and inadequate beyond words, and his cheeks and neck burst into flame.

"It means 'happy,'" she said, standing far away. "I don't like the lamp on, Martin."

"Please," he began. The pillowcase reeked of perfume and hair-oil. The beer surged back and forth in his belly like water in a tub.

At the edge of the light Felicia shrugged the blouse from her shoulders, and Spurling watched, mouth suddenly like sandpaper, as her breasts swung and her arms turned into wings, reaching behind her back. The skirt slid gently to the floor, billowing around her legs, a white parachute crumpling, and she held her pose, solemn faced an instant, while his mind staggered and ran, searching as always for words. Not good without words, not real, not yet.

She turned off the light and came to the bed.

Moments later she said, "That's nice." Her fingers curled around him, a limp worm slowly butting its head. Nor shall my sword sleep in my hand. The Durex slid down, clammy as a wet glove. Spurling turned her over, his cheeks and fingers rolling across soft flesh.

Hours later he awoke briefly to see Poole and Brissac coming through the door wearing only undershorts, carrying bottles of foaming champagne. When he awoke again both of them lay against Felicia's chest, each curled up to a stiff red nipple like nursing puppies, her hands behind their necks holding them in place. Poole opened one eye, yellow and bloodshot, wide as a window, and Spurling said, "Semi-moriturus." Poole's eyelid dropped like a shutter.

11 ━━━━━━━━━━

"His French is brilliant," the Group Captain said. He turned his deadpan face toward the man standing on the other side of his desk. The Group Captain's office was a room of exquisite Georgian proportions on the second floor of Milton Hall, its shelves stripped of all books now, but its polished furniture and oriental rugs still elegantly in place, supplemented by a row of olive drab filing cabinets and blackout curtains tacked to every window. In the whitewashed fireplace a small coal fire lay curled like a black cat. On a tripod nearby stood a map of the Dordogne valley, in southwestern France, marked with dozens of arrows, numbers, and inked notations.

"Absolutely brilliant," he repeated.

His visitor walked past the coal fire to the map and stood rubbing his jaw in an unmistakably American gesture while he studied it.

"This Colonel Verlaine," he drawled after a moment. "He code-named himself after a poet. He's got the largest maquis in the whole goddam Dordogne, right?"

Behind the desk the Group Captain nodded.

"And according to your reports," the American officer said, "he makes these wonderful speeches about France and patriotism

and General de Gaulle and Joan of Arc, and the peasants around
there would do anything for him. The Germans can't touch him."

"People live or die for him," the Group Captain said with his
strangely impersonal irony.

"Yeah." The American punched one big thumb at the map.
"Your *Das Reich* is an entire panzer division," he said. "Twenty-
thousand men, ninety-nine heavy tanks, sixty-four medium tanks,
seventy-five assault guns. Just returned from the Russian front—
these are seasoned, brutal soldiers, Captain. No one can say, of
course. But if the ball does drop in the north—" he stopped and
looked at the black and yellow arrows criss-crossing the map where
the Das Reich had been written in, thirty miles below the Dordogne
River. By summer 1944 at the latest, as everyone knew, landings
would have to begin somewhere on the European continent. American soldiers already overflowed London, spilling in long dark
streams across the fields of Kent and Sussex, running down to the
very edge of the Channel. And when the great invasion came, the
Resistance networks of France were to rise up together as a single
body and do whatever they could to prevent the Germans from rushing toward the beaches. The major's pipe stem traced a line north
toward London.

"His test scores in everything else are fine," he said, still looking at the map. "There was some kind of hitch with the parachutes,
but that apparently worked out. And his French, you tell me, is
great. So that leaves me one question. What do you think, Captain?
Is he ruthless enough?"

"Better than ruthless," the Group Captain said. He squared his
stack of notes with both hands and began painfully to stand up.
"He's young."

On the next-to-last day, thirty-six hours before the jump into France,
Spurling and Brissac were permitted a morning break for personal
business, and then at one o'clock required, as always, to join the
daily run.

Eight miles every day, no matter what the weather. They ran
through the forest paths of the huge estate, galloping out of sight of
the mansion's white walls and shuttered windows, nearly a hundred

men in black combat boots, heavy wool pants and shirts, and padded windbreaker jackets, led by the same mountainous sergeant who taught unarmed combat in the mornings.

"In the summer," Brissac panted to Spurling, "they say he still makes them wear the same clothes, to toughen." Spurling nodded, bowed his head, dug his boots into the gristle of the earth.

At mile four the path crossed an open field of great placid beauty, a scene out of an eighteenth-century painting, rolling away from them like a swell of pale green surf, over a ridge and vanishing. By then the group had strung out in a line a quarter of a mile long, and the sergeant sprinted to the rear, shouting at stragglers. In another five minutes they would enter the forest again, breath smoking in their faces, and begin a mile of uphill running before the last long easy grade back to the hall.

Ahead of him Brissac ran steadily, with monotonous competence, too heavily muscled to be graceful, too intense and single-minded to falter. Twenty feet behind him Spurling swung his arms for balance and paced himself.

But as they came into the open field, Spurling suddenly lengthened his stride and impulsively burst past Brissac and all the others, running as hard as he could through the waves of pale, rippling stubble. After the world of Harvard that had taken him in and made him, after the familiar gray enclosures of Widener Library, the safe path back and forth to Eliot House—this was a new and threatening country: trees, birds, the air itself were new and different, a foreign country where he had no childhood, no past, only the transparent continuity of a language. In France, not even that, nothing. Leaping into nothing. He stretched his legs and ran harder, running through time.

Over the last mile, feeling the air settle like a lump of cold brassy metal on his tongue, his lungs in tatters, he ran by sheer will. Around him the strange new English forest began to reel and blur, spinning.

At the end of the run he collapsed facedown onto the lawn behind the hall, soaked with sweat, panting and blowing into the dead grass, as if inaccessible spots deep within his body were burning like underground fires.

12 ■■■■■■■■■■■■■■■■■■■■■■

As he did every team from Milton Hall, the Group Captain escorted them to the plane for their drop, shuffling unsteadily across the tarmac on his splayed legs, pausing from time to time and ramming his upper body straight with a suppressed grunt.

Spurling and Brissac, heavy parachute riggings strapped to their legs, crabwalked awkwardly three steps behind, heads down and tense as if they were not staring at him. Behind them in the ragtag procession they could hear the radio man Poole struggling with the civilian suitcase of radio parts he insisted on carrying himself. Still farther back, as Spurling saw when he peered over his shoulder into the fading light, the pilot and copilot straggled, holding up a brown clipboard between them like a hymnal.

A Whitely Bomber, the Group Captain had told them regretfully in the briefing room. He had requested a Lockheed Hudson or a Halifax, newer planes with better navigational equipment; but only the workhorse, the old 1939 Whitely, was available. Still, the Whitely would do, he said, as if he were speaking of a nervous and unimpressive horse, patting a wet flank. A very long radius of action. Four .303 machine guns in the tail turret, one in the nose. An auxil-

iary fuel tank built under the wings to carry them to the center of
France and beyond.

At the far end of the runway the moon hung suspended between
two bars of cloud like a coin in a rack. Beside them the Whitely
looked long, flat, angular, its whole fuselage painted a dull black to
absorb searchlights and reflections.

At the front of the aircraft the pilot and navigator clambered up
a rolling ladder and began to inspect the engines. Poole swung one
suitcase into the open hatch above them, then bobbed to hoist the
second one with both hands. Spurling jammed his hands in the
coarse wool pockets of his suit, the first civilian clothing he had worn
since coming to England, a threadbare French suit issued to him in
an English mansion by a sergeant with a Cockney accent and a blue
and white Brooklyn Dodgers cap.

"All right," the Group Captain said. Across the great black carpet of concrete other planes were already starting their engines; two
or three little Lysanders, like parasitic birds around rhinos, were
taxiing up and down pointlessly. Brissac, bullnecked and stockier
than ever in his overcoat and a dark blue watch cap, grasped the
metal rail of the ladder with his good hand and heaved himself up
through the black hatchway and was gone.

Spurling reached for the ladder and felt the Group Captain's
hand on his shoulder.

"You're all right with this now?" His curt nod indicated the
parachute on Spurling's back.

The starboard propeller of the Whitely kicked to life and roared
up a scale before cutting off abruptly and leveling to a steady fan.

In its backwash Spurling simply imitated the Group Captain's
curt nod and turned back to the ladder.

Inside, when he had backed onto the wooden bench running
halfway up the fuselage, he rubbed his parachute hump against the
metal skin and tugged his harness straps tight. Through the gloom
Brissac and Poole were picking at each other's rigging like chimpan-
zees at fleas. Then the fuselage swayed and the Group Captain was
on the plane, stooped in what Spurling thought must be unbearable
pain and moving slowly from man to man, saying something quietly.

"All right," he said to Spurling when he reached him. And almost inaudibly: "I'm depending on you, personally." In rapid French: *"Nous sommes confrères, n'est-ce pas?"*

"Confrères."

He balanced himself with one hand overhead and turned to go. Then he stopped and reached over Spurling's shoulder. "The static line," he said in a harder voice altogether—the canvas cord that automatically twitched the parachute free and broke away. "You know you can't jump without your static line." Quick, competent hands: the click of metal just behind his ear. "All right," the Group Captain said again and disappeared without another word through the navigator's hatchway.

"Jesus Christ, you go out of here like a bomb without that static line, Lieutenant." Poole was groping hastily over his head to check his own line. Spurling jerked the canvas straps hard, his face blinkered by the hot flush running from jawbone to ears. He jammed his thumbs under the straps and twisted them tighter still, until the circulation stopped; sweat rolled in rivers from his brow, his eyes. Brissac reached his mutilated hand over the bench and patted Spurling on the knee. Like every other creature born of the war, the Whitely screamed to life and began to run.

Against the rules, they carried no dispatcher—shorthanded, the navigator had explained with a rueful County Mayo face—they would have to start their own jumps, with no more than the aid of the lights on the bulkhead. One gloved hand waved jauntily. Two four-inch circular bulbs had been attached to a slat of plywood and tied vertically with clothesline and electrical wire, just above the covered jumphole, like a traffic signal: red to mean they were approaching the jump area. Green to go.

Brissac and Poole dozed minutes after takeoff, slumped in their parachute riggings, occasionally scratching sleepily through their coats to the coarse woolen underclothes they had all been ordered to wear for the flight. Spurling sat upright as far as he could, holding his chin forward over his knees to ease the pressure of canvas behind him and the stiff crisscrosses of leather that trussed him from crotch to shoulders. In front, at the other end of what seemed a flying barn, the navigator and pilot smoked endless Gold Point cigarettes and talked by radio to the tail gunner. Occasionally, preternaturally clear flak bursts appeared in the distance, harmless showers of color that dropped away like Roman candles, first over hard, black water, then over France.

After a time Spurling dozed too. His mind spiraled slowly down out of his grip. Patches of unconsciousness drifted, like shadows in a placid ocean. They could not go to the toilet in their parachute rigs, he thought, stirring sleepily. Dispatchers were trained to snarl their comments, shouting the last *Go!* at the top of their lungs. At Harvard his first year the snow would fall for days, shrouding the Square, the dark Georgian roofs, and the sensual curved mounds of the bridges; Eliot House would stretch its arms protectively around its courtyard, like a fat man holding his belly. They read James Joyce's story "The Dead." *Nos morituri. Iam, iam, nulla mora est.*

When the red light blinked on, they had all been awake for half an hour, checking their equipment in tense, irritable monosyllables. Spurling slid instantly from the bench and knelt beside the covered jumphole.

"First me," he said, repeating once more the orders he had told them a dozen times since they had awakened. Brissac's mouth curled in disdain. "Then the Type Cs." He lowered his hand to one of the four Type C containers, sheet-metal cylinders reinforced with wooden ribs, which held radio equipment, batteries, extra sidearms. Each cylinder was the length and volume of a human body—"Use them for target practice if you can't find any Jerries," the supply sergeant had said sardonically—and linked by web straps to a parachute.

"Second pass, Brissac; then Poole with his radios."

He released the three latches on the oversized tin saucer that served as a cover, lifted it free, and shoved it quickly into the shadows as cold air sucked up, making a geyser of shrieking canvas and wind, and through the jumphole they saw the black and gray landscape of occupied France, flowing sluggishly beneath them like the tide at the bottom of the sea.

From his forward bench the navigator shouted something over the roar of the engines and wind. Spurling eased himself around the wooden bench and crawled to the other edge of the jumphole. The red light stuttered and held.

He swung his legs into the turbulent air and braced his hands on the rim. *Nous sommes confrères.* We are secret brothers. He had jumped six times all told at Inverness. Each time he had set his face with a furious effort of self-control, closed his eyes. Dropped like a body into a grave.

At a hundred and seventy-five miles an hour the Whitely would be past the clearing in seconds. He felt his stomach doubling over, folding. The navigator shouted again and Spurling lifted his eyes.

Too soon!

Spurling knew the instant he moved that he had jumped too soon—misread the flickering light.

Sideways, dropping into a river of darkness, tumbling away on unseen currents of air, he plunged, bucked, fell. Brissac's shout was strangled and gone. Three seconds, four—the static line yanked and grabbed and the pouch of white silk flew from behind his head like a ghost and the parachute thumped open.

Beneath him as he swung there was nothing to see: no line of four lights shaped like a capital "l," no torches or beacons or house-lights, only a slow rippling blankness where the reception committee was supposed to be. He twisted in the harness and craned his head toward the waning drone of the Whitely, but its flat black fuselage, its black oversized wings had simply pulled away into the French sky like the shadow of a great hollow-boned heron, all feet and wings, empty of its load.

Now Brissac and Poole would be jumping, miles farther ahead, where they should be.

The ground sailed up. In the cold rush of wind the black masses beneath his feet writhed and metamorphosed—bushes, trees, roads, blind mouths in the bottom of a pit. He would be hopelessly off target, lost without a trace in the back country of the Dordogne Valley. There would be German troops waiting, French Milice. On his left the landscape seemed to rise faster, spilling rivulets of white from its knuckles that might be hedges, might be snow. Like jumping off a fourteen-foot wall onto pavement, the British sergeant had said. You trained daily for this, tumbling off the backs of jeeps at thirty miles an hour: *bend your knees, bend your arms*. The last thing he saw before he hit the tree was a sudden vision of the Group Captain's hands on either side of his stack of notes, motionless as chunks of quartz.

13 ▬▬▬▬▬▬▬▬▬

Too soon, too soon.

When Spurling blinked himself suddenly, instantly awake, the first thing he saw was the face of a slender middle-aged man sitting in a chair beside the bed. He wore a neat blue civilian suit, a snap-brim fedora, a yellow silk tie, and a fawn-colored military cloak, unbuttoned and draped behind him like a surplice. He was astonishingly handsome.

Spurling blinked again and turned his head.

A wall of books.

Spurling lifted his cheek from the pillow, straining to see the books as if he were at home again, at Harvard again. Vertical rows tightly squeezed together, more books flat on top of those. Paperbacked, leatherbacked, yellow, blue covers, thin, fat. But the words and letters swam away and out of reach and dissolved like specks in his watery vision.

He turned his head back to the man in the chair.

"*Bienvenu à la Dordogne, Lieutenant. Bonjour. Je m'appelle Colonel Verlaine.*"

Spurling watched him rise to his feet with a grave smile.

"We sat by you all night to be sure you were recovering," Colonel Verlaine said in beautifully precise English. He adjusted his hat and coat and began to walk toward an open door. A maddening, inexplicable ticking sound reverberated in Spurling's ears. He raised himself higher on his elbow and tried to speak, but his tongue was swollen and unresponsive. In the corner of his eye, through the haze of returning pain, he had the impression of a young woman, brown hair, heavy sweater, swaying breasts under the sweater.

"I'm sorry," Spurling began to say.

"I leave you," Verlaine interrupted, "in the capable hands of Madame Gabaussau." He smiled again, made a gesture with the hat, and despite Spurling's attempts to call him back, disappeared through the door.

"Welcome here." Another woman, much older, had materialized as he spoke and was easing Spurling now into a sitting position on the bed. She fussed a hard bolster into place behind his shoulders and stood back, hands on hips, to admire it.

"Colonel Verlaine," he began.

"Colonel Verlaine comes back later," Madame Gabaussau finished the sentence for him in a heavily accented dialect, nodding for emphasis at almost every word. "This is the Hotel du Commerce in the town of Lalinde, my hotel. 'Safe house!'" she added gaily in English. Through the laced curtains of the window Spurling could see the gray needle of a church spire, and beyond it, lower down, a wide brown river curving under hills and a cloudy sky. "La Dordogne," she said, following his gaze.

He took the bread and thin white coffee she produced from a tray, and as he drank and chewed, tasting nothing, he slowly became aware of the clocks. The cabinet with Verlaine's books was directly beside him, at the head of the narrow bed. Around the rest of the tiny room, in every corner and at every angle it seemed, he saw nothing but tall wooden-cased grandfather clocks, pendulums swinging, their dials ornamented with scene after scene of cows grazing or peasants harvesting or oxen under yoke in yellow fields of grain. She was a Norman, Madame Gabaussau explained as she bustled over cups and pots, and in Normandy, according to tradition, every bride brings a clock to her husband as dowry. Downstairs in the hotel cafe she had dozens more clocks, inherited from her two grandmothers, her aunts, her cousins.

Spurling looked anxiously from the door to the window, searching for Verlaine or the young woman who had disappeared with him as mysteriously as a shadow.

Every clock kept a different time.

At noon by the church bell, Verlaine did return, but only for a moment.

He was accompanied by the young woman in the sweater, who stayed tantalizingly just in the outline of the doorway, and by a doctor, a short sad-faced Italian, thinly mustached, who presented himself with comic formality by pulling a photostat of his medical license from his black bag and insisting that Spurling read it aloud. Mirko Caduta, MD. Diplomate de Gynécologie, Université de Paris.

"Gynécologist." He shrugged apologetically.

Verlaine smiled and murmured something too low for Spurling to hear. Beneath the brim of the gray fedora that he seemed to wear indoors and out his face was smooth and slightly ovoid, a beautiful pale horse's face; his eyes so dark that Spurling's first thought was that he wore mascara and powder like an eighteenth-century fop. Before Spurling could speak, he had departed again, with a quick, distracted salute, already looking elsewhere. Groggy, uncertain, Spurling watched the cape and hat fill the doorway and then vanish.

Of course, Caduta told him, rummaging busily in his bag, as a doctor he should have waited until after nightfall to come. Far safer to visit a place like this unseen by anybody. He sat on the edge of the bed and tugged Spurling's trousers and underpants down around his ankles. The young woman reappeared, carrying a tray with hot water and a bar of coarse white soap. The Germans were fanatically strict about curfew, Caduta said, but as a doctor he had special permission to travel at night—doctors and gamekeepers, nobody else! Even so it was risky business. The Milice followed you constantly. The patrols appeared in the road where you least expected them, and they checked every document with Teutonic thoroughness.

Tall and fair-skinned, perhaps thirty, the young woman wore

her hair high in a careless bun, a chignon. Who? Her nose was slightly hooked where the bone must once have been broken, and when she turned to look at the nearest Norman clock her profile had the stillness of a painting.

Spurling's eyes fastened on her, but with scarcely a glance at him, she put the tray down beside the bed and left again, and Spurling was suddenly crying out in pain as Caduta's strong fingers began to knead the swollen flesh behind his knee. The sky was oyster-colored through his tears, his leg was in flames. Still, nothing was broken, Caduta said after a moment, with melancholy satisfaction; except, the triceps ligament in the knee was badly torn, and the hematoma above it was severe. The high fever came from the cut, which was infected now despite their efforts to wash it clean, and would simply have to run its course. The ribs had been massively bruised, but not broken. Compresses, soap and water. Youth was the best healer.

With one fingernail he scraped absently at the swastika embossed on the bar of soap and watched as Spurling struggled to pull up the trousers again. He had no painkillers, Caduta told him with a shake of the head, not even aspirin. The Germans had "requisitioned" everything; he ran his surgery on bandages ripped from sheets and whatever antiseptics he could find or improvise. Herbs, wine—he used red wine sometimes as an antiseptic, warm wine splashed on open wounds, red on red. It was all terrible in the Dordogne now: the shortages of food and clothing, the lack of the simplest things, like leather or coffee—had he drunk the acorn coffee? The Germans rationed only a few gallons of gasoline a week, some to doctors, most to farmers. You could buy more gasoline on the black market, and other things—Swiss watches, amazingly; he had a desk full of Swiss watches that his patients had used to pay him early in the war—he pulled the drawer of the bedside table open as if in demonstration, then rammed it shut.

Spurling listened with dazed inattention. The room revolved slowly around him. The demented clocks ticked unceasingly, snapping like teeth.

"Colonel Verlaine," Spurling said, concentrating hard, frowning to appear older. "Colonel Verlaine is not what I expected, from England. They told us he was a local landowner, a farmer."

"Colonel Verlaine," Caduta said intensely, "is a very great man." He closed his bag and stood up from the bed. "A patriot. The peasants here love him. Except for Colonel Verlaine, the peasants are sick of the Resistance, you know, they can't stand the word. They cower behind their curtains when the maquisards bang on the door—and you can't blame them, can you? The maquisards are thieves, they're magpies, half of them. They only come to demand food or gasoline or money 'in the name of the Resistance.' And whether the peasants give anything to them or not, they know that the Germans—worse yet, the Milice—are only hours away, on their trail. The 'other terrorists'—that's what the peasants call the maquis. But Colonel Verlaine—he protects them, he keeps a grip on the thievery and the blackmail; the peasants know he would give his life for France if he could. They hold back now, but if the Germans ever touched him, simply touched him, you understand, the Dordogne would go up like a match. They don't have enough guns and tanks to stop the people if Colonel Verlaine were harmed."

He had reached the door and pulled it halfway open. Now he closed it again and stood with his hand on the lever, working his mouth.

In France, levers instead of knobs open the doors, Spurling thought. His head was muzzy again with fever.

"Life cracks people open," Caduta said abruptly. "Most people are boxes of bones, you know, shells around nothing. Not heroes like Colonel Verlaine. You're twenty-something. I'm fifty-three years old. I studied at the University of Genoa and the Sorbonne. I used to have a practice in Souillac. When the Germans crossed the Demarcation Line and came to Souillac, they called me out one night, some drunken sergeant pounding on the door."

Spurling sank back on the bed and closed his eyes, too feverish and exhausted to sit up any longer.

"They took me to one of the hotels in town." Caduta's voice went on remorselessly, confessional. He tells everyone this, Spurling thought. Or only me. Where the hell was Brissac? Poole? "They'd caught a young girl, a maquisarde, fifteen years old; I knew her, I knew her mother. I delivered her, for God's sake. They had caught her stealing gasoline—the boys all got away. They called her the 'little terrorist' and they tied her by the wrists and ankles to the bed and raped her. Twenty soldiers. They took turns raping her on the bed all night long, and they wanted me there to hold her pulse while they did it and whenever she fainted to bring her to again."

Spurling strained fiercely to hear, but his mind drifted irresistibly out, on unending ticks, floating on words.

"What was I supposed to do?" Caduta asked loudly. "Did I have a choice? They threatened me with a gun; I have my family. But every day of my life I feel like a traitor." He pulled the door open with a violent bang. "Some wonderful doctor," he said.

When Spurling awoke again it was to a thunderous hammering of fist on wood in the hallway. A hand snapped on an overhead light, and a man he had never seen before was shaking his shoulders to rouse him.

"Milice!" He swung Spurling's legs free of the blanket—a gray head dipping—and yanked at his belt trying to pull him upright. *"L'inspection juif! Pour les circumcisés."* Circumcised men; they check for refugee Jews!

"But Colonel Verlaine—!"

"Viens!"

Outside the door other French voices came closer, shouting. Distant doors opened and slammed. Spurling hobbled after the gray-haired man, dizzy with pain and fever, groping over a carpet, down a narrow stairwell smelling of paint. In a dimly lit corridor that ran the length of the building other men were all on their feet, undoing their trousers or pajama buttons, muttering sleepily. At the far end of the corridor men in French police uniforms were shoving more sleepers into the line. Nearby two Milician officers, monstrously big in black raincoats and helmets, gestured with heavy batons at the stragglers. Brissac emerged from a room in the center, his torso covered by a crude brown sleeping shirt, his legs and genitals completely bare.

"Vite, vite!" The Milice motioned impatiently toward the floor.

Brissac looked at Spurling and moved his hands. All of the men were naked now from the waist down, shivering. "Drop your pants, wag your pricks!"

Spurling swayed and braced his shoulders against a doorjamb. The light overhead seemed to splinter into fragments. Verlaine had disappeared. He lifted his head at new voices. From the far end of the corridor women in housecoats and robes were being herded in to watch—Madame Gabaussau, two places behind her the woman in the sweater. Verlaine was nowhere in the corridor, nowhere to witness whatever the Milice were doing. A figment of his imagination, Spurling thought wildly, Verlaine was exempt from failure. The gray-haired man beside him crossed his hands in pathetic modesty and the nearest policeman snickered.

Reluctantly, disoriented and light-headed still, Spurling lowered his trousers, peering toward Brissac for a sign, seeing instead six feet away the young woman's pale face and Madame Gabaussau's clenched, whisker-lipped mouth. To his left one of the officers grunted and lifted a man's limp penis with his baton and spoke to the sergeant behind him. In nightmarish leisure the sergeant wrote on a clipboard. The officer moved to Brissac and stared at his mutilated fingers before repeating the inspection, prodding the baton into his groin until Brissac, suddenly vulnerable for once, suddenly younger-looking even than Spurling, gasped and sagged and the Frenchman nodded in satisfaction. The sergeant behind him made obscene kissing gestures toward Brissac's penis, then to the watching women, and swung the clipboard down in a mock slice of circumcision.

Spurling fastened his eyes on the wall. His bruised leg was a stump vanishing into shadow. The officer glanced at his face, then down. Spurling felt the cold slickness of the baton slide across his belly, down one thigh. In the bad light of the corridor the officer's face bent close. Over his shoulder, two feet away, he saw the young woman's hooked nose, her eyes hard and unblinking. The officer's scalp ran out from the back of the helmet like an oily rug of black hair. The baton rode erotically across his testicles, probed, lifted. An insane stirring. Spurling gritted his teeth, closed his eyes. The Frenchman's breath ran down his chest like a fire.

"Foutez-moi le camp, salauds! Vous êtes Français ou Sch-leuls?" Get the hell out of here, you bastards! Are you Frenchmen or Germans?

The officer, the sergeant, all of the Milice jerked to shocked attention. Verlaine came striding down the center of the corridor. The soldiers stepped backward rapidly and stared. His broad, angry gestures scattered them to either side of him. His voice was pure, cold, witheringly scornful.

"Frenchmen? Frenchmen who work for Nazis? Get out! Get out!"

They backed farther away. The nearest officer turned to reach for the stairwell door.

"Sortez! Sortez!"

Without warning, Spurling fell to his knees on the carpet. Eyes closed, swaying as if he would topple completely over, in the darkness he heard Verlaine's furious voice cursing traitors.

In the afternoon Brissac and Poole came into his bedroom to see him, Brissac to announce firmly, as if he were now the officer in command, that there was no question of leaving the hotel until the injured leg was healed. Poole stood at the end of the bed, hands in his overcoat pockets, and nodded.

"Hey, don't be in a hurry, Lieutenant," he said; his thin mouth twitched in counterpoint to the clocks. "I already spent the day out in the goddam field. My radio tent out there's got hot and cold running spiders. These crazy maquisards eat more kinds of acorns than a fucking squirrel. Myself, if I thought of it, I would of bailed out over fucking London."

In the evening of the same day Verlaine himself appeared, bringing with him the young woman, whom he introduced by her code name, "Hugo."

"He names us all after the great poets of France," Hugo said wryly. "To edify the Germans."

Verlaine paced from one side of the room to the other, among the clocks, looked down at Spurling, made no reference whatsoever to the scene in the hall the previous night.

He agreed with Brissac, he said simply and firmly, taking a

chair beside the bed. There was no question of going out into the field yet. He could understand it if Spurling were impatient, if he were eager to prove himself. . . . There was nothing to prove, he added kindly.

And as if to forestall Spurling's objections, he leaned to one side of the chair and casually pulled a narrow blue-jacketed volume from the wall of books.

Did Spurling know Auden, the great English poet?

Spurling shook his head, dazed, fascinated.

He ordered his books from Blackwell's store in Oxford, Verlaine said, turning pages; and war or no war, believe it or not, they shipped them to Switzerland, and the busy, neutral Swiss collected their duty and shipped them on to him here.

"Colonel Verlaine himself has published three books of poetry," Hugo told him. She was kneeling by a little potbellied stove in one corner of the room and feeding it balls of rolled-up newspaper. As she stoked it with a long, mossy branch the fire rushed to climb the twigs like blood lighting up veins.

Verlaine modestly waved aside the idea of his own books. In Paris, he said, to everyone's amazement the war seemed to have brought about a renaissance of French culture—there was a young friend of his named Sartre whose plays were being performed in the theaters. There was a Resistance journalist named Camus who wrote wonderful, eloquent essays for the underground papers. Picasso had reached Paris. So had a refugee painter named Max Ernst. With his rare, grave smile he described how a new sculptor named Giacometti had produced wire figures Spurling should see: utterly original but somehow classically timeless, disembodied, tragic; space and volume created precisely by their absence in the wire.

Verlaine's pale hands grasped the edges of the book and while Hugo served them glasses of a sweet-tasting soda drink called Pschitt, he read passages of poetry aloud in a hypnotic rhythm.

After a time Spurling's eyes drooped, his mind clouded.

"In the limestone caves where we store our weapons sometimes," Verlaine was saying, "you find prehistoric paintings on the walls. Thousands of years old. Once in a while, beneath a painting of a buffalo or a deer, there will be rows of vertical lines with a diagonal slash across them, after every ten or twelve marks, as we would mark off the passage of time in a makeshift calendar."

As he talked, Hugo refilled Spurling's glass and drank from her own, her lips partly open, her eyes heavy lidded, as if someone were rubbing her hips and lower back and she were a cat.

"I like to think that the origin of all art is the calendar," Verlaine said. He inhaled smoke from his cigarette. "The great impulse of art is to drive an arrow through time, so that nothing ever changes. Art is the enemy of metamorphosis, is it not?"

And then before Spurling realized it, Verlaine was rising on his feet, putting out the cigarette, promising to return but already looking toward the curtained window, and for an instant Spurling saw himself as he thought he must appear to Verlaine—skittish, incompetent, baby faced. Twenty-two years old, a student to lecture and pacify.

Hugo stayed for a moment longer, blocking the door in an unstudied fashion to let Verlaine pass first. Spurling watched with burning eyes as she walked down the corridor after him.

In the night, half dreaming, he thought of the Group Captain's last whispered words. The plane roared in his ears and rose. Spurling turned, sweating, on the narrow bed. He was always loyal. He worshiped his teachers. He felt his mind circle closer and closer to Verlaine's brilliant, glowing face, as a moth circles close to a candle.

Some wonderful soldier.

14 ▬▬▬▬▬▬▬▬▬▬▬▬

The parachutage from England had been scheduled since three weeks before they'd left London; scheduled, rescheduled, postponed twice, finally set again, by sheer coincidence, for the first day that Spurling left the hotel in Lalinde and joined the maquisards in the field.

"So much for your return to 'action,'" Verlaine said with weary irony as Spurling hurried to catch up with him on the edge of the parachutage meadow. Spurling slowed, trying to match pace for pace in the darkness, secretly wincing at the strain on his bruised leg.

"It's three hours late now, yes?" Verlaine said, still walking. He appeared to be patrolling the circumference of the meadow even in the darkness, weaving in and out of the gasogene trucks the maquisards had parked near the fences.

"Three and a half, in fact." The first sight of the maquisards that afternoon had shocked Spurling—teenaged boys, elderly men, scarecrows in baggy clothes and scraps of military costume. "Naphthalards"—named for the mothball smell of the old army uniforms they had dragged out of storage. There were a few square-jawed men in their thirties who carried hunting rifles and wore mismatched ammunition belts crossed over their vests like banditti.

Ragamuffin soldiers. They talked with a curious, stilted formality that made Spurling's ears ache, as if they were imitating their hero Verlaine.

"The war." Verlaine stopped and appeared to be resting his weight against the fender of one of the gasogene trucks. "The war is nothing but wasted hours, waiting, waiting." He cupped one hand around his watch. "Two o'clock. Two more hours at best, and then—" He gestured toward the sky behind Spurling, still oily black and on fire with stars. In another two hours it would be too light for planes to approach unseen and release their parachutes. In another day, it was obvious, the moon would be too faint for planes to drop at all; they would have to wait three weeks at least, almost to the beginning of July, before London could schedule them again.

Far to Spurling's right, shadows detached themselves from the surrounding blackness and floated across the field, carrying more wood for the signal fires.

"Modern warfare," Verlaine said. "Have you ever noticed, as a Harvard scholar, Lieutenant, the primitive mentality of modern warfare?"

My youth amuses him, Spurling thought. He worked his jaw in frustration.

Verlaine let his cigarette trace a slow, elaborate arc in the air. "Airplanes that fly five hundred miles to bomb a city, radios that cross the oceans—and we still squat in the dark and study the moon and stars like Babylonian astrologers, hoping for a sign."

"I hope for supplies, guns," Spurling said, "to win the war."

"Those fires have gotten way too goddam small!" Brissac materialized out of nowhere, waving his flashlight toward Verlaine.

"No."

There were five signal fires arranged in the clearing, meant to be visible at least twenty miles away by air.

"The pilots will never see them between these bloody cliffs—I've just been up to the top. You need to make bonfires now, *enormous* fires to bring them in."

Spurling listened in amazement, marveling at Brissac's effrontery.

"Never." Verlaine's voice was all iron. Pilots would see them,

German patrols would not. He had chosen the drop point himself. He knew every inch of the Dordogne; he would do nothing to risk reprisals to the farmers.

Brissac planted his feet to block the way and argue, but Verlaine simply walked around him and disappeared into the darkness.

"Bugger the farmers!" Brissac spun angrily toward Spurling. From the cab of a truck Hugo had emerged. On cue, Spurling thought. He watched her hurry through its cat's-eye headlights after Verlaine. Spurling shook off Brissac's arm. Verlaine was the colonel. Spurling was the next in command. A "marriage" was drawn up along lines of power, wasn't it?

"The new Group Captain, yes, Spurling? Somebody new to be loyal to?" Brissac mocked him.

"You follow orders," Spurling said coldly. "To win the war you follow orders."

In the flickering light of the fires he saw Brissac jerk a small square of cardboard out of his jacket, roll it into a tube, then jam a cigarette between his lips. "Take a good look at him, then," he mumbled around the cigarette. "Our leader. The colonel-poet who fights the war in his fedora hat. Look at his pitiful maquisards, incompetent, hopeless."

Spurling moved a step away but watched the faces of Verlaine's men as they ran back and forth around the fires, in and out of shadows, with no more idea of security than the man in the moon.

"Reprisals," Brissac muttered contemptuously. The match caught and he inserted it quickly into the cardboard tube and lowered the tip of the cigarette. "Verlaine pisses down his leg when you say 'reprisal'—what does he think the war is? A bloody poem? 'Civilians safe at all costs.'" He mocked Verlaine's sonorous voice and Spurling grimaced in indignation. "'Military targets only—never, never anger the Boches for fear they'll shoot a farmer.'"

It was Brissac's obsessive refrain, from the moment he and Poole had left Lalinde on their own, without Spurling, and begun to organize the outlying maquis: Verlaine's unshakable policy of protecting civilians from German reprisals, his agonizing caution in choosing targets for sabotage. "Jean d'Arc," Brissac sneered. He was rumored already to have become an "executioner" for the Resistance, Madame Gabaussau had whispered to Spurling: "He kills traitors, he assassinates collaborators." No trials, no judges or jury. He was quick, cruel, deadly, not merciful like Colonel Verlaine. But it takes both kinds to win a war, she had also whispered.

"The flashlight!"

Beyond the fires, on higher ground, where the black silhouettes of the limestone cliffs stood just over the tops of the trees, there were suddenly voices and the sounds of feet stamping into the mud.

"Listen!" Verlaine was approaching from another direction. One hand appeared suspended and disembodied in the darkness, illuminated by a sweeping flashlight, palm out for attention. Across the meadow, like a dog's low growl, they heard the sound of engines.

"Signal! Signal!"

A shadow ran past them whooping and a moment later they saw the rapid flashes of the signal light from midpoint between the bonfires, blinking out Morse for the RAF pilot. Around it other shadows swirled and circled, heaping wood on the fires so rapidly that they blazed up, skyward, like jets of gas, and the shadows became silhouettes in a pagan dance. Closer, men were running in a frenzy of pointless action, shouting at the top of their voices.

"Mon colonel!"

"Les avions!"

"Encore de bois! Encore de lumière!"

Across the western sky now, the outlines of wings and a sluglike fuselage were coming into focus. Thin clouds drifted purposefully away from the moon. Nearby, the man with the signal flashlight turned to shout and lowered the beam until it raked across Spurling's eyes. Twenty voices rose in protest and the flashlight soared again. The engines now filled the forest, the meadow. Spurling and Brissac were racing toward the center of the field when the first Lancaster rode over them, five hundred feet above the treetops, its wings and body making the shadow of a giant bird in the faint moonlight, its engines booming over the clamor of the men. In every direction Spurling heard cries of encouragement, incoherent instructions; beside him someone was leaping off the ground in delight. But in an instant the giant shadow had passed and the shouts turned to groans of dismay. Under the black canopy of sky there were no parachutes, no other planes, only the burning stars, looping whorls of clouds, the small white face of the moon, smiling.

"*Mon colonel!*"

"*Pas de parachutage!*"

"*Vraiment Américains?*"

"*Bois! Encore de lumière!*"

But the Lancaster was simply obeying general directives: a first pass to check for the blinking code light, to test for wind and perimeters. As it cleared the meadow and began to bank northward over the cliffs Spurling picked up the sound of other engines and, straining, saw two more great shadows moving across the murky western sky. In a minute more the first plane had returned, louder, lower than before, and its bomb bays were spilling dark spinning circles of parachutes and supply boxes that swayed and drifted in the breeze and hung above their heads, tantalizing and flirtatious, while all below them men rushed about with their arms spread open as if to embrace.

Within moments the second and third bombers had passed over, the sky had metamorphosed into a field of falling flowers, and Verlaine's men were rushing from parachute to parachute, cheering like schoolboys when one landed in the clear, or groaning and shouting orders when others snagged in a tree or blew past the fires and meadow altogether. Then the motors of trucks and cars were turning over, making the ghostly hiss and rattle of the gasogene attachments, and men and bundles were converging on the trucks. In twenty minutes the field was deserted, the signal fires kicked over and smothered with mud, the parachutes and riggings cut away from their canisters and everything headed toward their farmhouse rendezvous miles away.

Verlaine made them count off in the dark, Spurling noticed, so that no one would be left behind, something he himself would never have thought of doing. And in the farmhouse, while the exuberant maquisards celebrated with bottles of wine and loud toasts to the Americans and British, Verlaine paced up and down between the canisters, supervising the removal of the layers of sorbo rubber the packers used for cushioning. Over Brissac's protest he insisted that every canister be opened in front of him personally, to prevent theft, he said coldly, and he watched with arms folded as men strolled gaily among the bundles, laughing, passing out the cigarettes and chocolate that the RAF stuffed alongside the rifles.

Toward the end, when the gray clouds had turned dark against the new background of pearl, Spurling found himself slumped on the floor of the living room, yawning, as Verlaine still worked tirelessly among the canisters. Sleep rose in a slow tide. Spurling's leg throbbed with old pain. In a far corner a fat boy, no older than four-teen or fifteen, lay curled in a spongy ball, half covered with para-chute rigging. Spurling glanced around the room, appalled. Verlaine was a great man. But Brissac was right. They were going to war with drunken teenagers and old-age pensioners. In the morning they would learn how to fire machine guns at trees and squirrels. From another room he heard murmurs of adult voices, smelled food cook-ing. His eyes closed, opened.

"Tomorrow morning," Verlaine was saying, bending over him. "Tomorrow morning you go with Hugo into the hills to bring back the German ammunition we stored in the caves."

His last memory was of Hugo wrapping the bright red and green silk of a parachute around her waist and dancing across a row of canisters toward Verlaine, one bare leg flashing, naked from hip to toe.

15 ▰▰▰▰▰▰▰▰▰

A psychic phenomenon: he was conscious now of Verlaine's physical position no matter how far away, his slightest motion, as if they were opposite poles of one magnet, two sides of one coin. On a map the next morning Verlaine was not quite five miles to the south, still in the farmhouse where they had slept. Spurling was on a straight line above him, on a narrow stone path halfway up the side of a limestone cliff.

Ahead, Hugo slowed and pointed out the Vézère River some two hundred dizzying feet below, running through a valley of trees and new green grass. It had rained briefly in the late morning, and now over the river sunlight fell on wet branches and broke apart in bright showers of coins.

"Le pays des préhistoriques," she told him cheerfully—the land of prehistoric men.

Spurling grunted in acknowledgment and shifted his knapsack. This was cave country, he knew from their briefings in England. The shaggy limestone cliffs were supposed to be riddled with undiscovered caves. Ten thousand years ago Cro-Magnon men, in bands of hunters and shamans, had lived in them and worked up and down these same paths, or hurried unseen across the floor of the forest. Hugo smiled and resumed the climb.

Before they reached the cave it was midafternoon and rain had started to fall again. For the last hundred yards they scrambled inches at a time along a muddy ledge over the river, clutching at slick roots and stones to keep their feet, pawing at the wind and the chalky limestone. Twice as long a trip as she had told him, Spurling thought with sudden anger. A boy's errand. Donkey work. His anger amazed him; he had no idea where it came from. Emotions seemed to spring up and rage through him now with the speed of a fire through a forest. He clenched his teeth against the dull pain in his leg and watched her brown sweater disappear around a curve in the trail.

When he stepped around the curve himself, she was gone—he stood straight in disbelief and sudden panic, and then she appeared again, grinning, a face growing out of the wet stone, holding back a long green mustache of hawthorn bush.

"La grande moule," she said mischievously as he reached the bush and crawled through the space she held open, and Spurling's jaw dropped and he turned to stare. "The maquisards call it the grand cunt," she said, translating. Then she brushed by him into the cave, leaving her smell of damp hair, soap.

Head lowered, blushing, he began to follow.

Not more than twenty feet from the entrance all light vanished and the air had turned icy cold. Flashlights looped into their knapsacks, they groped forward on hands and knees until they reached a low-domed chamber of rock, not quite high enough at any point for either of them to straighten and stand. The slick walls of the cave moved in their lights like a gigantic maw, ready to swallow them whole. When he stretched out one hand to touch the walls Spurling felt a rubbery dark moss, cold trickles, and patches of moisture. Membrane turning to stone.

"Tout au fond," Hugo ordered. All the way in.

Her voice came from behind her flashlight, deeper in the chamber, and she ran a quick finger of light up and down one wall to show where the cave shrank again to a slit.

Then her light dipped and vanished, evidently down a path, and Spurling stopped for a moment, lost. His mind floated in an eggshell of utter darkness. At his feet his flashlight beam curled sinuously over irregular stones and surfaces like a luminous snake. A limestone gullet, a frozen throat. There were noises everywhere, plumbing noises, he thought, like the noises that must go on in the center of your body, tiny metallic plinks of water striking stone, wearing away stone, building up rounded ulcerous accretions.

Her light reappeared, much farther away than he would have guessed. He saw the curve of her cheek and stumbled after her.

"Les peintures faites par l'homme préhistorique," she said when he finally caught up, another fifty yards down into the blackness. She was kneeling on a pillow of frigid earth, in front of what seemed to be a narrow trench. Nearby, or miles away—he had lost all sense of distance, he was cut loose in outer space—an unseen trickle of water made a slow, measured clicking sound, like a sleeping clock. At the end of Hugo's flashlight beam, in a perfect circle of light, marched a series of rounded and sticklike figures on the stone—the paintings Verlaine had described in Lalinde: brown and yellow buffalo and deer outlined over the contours of the rock, a red arrow in flight, black dots and criss-cross patterns like numbers—calendars becoming art.

The limestone cliffs were indeed full of caves, she told him as he knelt beside her, and the caves were full of prehistoric paintings. Nobody knew how many. As a girl she had spent summer vacations in the valley with her grandmother, and all of the children had been instructed by the famous Abbé Breuil, who traveled back and forth over Périgord in search of caves and also bones, tools, pieces of carved rock—he rewarded the children for finding them and sometimes set up miniature excavation sites, just as he had done near Cro-Magnon in Les Eyzies; demonstrating, she let a handful of white grit sift between her fingers to the floor of the cave, as if she were prospecting for gold.

"Now look down there."

She lowered her light to the corner, where the prehistoric artist had used a bulge in the rock to make a three-dimensional stomach for a deer.

"And below it, there."

Spurling followed the light as it traveled six inches farther downward to the outline of a human hand, fingers spread open, set within a black semicircle on a flat area of the wall. She stretched out her own fingers to match the outline of the hand, an inch above the rock.

"He made it by holding up his hand just like that and blowing black paint through a hollow bone," Hugo said out of the darkness, close to his ear. "He probably used a bird's leg, like a straw. The Abbé called it his signature." Slowly Spurling placed his hand just above hers, not touching. "You see his finger," Hugo said and lifted the light to show how the middle finger of the painted hand was cut off at the first joint. Spurling squinted to be sure that the missing finger had been deliberately painted this way, not lost in a break or discoloration of the rock.

"Mutilated," Hugo said. "He cut off the tip of one finger."

"But why?"

In the chilly darkness he heard the rustle of clothing. She had shrugged. "A ritual to become a painter?" He was conscious again of her hair, the illicit feminine odors clinging to her sweater and skin. She moved again. "The Abbé Breuil said that to paint animals was a magic act—you did it to bring animals for the tribe to hunt—you sacrificed yourself for the tribe."

Furiously, inexplicably, his anger rolled back and he sat up straight in the dark, as if to distance himself from her. She meant Verlaine, of course, Verlaine sacrificing himself for the tribe. Whatever she said or did, it all flowed back to Verlaine. Wherever he stood to see Verlaine, she was there first, interposed, opaque.

"De la cravate," he said coarsely—bullshit. He bent his thumb and forefingers back until his shadow cruelly resembled Brissac's mutilated hand, hovering above the whole painting. *"L'homme pré-historique* was only a German."

The boxes of German ammunition had been stored just past the paintings, in rows of wooden crates topped with more rows of moldy knapsacks that looked as if they had come from the first Great War rather than the second. Spurling sorted out hundreds of the .303 shells that fit their new Bren guns, and together he and Hugo stuffed them to the bursting point in their own knapsacks, then draped heavy canvas bandoliers with more bullets across their chests.

By the time they reached the front of the cave again, rain was blowing in cold, hard sheets from the west and the pale sun had vanished. Hugo led in the opposite direction, a shortcut over the cliffs, she said, and across a ridge to a second little wooded valley. But halfway down the new path, they dragged to a halt. The knapsacks were soaked and twice as heavy as before, and the ammunition becoming dangerously sodden. They waited indecisively beneath an overhang, shifting the straps on their shoulders and checking their watches, squatting in mud and watching the rain come down harder and blacker than ever. From the silent cliffs rising skull-like in front of them, Spurling had the sensation of eyes turning toward him, watching.

Just before seven, long after they should have returned to the farmhouse, Hugo called out something indistinct and led him at a splashing trot through the trees until they reached the gnarly base of a hill. There she suddenly stopped and dug with both hands puppy-fashion at a screen of woven ferns. When the cave entrance finally appeared two minutes later, she stepped back and used her flashlight to wave Spurling swiftly in.

"Voilà!" Playing the flashlight beam on the walls: "Welcome to Hugo's house."

Pink-gray stalactites rippled in and out of the light as she moved around him, outlines of crates, rocks, unexplained angles and colors. "My own retreat, my bolt hole," she added. "I've known this cave since I was a girl. I hunted stone carvings in it for the Abbé Breuil. Once I turned up bits of a painted bowl that he said must have been here for two thousand years. Two thousand years! After I left Sarlat and joined Verlaine's camp, the first thing I did was hike out on my own till I found it again."

He shivered and flapped his arms against his sides and followed her voice as it moved closer and then farther away.

"No point trying to get back now in the dark and ruining the ammunition," she said from somewhere unexpected, and he turned to see her hand, ghostly at the end of the light, extending the corner of a blanket toward him. "Better change your clothes. You'll freeze to death." Gone again. "These caves are colder than ice."

Slowly, carefully he took off the knapsack and bandoliers and sat down on hard mud. In some new time warp of anger he saw himself bent over his desk at Harvard, dreaming of women. He saw himself at the airfield near Milton Hall before they took off, where a ground crew was hosing the body of a gunner from the turret of a B-17. You see somebody hit by flak in a turret, the pilots had told him, what you see is a young man blown apart like a can of paint.

"And you need a bedroll too," Hugo said, returning. "The walls in here are like rivers sometimes after it rains."

Abruptly he wished she would shut up. Would disappear. Would vanish and leave him. His hands trembled. Verlaine's long face was everywhere in the shadows. He couldn't keep track of where she was. He shoved his hands under his sore legs, yogalike, on the blanket and watched as her flashlight bobbed busily from place to place in the darkness, rising and falling in a lightless ocean.

A housekeeping voice: "Everything's filthy," she grumbled. He heard the thump of boxes, the crinkle of clothing. Her tone was absorbed, infuriating. The flashlight beam, drifting apparently at random, caught him full in the face, revealing his wet hair and shirt, the mud streaked and caked on his collar.

"Freeze if you want to," she said. As the light dropped away he glimpsed her shoulder, white and sloping, and the fringed edge of a blanket.

"Lantern," Hugo said and set down between them a rusty kerosene lantern, which she lit with a long wooden match. *"Et du vin."* The lantern glinted off a bottle of red wine. She worked out the cork with the filleting blade of a fisherman's knife. Then she poured into two thick glass tumblers that she had wiped with a cloth and placed on the ground.

"I stocked it with food too, tins of meat somewhere." She looked doubtfully into the darkness.

"I'm not hungry."

She nodded and continued to arrange unseen bundles, so that when she finally stopped they were sitting on bedrolls facing each other, separated by the bottle of wine and the kerosene lantern and surrounded by lumpy shadows, and each of them had a blanket draped from head to shoulders like a hood, and another blanket wrapped loosely across their bodies. Around them, just above the flickering corona of the lantern, the darkness of the cave seemed to go on forever, and inside it from every direction they heard only the steady dripping and clicking of water.

"We look like two monks," she said with a laugh, "preparing for a black mass." She drank her wine and glanced to her left, toward the rear of the cave, making her profile look for an instant just as it had when he first saw her bending over his bed in Madame Gabaussau's room: the slightly hooked nose, with its suggestion of distance, intelligence; the high cheekbones, heavy-lidded eyes.

"There are paintings in this cave too," she said. "Small ones of buffalo and deer." Then she bent her head forward and touched his knuckles with her glass. "Spur-ling," she said, giving both syllables equal stress in the French manner.

"This was all planned," he said abruptly. "You two wanted to keep me out from under Verlaine's feet and let him work, yes? Keep the boy out from under the great man's feet?"

Hugo shrugged and finished her wine. Discomfited, uncertain, he picked up his own tumbler and gulped, the raw oily taste of new Bergerac that he would forever associate with his youth.

"Brissac thinks that after the Allies invade, Verlaine will have to turn the maquisards loose," he said after a long, uncomfortable pause. It was Brissac's other obsession—what they would do at the moment the long-awaited invasion began. It could come any day, any week, Brissac insisted over and over to anyone who would listen. If it came in the north, the huge Das Reich armored division near Montauban would have to cross the Dordogne River somewhere, going to meet it. And then the whole valley should erupt to stop them—*if we have to throw our bodies in front of the fucking tanks,* Brissac would cry, raising his fists. *Foutre:* to fuck. *If every fucking peasant in the Dordogne pays in reprisals,* Brissac said. The first thing to save, Verlaine always replied, was France, not the army.

"'There is no liberation in becoming tyrants ourselves.'" Hugo quoted Verlaine. Spurling watched her pour herself more wine. The whole camp had seen her emerge from Verlaine's room in the farmhouse. After she had bathed under a makeshift shower beyond the trucks, Verlaine had come to her carrying clean clothing and smiling like a young husband, and they had walked back arm in arm, the fresh blouse still clinging in damp spots to her body.

"Verlaine is the greatest man I've ever known," she said. The blanket hood had slipped from her bun of hair and the glow of the lantern caught her eyes: brilliant white eyes, glowing; in the black shell of the cave they seemed to be lit from within.

"And you're twenty years old and you'd gobble him up if you could," she went on after a moment. "You know that you're two of a kind, you and Verlaine. Word-crazy little boys. In another life you two—" She stopped and wagged her empty glass back and forth in her hand. "Verlaine says we hate change. Do you remember that? He also says, 'The one unbearable fact is that death has absolutely nothing to do with life.'"

She poured herself new wine, splashing it onto the black ground. "Do you think Verlaine really expects to survive the war?" she asked. "Martyred for France would be better, no? Like Jean Moulin? *Mieux la mort que de beurre au cul.* Better dead than butter up your ass." Spurling thought she might be drunk. Her eyes were white points of fire.

"Verlaine and his metamorphoses," she said. "I hate what the war has made me." She drank the wine in one swallow and bent to poke under the bedroll. "*Merde.* No cigarettes." When she straightened, the blanket fell partly away from her chest, and Spurling saw one heavy breast and a dark crescent of areola before she closed the blanket again with one hand.

"After the war," Spurling began.

"'After the war,'" she interrupted. "Nobody can imagine after-the-war, least of all word-crazy boys."

She took his left hand and slowly balled it into a fist.

"Something has made you so angry," she said softly, in a different voice altogether. "Some secret." She brought his fist to the point of her chin and held it there. "In war anger protects us. In war it keeps us alive."

The war filled his mind like an explosion. When he reached toward her, he had never held anyone so hard. His hands gripped her shoulders until she cried out, falling away, and his body came out of the blankets as if he were riding the crest of a wave. Her mouth opened to him, her tongue drove in and out like a snake. If he touched the tips of her breasts, they were blunt and hard, like bullets. If he took his eyes from her skin, the two of them were dropping through blackness, bodies flung into the sky.

The lantern clattered away, sending the black shadows reeling. Her hands pulled him into her, while her legs came around him, thrust, and locked.

The second time she lay on her back, and his hands rose from knee to pubis, back and up, again and again, so that her thighs parted, spilling honey. As he entered her she arched in slow motion, turning her face to one side toward the overturned lantern and the shapeless black walls of the cave. For a split second only, before he cried out in triumph, he wondered who sacrificed what for the tribe.

When they returned to the farmhouse at dawn, no one paid the slightest attention to them.

It was June 6, 1944, and hundreds of maquisards had flowed out of the forests to gather around a radio tuned to full volume and set on a stump in a clearing. Over and over, the farmhouse and the clearing shook to the sounds of "La Marseillaise," "God Save the King," and "The Star-Spangled Banner." Jubilant French voices cheered each new announcement of the invasion, each new call to arms.

From the edge of the clearing, stunned, Spurling watched Verlaine mount to the back of an elephant-hipped gasogene truck, spread his arms wide, and begin to speak to the crowd, passionately, eloquently, his long face glowing.

At Spurling's side a fierce hand gripped one elbow.

"He's not your bloody father!" Brissac hissed.

PART 3

Washington and
Boston, December 1982

STEFAN ANDERS

16 ━━━━━━━━━━━━━

The man behind the desk swiveled to glance out the window and cursed when he saw that it had begun to snow lightly. Every cliché about Washington was true, but those about Washington drivers and snow were truest of all. It would take him at least two hours tonight to cross Memorial Bridge into Arlington.

At the first high-pitched murmur he swiveled back, completely alert, and automatically checked his watch. He hated the new telephones that chirped instead of ringing, but otherwise he loved electronic gadgets. In this office, in addition to the inevitable personal computer to one side, there were three separate miniature control panels lined up across the front of the desk, each equipped with a telephone receiver of its own. He reached for the middle telephone and kept his eyes fixed on a palm-sized LED clipped to the base of the panel, which flashed red digits on and off while an automatic listening detector continuously swept the line.

"You keep track of the fucking weapons yourself," he said after a moment. "Wait till you're alone to take them out of the courier bag. Those came straight from the kid in West Berlin—right, the terrorist who wet his pants—and the last thing we want is some son of a bitch from the *Post* coming in here three weeks later and saying *our* kid bought it at the White House commissary. . . . Of course it's not normal channels. That's the point."

He looked up at the falling snow again, framed by thick blue window curtains. With the cases of green and brown legal reference books floor to ceiling on the left, the wall maps and dark leather chairs, the muffled teleprinter in the corner, to the casual observer the effect was that of a slightly old-fashioned stockbroker's office, a place where someone behind the desk might still hold a phone to each ear and bark buy and sell orders into alternate mouthpieces like a man in a cartoon.

"I know it would be better to do it while he's still in Europe. It would be better if fucking Brezhnev did it himself on the six o'clock news. You got anybody in place in Paris? No. Warsaw? No. So you work with what you can."

He grimaced in annoyance at the lighted button on the first telephone, which meant his secretary was now holding more than one call.

"Two complications you're not allowed," he said impatiently. "Choose one. . . . All right. All right. No names. No names even on this line. . . . What is he, a regular cop? What kind of regular cop? Where from? . . . So find out what the disability is. . . . I would much fucking rather not take out a cop, but you're the one who's going to be on the spot and have to decide. I don't want to know a thing about him."

He swiveled again and looked up at the huge custom-made map of western Europe on the wall, NATO countries bordered in blue, Warsaw Pact in red. When he swiveled back, buttons on all three telephone panels had begun to blink angrily on and off.

"That's right," he said with satisfaction. "If we do it right, the Russians won't have any choice at all, will they?"

17 ━━━━━━━━━━━━━━━

"I would find the punk kid first," Fahey said, "just like Vico told you." He planted himself in the graveled parking lot of the Blue Grill and flipped his cigarette butt at the sidewalk ten feet away, a big Falstaffian man in his early sixties, even wider and heavier than Gilman, with whorls of fine white hair and huge buttery jowls that hung like saddlebags from his jaw. Fatter than King Farouk, Vico had said; you can't find Fahey in the Blue Grill, forget about finding your whatsis.

"You thought of it yourself, Gilman. There's no percentage looking for anybody else but the kid. What's the big problem? You're a cop."

"The name and address are the big problem, just to start," Gilman said sardonically, looking up Dorchester Avenue toward the broken teeth of the downtown skyline. He adjusted the knob in his right ear until it squawked like a finger rubbing a balloon. How the hell could you find anybody in Boston? It was nothing but a scramble of run-down, hung-over, convoluted streets laid out by wandering cows in the seventeenth century. "I already spent a little time on looking for the kid. He's not in the phone book, and Vico called his friend at New England Telephone for me. There's no Turelli listed or unlisted in the Boston area except a pet store over in Chelsea."

"You got the arrest sheet," Fahey said impatiently. "You can't find him in the phone company, you go back to the files in juvenile court. When was he busted? Three years ago? You look on the sheet for the parents, the next of kin, whatever."

"I saw the sheet this morning," Gilman said. "Next of kin is a law firm on State Street that hung up politely when we got to that question."

"The arresting cops should remember. They all keep a note-book for the courts."

"Yeah," Gilman said. "This one was a solo arrest, and the guy resigned from Boston six months ago to join the army. I called his house—he's en route to Wiesbaden, West Germany, for the next two weeks."

"Anybody arrested with him?"

"No, just Turelli by himself one evening down on Essex Street, trying to sell a jar of crank and carrying an unloaded Army Colt."

"A rookie narc," Fahey said in disgust and opened the door of his car, a late-model Buick that looked small beside him. "Who the hell bothers with one punk crankhead these days? Half the high school kids in Boston put it in their Slurpees for lunch." He scowled at the wooden cane in his hand and threw it across the driver's seat of the Buick as if he were throwing it away for good.

"So I figure I'm down to the kid's probation officer," Gilman said, and for the first time Fahey let a pained smile break through his crust. Archie Bunker and the Meathead.

"They teach police work in California after all," he said and pantomimed applause with his pale fat hands. "But lemme tell you something—go see him in person; don't try to get him on the phone. You try now, he'll be out seeing cases or he'll be in a dugout some-where in the South End drinking beer and feeling overworked and sorry for himself. The commonwealth assigns a minimum four hun-dred cases a PO now. You do that, I tell you what. I'll check some hotels for you this afternoon. A lawyer's wife with a lot of credit cards is going to be in one of the good ones, right? Not the Bradford or some other dump. In Boston that leaves you probably a dozen, maybe six or seven more in the suburbs, the Sonesta over in Cambridge."

Gilman began to thank him and Fahey waved a dismissive hand. "You don't know the house dicks in any of the good hotels," he said. "And walk in, you're a wired-up looking cop from out of town in a mousehair suit he looks like he slept in?" Fahey shook his head. "Sexy picture of the lady or not, they wouldn't let you read the meters." He eased his bulk into the car, sagging the springs.

"You wanna know what I think?" he asked. He started the engine and bumped the car into reverse. "She's smart enough, she's gonna waste two or three days farting around Boston being miserable, then she's gonna hire some slimeball private jamoke to find the kid for her. And this town is lousy with PIs—ex-cops, ex-lawyers, ex-dogcatchers. I got my own list from when I ran missing persons. You can use that if the probation guy flops. But don't expect too much, Gilman. I can just barely fit you in my schedule, now I'm disabled and retired. If the Polacks don't send us all to war, I got to walk my Jack Russell dog twice a day, I got to watch *Wheel of Fortune* at noon with the old lady. Call me early tonight, before I pass out from excitement."

He backed ten feet and pulled away with a wave and a spurt of gravel. The left rear bumper had a sticker with a picture of a black and white dog and a kennel club logo. A second sticker on the right side said "Gun Control Is A Steady Hand."

Across the street another heavy American car, a Mercury Grand Marquis with a hood the size of a flight deck, sat parked by a bent meter. On his way to his own car Gilman reflexively glanced down at the two men sitting in it. The driver lit a cigarette, his face hidden in shadow. His passenger twisted in his seat and glowered. Welcome to Boston. Gilman remembered he was hungry and turned back toward the Blue Grill with an involuntary shiver.

18 ▬▬▬▬▬▬▬▬

"Stefan Anders to Speak at Harvard"

Gilman crumpled the newspaper and shoved it onto the right-hand seat of the car, along with the hamburger wrappings, the cup of watery cola, the french fries that tasted like shirtboard. The Mercury was gone when he came back from the grill with the food. To hell with Stefan Anders. He couldn't even remember buying the paper, let alone reading yet another story about Cassie's hero. He started the car with a hard turn of the key and let the protesting engine idle for a moment. Say he was jealous of her heroes. Say he felt her political passion was an unfair criticism. Was that enough to drive him out of the house and straight after Nina? He grimaced in annoyance. Who was he doing this for—Nina? Donald Kerwin? Himself? The crumpled newspaper slowly unfolded and he saw the headline of the second lead story emerge: "New Man Held in Plot to Assassinate Pope; Mehmet Agca Linked to Bulgarian Killer." The world now was one big assassination junkie, Cassie said; score another point for Cassie.

He jammed the car into gear. The tinnitus in his ears whistled and gained a notch in volume. Squeezing his eyes shut, he forced his mind to concentrate on police work. When he had called the Suffolk

County courthouse from the Blue Grill, the probation officer had been out in the field on cases, just as Fahey had predicted, but he lived only ten miles away in Medford according to the phone book, and everybody, even Gilman, had to come home sooner or later.

He took the Fitzgerald Expressway up the eastern edge of the city, where the North End juts like a stubborn chin into Boston harbor. On the other side of the Charles River he found the Bunker Hill exit and peeled away from the bumper-to-bumper rush-hour traffic, winding through Charlestown toward the Mystic River. He could find the neighborhood from memory. His father was a colonial history buff and weekend after weekend used to drag the family off on historic walks or drives—Cambridge, Lexington, Paul Revere's house, the goddam Freedom Trail. Gilman hated them all. Medford, he remembered, had been briefly famous in the seventeenth century for shipbuilding and rum. Afterward it had blended indistinguishably into the other industrial towns on the north side of the river—Medford, Somerville, Everett: bleak gray suburbs that circled Boston like a dirty collar. Geography was destiny, Donald Kerwin had liked to say.

At Mystic Avenue he turned north and plunged into a maze of brown and green wooden tenement houses that he had long ago learned to call "triple deckers," like a Dagwood sandwich. His father had lived in one, he claimed, just after law school, and he had driven the three of them from Brookline on a Sunday afternoon to take a nostalgic look. Gilman had been six years old, and he remembered the leather smell of the car's upholstery, his mother's hat with colored feathers, and his father's voice rising in anger at his mother.

For all he knew, Benjamin C. Ferraro lived in the same place. Gilman parked half a block away, in front of a brightly lit Dunkin' Donuts shop, and walked up the inside staircase to the third floor.

Mrs. Ferraro was too quick to open the door for him, and too obviously disappointed that he wasn't her husband. But she remembered that he had called, and after he insisted on showing her his badge and ID card she was happy to lead him into the front room and bring a cup of instant coffee.

"He works so late," she said, sitting down on the chair opposite him and brushing hair away from her eyes with a girlish gesture that made Gilman feel avuncular and old. "And there's nobody here all day except this deaf widow down on the first floor and the two cats." She smiled and pointed toward two fat marmalade-colored tabbies lying warily under another chair.

"Not for long, I guess," Gilman said kindly, and she blushed and smiled even more broadly than before. She was no more than twenty-two or twenty-three, had brown, shiny hair and a thick Massachusetts accent, and she was obviously in the last few months of pregnancy.

"January," she said, still smiling. "I'm so scared." But she didn't look scared to Gilman; she looked absolutely radiant, as if she could light up Medford with her happiness, and when her husband still hadn't arrived by seven-thirty, she looked as crushed and fragile as she had looked serene an hour ago. She brought Gilman two more cups of coffee, till he held up his hands and swore he couldn't drink another drop; then she slid pots and pans around in the tiny kitchen and worried about the traffic and the latest Tylenol scare and the rough neighborhood and told him that Benjamin was very idealistic, and after he had graduated from Suffolk University five years ago he'd gone straight to work as a probation officer for the Massachusetts Corrections Bureau and had been promoted three times in the last two years. When the baby came, she said shyly, patting the arrow on her sweatshirt that said "Baby Under Construction," they would try to move farther away, to Winchester or Stoneham, near her parents, so they could have a lawn and a dog. She made a polite, unseeing face when Gilman answered her question brusquely, no, he didn't have any children himself.

Ferraro appeared at ten minutes to eight, out of breath from running up the stairs, and he hardly glanced at his pregnant wife before he saw Gilman rising from the couch and snapped angrily, "Who the hell are you?"

He was late because of work, he said, by way of apology to them both. He had been driving around Roxbury since three, looking for a black kid who was out on probation for three counts of armed robbery, and the kid's mother kept promising he would be back every fifteen minutes until Ferraro had finally served a violation and left in disgust.

And now he was so far behind, he said, blowing his nose on a wad of Kleenex, he had to go out again that night and finish his cases. His wife groaned and bit her lip, and then went into the kitchen for the dinner she had been warming since five-thirty. Ferraro prowled around the room, touching knickknacks on counters and tables, straightening a pile of magazines in a woven basket. He sat down at one end of the bright maple dining table and settled his scowl on Gilman.

"It's a zoo out there," he said too loudly. "I got a paycheck to earn, for chrissake."

"You got maybe half an hour to talk with me?" Gilman asked. "Tonight before you go? Tomorrow morning?"

"You wanted what?"

Gilman began to explain and pulled out his picture of Victor Turelli to show him, but Ferraro was already waving him off with one hand and saying through a mouthful of salad that it was impossible. "That's confidential information, Mister Gilman—it's against the law."

"I'm only asking for an address. He's not in the phone book. The police records just show a lawyer who won't talk to me. The man was accused of shooting my brother-in-law back—"

"*And* released, no charges. I got all the paper on that. Listen, Mister Gilman, I don't know what you people do in California, but in the Commonwealth of Massachusetts there is a law that prohibits release of information on probationers except to another government agency that makes a request *in writing*. Am I clear?"

Gilman pushed the coffee cup back and forth on the coaster Ferraro's wife had gotten for it, a square slice of cardboard with a color photograph of the State House, where the laws were made. He shoved Turelli's picture back in his pocket and stood up. The last time he had been in Boston, he thought of saying, they were about to let the whole membership of the Massachusetts Assembly appear on *The Price Is Right,* but he looked past Ferraro's red, unhappy face and saw his wife's face peering around the corner from the kitchen, and he picked up his raincoat and walked.

When Ferraro came out fifteen minutes later, Gilman was still sitting in his rented car opposite the Dunkin' Donuts. Ferraro hurried past, shoulders hunched, and climbed into a green Plymouth Reliant three places farther up, then hit the horn twice and leaned over to push the curbside door open.

In the Dunkin' Donuts a woman in a tan loden coat stood up from the counter, said something to the waitress, and headed for Ferraro's car. If she hadn't dropped her purse at the curb, Ferraro might never have looked to the rear. But she lost her shoulder bag as she stooped to get in, and while she fumbled for whatever had spilled, Ferraro swung his own door impatiently open and strode around the back of the Plymouth, and that was the moment he saw Gilman, hands folded across the steering wheel, staring straight ahead.

In the harsh fluorescent light from the donut shop Ferraro looked older than he had upstairs. His skin was pale and drained gray like all the other skin in Boston, prison pallor, and his eyes were recessed black smudges that looked like tar spots rising out of sand. Bankable sunshine, Gilman thought: one of Donald Kerwin's favorite phrases for the lure of California.

Ferraro had a choice then: he could have driven off without acknowledging Gilman or without giving a damn whether he was seen or not; but he was really very young, Gilman realized, watching him turn first to the woman, then to him, then back to the woman again, and finally start to walk up the sidewalk. And very guilty. You don't leave your pregnant, pretty wife upstairs alone while you ride off with another lady. It's the law.

"Are you trying to make trouble?" Ferraro got in on the passenger side and slammed the door, but his heart wasn't in it and his face up close was trembling and close to tears.

Gilman rolled his shoulders back against his door as if he were scratching his back. "Just watching the passing parade," he said. The whine in his ears grew louder moment by moment. "The men and women of Boston."

"I know what you're thinking," Ferraro said. "You're thinking I must be a shit leaving Dianne up there—" He hesitated and swallowed. Ahead of them the woman in the loden coat had turned their way for a moment—wide hipped, broad shouldered, a mouth like a dot of blood—then stepped into the car. "And going back out to work," he finished weakly.

"What are you, Ben, twenty-four, twenty-five?"

"Twenty-six."

Beginner's luck. Gilman thought of Cassie and Cassie's doll-house. He sat still, saying nothing, and let his face go hard.

Ferraro squirmed on the seat. Bony fingers worked the door handle up and down. "You're not going to start something with Dianne? She wouldn't believe you anyway."

"I'm just looking for Victor Turelli."

Ferraro pulled a cigarette from his shirt pocket and stuck it in one corner of his mouth. "I'm not supposed to smoke in the house," he muttered. "Bad for the baby, she says." He lit the cigarette with a paper match from a book and rolled down the window a few inches to blow smoke out. A polite boy, Gilman thought. A father-to-be. With a rabbit chin and shaking hands and a conscience bleeding all over his marriage. "Victor Turelli lives with his mother," he said, "out in Framingham. She's got a different last name; that's why you can't find him. She's been married twice. After the second divorce she went all the way back to her maiden name, some feminist idea, but Victor's last name had already been changed when he was little to the second husband's and they didn't want to change it back."

"You remember all your cases like that?"

"The ones that don't live in goddam Roxbury I sure as hell remember," Ferraro said, regaining some of the earlier bluster. "Look." He wrote rapidly with a mechanical pencil and handed the sheet of notebook paper to Gilman. "Look. Vic Turelli gives me no problems. He's a strange kid, he's a real strange kid. He probably needs a lot more counseling than I'm going to give him, but the only actual trouble he ever got into was trying to deal amphetamine—crank—down in the Combat Zone to a cop. He goes to school part-time now, he travels a lot—that's OK; he's been clean since he was busted. I see him every couple of weeks out in Framingham, we chat, he's fine, and it sure as hell makes a break from walking up and down housing projects in Roxbury and dodging winos and rats and shit on the stairs. Out in Framingham they don't put wire grills over all the light bulbs and they don't shit too much in the hallway, so yes I remember Vic Turelli. But I don't think you're going to find anything wrong out there."

"How's he strange?"

Ferraro yanked the ashtray open and stubbed out the cigarette. "He's one of those political rich kids," he said. "A *demonstrator.*" Ferraro pronounced the word with working-class distaste. "You name it, he marched against it."

"That's not on the sheet."

"He's been busted ten, twenty times—he went down to the Russian consul last year; he marched in support of this Polish guy Anders and started throwing brickbats through the windows—nothing stuck. Nothing ever sticks once the TV leaves. No DA in his right mind wants to prosecute five hundred students for trespassing. In Boston they've got immunity, like diplomats. You know how many colleges there are in this town?"

"He's a leftist, an anarchist, what?"

Ferraro took a deep breath, as if to draw the smoke back into his lungs. "You wanna know the truth, he doesn't make any sense; he wants to change the world, but the kid's about as political as a lamppost. He wouldn't know the Constitution if it sat on him. He just wants to piss off his family. Same with the crank. It's all his family. Last year he dropped out of Harvard and started traveling. He went to Europe—he's got money, the whole fucking world's got money— and he came back a lot cooler, calmed down. Determined. No more politics, no big problems. Then he went skiing and this Tahoe horseshit blew up—I got to go."

He opened the door and stepped out, then hunched his shoulder and leaned back in. "His mother's a psychiatrist," he said. "You want to know something, I think she's even crazier than her kid." And he shook his head and walked quickly away.

Gilman called Fahey from the Massachusetts Turnpike toll booths at Weston, and Fahey came on the line with a growl, as he expected: "Who's this?" In Boston, Gilman thought, staring out at the white river of car lights, politeness is taken as a sign of weakness.

"I got an address in Framingham from the probation officer," he told him, when Fahey had changed to the phone in his den.

"It's what, nine o'clock?" Fahey said.

"Ten past."

"You going out there now?"

"Yeah."

"All right. I already called three hotel dicks I know; nobody heard of anybody her name or description. You wanna meet me somewhere tomorrow morning about ten and tell me what you got?"

"The Blue Grill?"

"Hell no, Gilman, you're buying. Meet me in the Ritz bar on Arlington Street. There's a Dorchester girl I know waitresses there now, I wanna see her face when I walk in the Ritz."

"The PO told me the kid's political more than a dopehead; he's a demonstrator."

"They all are. They own the world. They're ready to go to war about a fucking Polack. I'm sitting here right now watching Stefan Anders on the tube, demonstrating. Listen, Gilman, I knew there was a question I didn't ask you. What the hell's a streetwise kid doing hitting on a 7-Eleven? You know what I mean?"

Gilman pinched the bridge of his nose and watched the lights move hypnotically back and forth. "It was there," he said.

"Fuck it, Gilman. Every shag head in America knows 7-Eleven invented security—they got the cash register practically out in the parking lot so people can see it, they got the four cameras in the corners, the time-locked cash box, the big measuring tape strip up the door for the clerk to give you a guy's exact height. They hired some ex-con three years ago to tell them how to robbery-proof the stores; since then nobody but a blind drunk touches them. So how come a kid tuned in enough to be selling crank in the Combat Zone goes in to knock off a 7-Eleven?"

"I don't know."

"Think about it," Fahey said, and hung up with a Boston bang.

I don't have *time* to think about it, Gilman told the dead line.

Massachusetts Route 128, running in a huge semicircle from northeast to southwest, links all the electronic ganglia of Boston and Cambridge. Silicon Circle. After Gilman left the Mass Pike he passed first a gigantic IBM building, silent but lit up like a landing spaceship; then a smaller wedge-shaped Digital Equipment lab; then Sperry, Genentech, Wang, Osborne. From 128 he took the Natick exit and headed west through wooded residential areas toward Framingham. "Framlingham" it was when they first settled it in the eighteenth century, he remembered. But crunched between the Bostonian jawbones, the "l" had gotten spat out and the "a" stretched long: Framingham. The way Bedlam was first Bethlehem, his father said.

In Framingham, Angela S. Freeling, MD, lived on a crescent-shaped street that dead-ended against a huge backdrop of trees and sky, and when Gilman got out of the car, stamping his feet and puffing scraps of breath, he was impressed to see that the houses were all bigger than he had expected, bigger than California houses, two-story colonials and white brick ranches, set back from the street on generous one- and two-acre lots. The trees were mostly evergreen, aromatic and handsome against the stars. But the air sat on his skin like cold bricks, and in the morning there would be no bankable sunshine.

What the hell was he doing in Boston? He yawned and his ears popped and whistled, the air cutting his lungs like ice; he started up the walkway. In the morning he would go home. Nina would already be home, shamefaced, calm; Victor Turelli would turn out to be just a pimply kid with a lopsided smile and a perfect explanation.

"You are who?"

A woman's voice with no Massachusetts in it, and she was holding a straining Doberman back with each hand. Under the dazzle of the porch bulb her face was utterly invisible, a talking ball of light.

Gilman reached slowly into his jacket pocket and pulled out his badge and ID wallet. The Dobermans' growls seemed to come out of the earth, somewhere between their muzzles and Gilman's knees, and he held up the wallet very slowly so that the woman could see the glint of the shield and the official-looking photo.

"Police officer," he said. "San Francisco PD. I called twice this evening and left a message on a machine." The Doberman on her left came six inches closer, and the growl sounded like a distant truck changing gears. "I was hoping to talk to Victor Turelli or his mother tonight."

"I'm Victor's mother. Have you come about that trumped-up charge in Lake Tahoe? I thought my lawyers wrote you people a blistering letter about police incompetence. I'm amazed they'd send somebody all the way out to Boston to stir that up again."

"Could I come in, please, and explain?"

"It's nine-thirty at night. You certainly cannot."

"I'm from San Francisco, not Lake Tahoe, Doctor Freeling, and I've come here on my own, by way of private business. Could I come in, please, and explain?"

The Doberman on the left had suddenly sat down, halfway over the first step, looking up at Gilman with the equivalent of a homicidal smile. Brown fur and slobbering pink gums; Donald Kerwin had hated all big dogs, especially Dobermans. Make them into matched luggage, he liked to suggest to their owners. Demented animals, mutated ferrets. What do you think is the greatest threat to world peace? Donald's college reunion questionnaire had asked. Barking dogs, he had written.

"It was my brother-in-law," Gilman said, "who was killed."

Doctor Freeling looked down and jerked the dog to its feet with the choke collar.

"I would very much appreciate it," Gilman said. And on impulse added: "Now his wife has done something psychiatrically very strange."

The face was still invisible in the glare of the porch light. Only her hands and wrists could clearly be seen, thrust forward and keeping the short leashes tight, so that with the two dogs tensed in front of her she looked as if she were in a brilliant fiery chariot, riding it into the night.

"I'll give you five minutes," she said.

The house was too big for one person, or even two, but there was no sign of a husband in residence, or a lover, or a son. In the hallway, beside a table with a photograph of Victor Turelli, she stopped and made him bring out his ID wallet again, which she studied carefully before snapping together and handing back.

"We'll go in my office, Inspector Gilman."

She walked ahead of him, through a large living room expensively decorated in chic, cheerless earth colors and low-slung Danish furniture. The only personal touch seemed to be a strong, even violent abstract collage across one wall, over a teak credenza. The office itself, at the other end, had once been the side porch, now remodeled into an elongated room lined with gleaming chromium bookshelves. There was a short leather couch along one wall, to the left as they entered, and a facing wingback chair for the doctor. Behind it were a desk and matching cabinet filled with tape deck and radio and oddly shaped ceramic sculptures. On a narrow strip of wall above the desk a line of framed diplomas had been arranged perpendicularly. The top was from Radcliffe College, cum laude in General Studies, dated 1961; the next two going down were from Tufts University School of Medicine dated in the early 1970s, and at the bottom a certification from the Massachusetts Board of Psychotherapy. Learn to read a room, Gilman's first homicide sergeant had always told him; look for what they pick out themselves and put at eye level where they can always see it. On the desk beside the telephone was another oversized photo of Victor Turelli, a roundfaced ten-year-old boy holding a football to his chest and smiling into the camera.

Doctor Freeling gestured abruptly toward the wingback chair and went herself to the chair behind the desk. The door to the main house she left open, and one of the Dobermans took up a sphinxlike posture just on the threshold.

"Explain what my son has to do with your sister-in-law, please."

Gilman nodded. In ordinary light she was a sandy-haired woman in her early forties, trim, short, not quite square jawed. High breasted, long waisted. She dressed like the collage in her living room, Gilman thought—hard, bright colors, red cardigan sweater, black skirt—and she stared straight ahead at him, unfriendly, through oversized clear plastic glasses that made her brown eyes look distant and small.

"I'm waiting, Inspector."

Part of him wanted to get up slowly, stroll past the winking Doberman, and slap the professional snobbery out of her face. What her son has to do with Nina Kerwin is that he held a shotgun six inches from her husband's body and blew his chest into bits of bone and blood. And part of him wanted to please her very much, so that Victor Turelli would appear in the doorway, and Nina too, and he could wake up and go home. He told the story quickly, concisely, trying to match her brisk manner, but when he had finished, she had turned her head away from him, toward the chromium bookshelves, and her expression had softened all the hard lines of her jaw, her skin had sagged under her chin, and her brown eyes had grown darker and sadder.

"You don't have children?" she said.

"No."

"I'm going to need a drink to talk about this," she said, standing up suddenly. And with a flash of humorless irony, "I assume you're allowed to drink off duty."

Gilman remained in the chair, observed by the Doberman's pink eyes, while she went into a distant part of the big house and returned with a tray containing an ice bucket, two glasses, and a bottle of Glenfiddich single-malt scotch.

"Victor has a room upstairs here," she said, pouring them both three fingers over ice, not bothering to ask if he liked scotch. "I'd show it to you, but there's no point. He comes here once every few weeks for a couple of nights. He talks to the probation officer and charms him—some poor creature from Malden or Revere or somewhere—and then Victor goes off again, wherever he pleases. We all agree to the pleasant fiction that he's taking classes at North-eastern University." She smiled, still without humor. "If you ever have children, Inspector Gilman, don't make the mistake of giving them money as babies under the Uniform Gift to Minors Act. At eighteen Victor became entirely self-sufficient as far as money goes, thanks to his doting grandmother and the Old Colony Trust."

"And his father?"

Doctor Freeling drained her glass and poured another three fingers, then glanced at Gilman. He shook his head.

"They never see each other," she said shortly.

Gilman swirled the ice cubes in his glass and waited. She swallowed half of her new scotch and looked at the bottle.

"Most policemen despise psychiatry," she said. "What do you think of psychiatry, Inspector Gilman?"

Gilman shrugged and sipped his drink. He wanted to say he thought it was couched in jargon, but any policeman in the world can type a drinker after two minutes and his one unbreakable rule with drunks was never ever to joke, never to make them puzzle over a wisecrack and lose their train of talk.

"If you were to put me up on the witness stand," she said, "and ask me if, as a professional psychotherapist, I thought my son was capable of robbing a convenience store and shooting down a man in cold blood, for no apparent reason—" She stopped and looked at the bottle and took a deep breath. "I would say, '*absolutely not*.' He's not capable of such a thing. He's a very troubled boy, Inspector—I concede that. Very bright, very troubled, very angry. I've had custody of him since he was three—no lasting father presence in the household, not even any drop-in lovers. I know what that does to a boy." She smiled a tight smile that seemed to cost her effort. "Not *many* lovers. I spent most of his childhood getting married and divorced a second time—very fast, very amicable. Arcangelo Turelli gave my son his name legally when we were first married, one of his many possessive so-Italian gestures. Later, it didn't seem worth threatening Victor's identity by changing the name back. In prep school he refused absolutely. Besides, I was busy putting myself through medical school, internship, residency, all those patriarchal medical gymnastics that build character and destroy families. His father was no help at all— Victor felt abandoned by him, rightly so. When he began to have problems, I sent him off to boarding schools."

Gilman rubbed his jaw. After his mother's death his father had talked about the same idea for him.

"I sent Victor to dozens of them," Angela Freeling said, "stricter and stricter as he would get kicked out of each one and come back, two inches taller, grinning defiantly, like some poor mutt that's been in a fight, and I would get out the *Times Sunday Magazine* and look in the back and pick out the next military academy for teens in Vermont or South Carolina and try again."

"What kind of problems?" Gilman asked.

"I hired the best, the very best lawyers in San Francisco when this incredible arrest happened. Your people were very incompetent, *very* quick off the mark. And I couldn't stand the idea of him in jail," she added.

She held up the bottle and seemed to measure how much was

left. "I do *not* feel guilty," she said, either to the wall or to the photo of Victor Turelli. As Gilman extended his glass, the Doberman growled briefly, then put his head on his paws.

"Is that a hearing aid or a tinnitus masker?"

"It's a tinnitus masker. From the gunshot by my head at Tahoe City."

"That's often psychosomatic, you know; tinnitus is a common defensive reaction. The patient really doesn't want to hear anything that makes him feel guilty—it comes and goes with stress."

Gilman nodded and listened to the rising whine in his ears. She was right; he despised psychiatry.

"It can go away suddenly for good, without warning," she said.

"Or get worse."

"Anything can get worse," she said quickly.

She made a birdlike motion with her head, ruffling her shoulders, and poured them both more scotch; then she drank hers down and poured another, as far as Gilman could tell completely unaffected by it.

"By the time he was sixteen," she said, "Victor was six feet three inches tall, thin like his father, but wiry and strong. He likes to think he's a political activist. It's a stage, it's radical chic. He flirts with the CP. He protested against Reagan when he came to New Hampshire for the primary; he marches around for the anticommunist leader in Poland who's coming to Harvard. The 'righteousness of spring,' his father said the first time he was arrested; according to him students never demonstrate in the winter, when it's cold and wet. My own view is that Victor's fixated on dictatorships like Poland or Russia—places ruled by authority figures, father figures obviously. The paradox, of course, is that he's drawn to strong, authoritative men and yet wants to overthrow them. I can't control him, Inspector. I think your sister-in-law had a delayed hysterical reaction and she'll probably collapse in a day or two from sheer emotional exhaustion, and then you'll find her and take her home to her children. If there were any real danger—but I can't believe it's very likely she'll find Victor on her own, just wandering around a city."

Gilman looked at the row of medical textbooks on the shelves, big, the size of bank vaults. "I wonder if I could just see his room after all?" he said.

The unused room was on the second floor, at the front: ordinary American teenage eclectic, overfurnished, too neat, too small. As they stood by one end of the bed, Gilman could smell the scotch on Angela Freeling's breath and see her sway ever so slightly on her feet.

"His father is a complex man, Inspector Gilman." They had worked their way around the room, from Victor's collection of rock records to his old sports equipment to the combination nightstand and bookshelf under a poster of a Navy jet in flight; then worked their way from Victor's anger to his father's contemptuous disappointment in him. The bookshelf held a Time-Life picture series on the Second World War and a complete set of Churchill's memoirs. On the opposite wall, at eye level, there were other posters of World War II fighting men, warplanes, the Marines raising the flag at Iwo Jima.

"Made up of sealed compartments, like a submarine," she said. "Absolutely airtight. Most of us aren't so compartmentalized. Our subconscious is always leaking into our consciousness, like a frayed balloon or a gas bag, interfering with us in small, obvious ways, like bad dreams or Freudian slips, or harmless compulsions—people who won't leave their house until they've tried every door handle twice. But my ex-husband doesn't leak. Very stiff upper lip. He likes to say he's descended from Nathan Hale, who was hung by the British without a quaver. Hung. Hanged. Do you know he's the only adult man I've ever known who actually corrects other people's grammar."

"My father does the same thing," Gilman said, but she wasn't listening.

"Other professors never tell you, " 'That's a solecism, dear,' " she said. " 'That's a misplaced modifier, lover.' "

"Is that why you left him?"

She smiled and swallowed more scotch, her sixth by Gilman's count. Standing side by side, she barely came up to his shoulders: a compact body, with Nina Kerwin's small, elegant breasts. "That's why I married him," she said.

"I was twenty years old. My own father had spoiled me shamelessly—his little princess—and then run away with his fat cow of a secretary, frightened by debts, frightened by life, leaving his 'little princess' to reign over an alcoholic mother with no job, no prospects, two indifferent older brothers, and a five-foot shelf of Harvard Classics inherited from *his* father. When I met Victor's father the thing I wanted most in the world was a strong man who would correct my grammar, browbeat my brothers, and fuck me silly. That he was my Harvard professor just made it all perfect."

Gilman drummed his fingers against his leg and watched as she put her glass down and began to poke among the books.

"He doesn't leak emotions at all," she said over her shoulder, kneeling to see better. "Certainly not, for instance, affection. We should have been married in an ice house, my mother said. He's just exactly what they taught him to be in the war, except the war's been over rather a long time now, wouldn't you say?"

"What do you mean, 'in the war'?"

"You didn't know? Victor's father was a war hero. Oh yes. An OSS man—'Oh So Social,' they used to say. I'm looking for the famous book he wrote about his adventures. Victor loves it and he hides it. Of course." She rose unsteadily and held out a well-thumbed volume from a place deep in Victor's bookshelves.

Gilman looked at the title page without understanding: *The Making of a Maquisard.* After a moment he turned it over to the author's photograph on the dust jacket. "That's Victor's father?"

She didn't bother to glance, or to disguise the bitterness in her voice.

"Oh yes," she said. "Martin Spurling of Harvard."

19

"Back off the fucking car!"

Gilman's right hand froze over the door handle. He was twenty miles from Framingham, but his mind was still back in Angela Freeling's conservatory of neuroses, and he turned his head slowly, blinking. You don't get mugged in hotel garages, he thought, not when you're my size, not by middle-aged men in suits. But his left hand rose automatically toward the holster under his armpit.

"Touch the fucking piece you're a dead man, Gilman!"

Who knew his name in Boston? The taller man was coming at a run between the rows of parked cars, squeezing around fenders with practiced swivels of his hip, even at a distance anger in his red face, anger in his sharp Boston voice.

"Move away from the fucking car, Gilman—get over by the goddam wall!"

Gilman straightened and stood where he was, feeling Angela Freeling's scotch burn in his stomach. The other man, shorter, calmer, was coming from the direction of the elevator door, pulling the flaps of his overcoat fastidiously away from protruding bumpers and raising an open palm as if in reassurance. He was of average height, average blandness—conservatively dressed, a clean-shaven face, small features bunched together like the bull's-eye in a target, the faint tart smell of a fashionable cologne as he came around the trunk. Gilman's hand was already dropping from the holster, his shoulders relaxing. Cop knows cop even in the dark, he thought, the way bats know a wall is near.

"We checked out your hotel and then we picked you up coming in off the turnpike on Boylston Street, driving like an asshole." The taller one stalked around the hood on Gilman's left, breathing tobacco and coffee, and he kept his hands well clear of his overcoat pockets, gunslinger style. Under the fluorescent lights of the garage his red face looked as if it were wrapped in waxy paper.

The calm one was flipping open his wallet and passing an ID card in front of Gilman's face while his partner talked. He snapped it closed again and made it vanish.

"I couldn't read a thing," Gilman said. His buttocks touched the cold metal of the car behind him. "Perfect."

"You saw enough, asshole." The taller one had stopped inches from Gilman's left shoulder, leaning forward, violating personal space just the way they teach you in witness interrogation. Hardball, softball—when Gilman had to work this way in San Francisco, he thought, they always assigned him to be hard guy because of his size. He was never any good at it.

"Hastings," the bland one said, pausing and timing it an extra beat to register the full effect. "Federal Bureau of Investigation."

"Gilman, Canadian Royal Mounties."

"We know who you are, Gilman."

"Your partner forgot to show me a badge. Is he FBI too, or the Boston school patrol?"

"You're interfering with a major ongoing investigation," Hastings said. "Goddard and I have spent a lot of time trying to find you. We've been instructed to advise you to stop."

"In other words, to get your ass back to San Francisco," Goddard said.

"You were undoubtedly not aware that this was a federal investigation," Hastings said smoothly. "We understand you're on medical leave, you may be distraught. The bureau has communicated now with your office in San Francisco; everyone's been advised."

"Back off Victor Turelli," Goddard said.

Gilman jerked his head toward him, too surprised now even to protest. Goddard began to speak again, but a huge trailer truck moving on the dark street outside the garage suddenly hit its brakes and set them screeching at unbearable volume, and for ten seconds Goddard's mouth was open and moving, forming words, while Gilman heard nothing except the shriek of metal on metal and the echoing shriek in his ears.

"Are you all right?" Hastings asked.

Gilman shook off his hand and stepped past him, into open space. FBI. Irrelevantly he noticed that he had mud on his trouser cuffs from Angela Freeling's driveway in Framingham. Irrelevantly he noticed that it was twelve thirty-five now, making it only nine thirty-five in California. Martin Spurling. Every instant in the 7-Eleven was still clear in his mind, but not the words. The words had been flattened under the pressure of guilt. What was Donald Kerwin saying about a book before he died? Did Kerwin know Martin Spurling? The memory slipped away behind a wall of noise.

"Who sent you people?" Gilman asked over the pain in his ears. "I just got here last night to look for my sister-in-law."

"Sir fucking Lochinvar," Goddard hissed behind him.

"Boston PD tells it otherwise," Hastings said, beginning to circle briskly around to face him. "Boston PD says you're looking for Victor Turelli."

"What the hell does the FBI have to do with Victor Turelli?"

"We're not at liberty to explain it," Hastings said. Over his shoulder Gilman smelled Goddard's breath again and instinctively took another step forward. "But this could impact national security. You're definitely to stay away."

Gilman closed his eyes for a moment, letting the sound of the brakes drain from his ears. It comes and goes with stress, Angela Freeling had said. "Impact" is a noun, not a verb. He had no idea if he were thinking or speaking. Either way he sounded like his goddam father. He would get away for ten minutes and clear his head, then sit down with these two and clear up whatever horrendous bureaucratic mistake had been made. But when he opened his eyes again Hastings was already moving toward a Mercury parked by the elevator, unlocking its door, and Goddard was backing away and glowering as if he could barely restrain himself from throwing a punch.

"This is a mistake," Gilman started to say, but Goddard interrupted.

"Donald Kerwin did enough fucking damage to this country," he said fiercely, and turned and stalked toward the car.

At six Gilman woke with a start and sat for a long moment on the edge of the bed, cupping his ears. Then he got up slowly and began to dress while last night filtered back into his mind. The FBI had really come after him, he thought, shaking his head. The tag team of Hastings and Goddard in their black overcoats and plain white collars had really tracked him down in a hotel parking garage and told him to go home. All thoughts of Nina loose in the city, of Angela Freeling and her sad-sack son had to be shoved aside. He would have to call San Francisco in a few hours and straighten it out, or call Vico at Boston PD and see what kind of monumental screwup he'd started.

Who else could it be but Vico? Gilman's ears rang now without ceasing, and the faint underlying static that sounded like distant voices had returned. Goddard was a pathological cop, he thought, closing his door and heading down the silent corridor; you could see it in his face—one of those people twisted in knots by some unappeasable anger. A dime a dozen on big-city police forces, but a type that rarely got past the FBI's elaborate psychological screening. What the hell would a creep like Goddard know about Donald Kerwin?

What the hell couldn't he remember?

Outside, he impulsively stuffed the tinnitus masker and ear plugs into his jacket pocket, unwilling suddenly to wear them. Donald Kerwin had come west to make money, take care of his children. Gilman hesitated by the phone box at the entrance to the Lenox garage, where Hastings and Goddard had found him. By whatever loop and circuit in his brain, the FBI made him think of his father— his father the lawyer, his father who could be no possible help whatever in finding Nina. But his father did know every well-connected government lawyer and old boy in Boston. And sooner or later he had to be called anyway. Gilman stared at the empty street and pinched the bridge of his nose. After a moment more he felt in his pocket for change.

Five minutes later he steered the rented Plymouth down the ramp and onto Exeter Street. From Copley Square he made his way to Storrow Drive and turned west along the Charles River, by the jogging paths and the factorylike campus of Boston University, just beginning to reflect the early morning sun in its windows.

At the Larz Anderson Bridge across from Harvard he turned south and drove through Allston, over the turnpike and into the northeast section of Brookline. By six forty-five he was pulling up to Beals Street, looking for a corner house that he could have drawn with his eyes shut, that he hadn't seen in almost ten years.

I wake at five, just as I always have, his father had said when he called. I read the *Globe,* the *Times,* and *The Wall Street Journal.* I go into the office at eight. Come anytime before eight.

Gilman parked on the street and walked down to the familiar white wooden gate. He had helped to set it up one summer, he remembered. Could it be the same wood after so many years, he wondered, pausing to inspect. Wood rotted fast in a Boston winter. These would have to be replacement posts by now. The brick walkway to the porch he had also helped to build, when he was nine or ten. Typically, his father had got out a book on landscape architecture while they worked and made him learn the odd technical names architects use for each of the six sides of a brick. The only one he could remember now was "soldier."

When his father answered the door he was already dressed for work, the picture of a Yankee lawyer in his blue Brooks Brothers suit, his perfectly trimmed gray crewcut, his black wingtip shoes. He greeted his son with the single firm handshake he had used since Gilman was ten and going off to summer camp for the first time— demonstrative enough if you were a Bostonian, terminal repression in California.

So Gilman told himself, so he thought. Unlike wood, he told himself, feelings never rotted. Feelings burned like stars and lasted forever.

His father led him into the house, shuffling a little but otherwise ramrod stiff at seventy-one. He ushered Gilman down a hallway, straight into the old-fashioned kitchen that had always seemed too big for any normal family—the kitchen as big as a house, his mother had liked to joke while he watched from a stool, eating, and she hurried from one end to the other, cooking.

"You catch me at an interesting moment," his father said drily, and waved one hand in tight circles at the room.

Gilman stopped at the threshold and stared.

Everywhere, up and down each side of the long bright room were rows of neatly stacked cardboard boxes, taped and labeled with black Magic Marker. The dishes and pans had all come down from the beaverboard sidings, and though a few still sat on the table, peeking from wads of white packing paper like nesting hens, the rest were already sealed into boxes with Allied Van Lines insignia, ranged under the table in the center and piled shoulder high up to the back door. Every wall was bare except for curtains and a single lonely Tupperware skillet still hanging from a hook.

"You're moving!"

"The detective," his father said and turned off a tiny transistor radio on the counter. Your father is funny, Cassie said. He's ironic; he has a dry sense of humor, like you.

"Where the hell are you moving?" To his astonishment, Gilman was indignant. He clenched his fists in his pockets to keep from ripping the nearest box open and throwing the pans and dishes back into the cabinets where they belonged. Why the hell was he angry? Why should he care?

Calmly, his father threaded between boxes and began to restart his coffee machine, next to the stove.

"Beacon Hill," he said with his back turned, measuring more coffee with a plastic spoon. "Joy Street, of all places. An auspicious name, possibly. This place has been too big ever since your mother died. Eleven rooms. All that lawn out back. And without family here in Boston . . . ."

Gilman felt the unspoken accusation spread and fill the silence. He tightened his jaw muscles and said nothing.

"So a young associate in the firm bought one of those big Federal houses on Joy Street, just up from Louisburg Square, and divided it into condominiums, and two months ago I signed the papers on one. I was going to surprise you at Christmas with the new address, but—" He straightened and looked his son up and down, taking in the dirty raincoat, the unpressed suit, tieless collar. Gilman turned away impatiently to look at other boxes. "But here you are," his father said.

"I don't picture you in a 'condominium,'" Gilman said irritably. His father pronounced the word in an arch voice, with his amused, superior contempt for the decline of reasonable English that always set Gilman's teeth on edge. There was no point in asking for his help, about the FBI or anything else.

"Would you like tea?" his father asked. "Or do you drink coffee now?"

Gilman made an untranslatable gesture of disgust. He had begun to drink coffee when he was fourteen years old and working a morning paper route of more than three hundred houses—the biggest in Brookline—a grown-up boy, already paying his way. His father's memory for legal citations and precedents was legendary, but for over twenty years he had been unable to remember that his son drank coffee.

"Coffee's fine. Black, no sugar."

"Ah." His father made a doubtful face and bent to adjust the burbling machine. "There are no hot tubs in Joy Street," he said and poured coffee into a chipped navy-blue mug. "I trust all is well in the land of hot tubs and happy faces?"

"All well." Gilman resolved to keep his temper. He took the mug and glanced at his watch.

"And Cassie?"

"Cassie's fine. I called her last night. She's still working in the bookstore, still doing yoga every week. She sends you her love."

"You're here long?" Cool, moving away with his old man's shuffle.

Gilman sipped the coffee. Excellent coffee. He put the mug down for a moment on the marble-topped kitchen table and thought that he had breakfasted and, while his mother was alive, done his homework on that table, for one-third of his life. Since the day he had passed his police academy exams and begun his first stint as a patrolman, he'd said as little about his work as he possibly could, and his father never asked directly.

"A few days. I can't be sure. Business."

His father made it a point of Yankee pride not to approve of California. For as long as Gilman could remember his father had made it a point not to approve of whatever he did—a stubborn, willful personality, not easily given to compromise; two stubborn, willful personalities, if he were honest; face to face in a motherless nest. The fall of his senior year in high school his father had brought home an application blank for Harvard and put it down in front of him without a word, and Gilman had torn it to pieces in his face. The day after graduation, without looking back toward the house where his father might or might not have been standing, watching, he had driven away in his VW bug, going west in the great tradition, to find a job and to get as far as possible from his father. What the hell had they fought about all those years? Gray-haired, baggy-skinned old man.

"Where are the pictures?" Gilman moved to the other end of the kitchen and peered into the living room. Why did he still telephone? he once asked Cassie. Why haven't I just broken off completely and never seen the SOB again? First, Cassie said, because it goes against your nature: you're a loyal person. Second? Because he loves you.

"The packers took them down. The truck comes tomorrow morning. Most of them are going to storage anyway. There's nobody here who wants to use them."

Fairly or not, after only ten minutes Gilman heard everything he said as an accusation, one more critical voice along with all the other noises in his head. Abruptly, he stood up and carried his coffee into the living room. His father liked photographs better than paintings, naturally—hard New England facts, no impressions, no subjective distortions—and had long ago covered the walls of every room with framed photographs. What of? He pinched his nose and tried to remember. His mother, of course. Dozens of photographs of his mother, moving gracefully from girlhood to bridehood, motherhood, a plump, sweet-wrinkled middle age. The photographs had stopped abruptly in 1955, before the hospital weeks, freezing her at thirty-eight, in a sun hat and summer dress, outside by the grape arbor. And of himself, he conceded. Himself marching up the years, a miniature chart of human evolution, from fat-bottomed infant to stoop-shouldered, slack-jawed adolescent, leaping from black and white to color one spring when he was eight or nine and caught in the act of diving headlong, dangerously, into a breaking wave at Cape Cod, the water all blue and white exploding, his body brown as oak, suspended in air, beginning to disappear.

"They packed all the books, too," his father said, coming into the room behind him. "I could never have gotten through them by myself." Gilman nodded curtly. For the hell of it, he had counted up his father's books one summer and arrived at the staggering total of three thousand one hundred and seventy-two hardbacks. He still remembered the number; he had written it down somewhere in awe. Politics, history, biography. Like Nixon, his father never read fiction. And never bought paperbacks. But he wrote sonnets to your mother for years, Cassie had once told him; Gilman had never known. How could she know more about his father than he did? Apparently he would write them down in the car, at traffic lights and stop signs, while he was going to State Street to work in his firm. Like everything else his father did, it made Gilman obscurely, childishly angry.

"Will you be free for lunch today?" his father asked, clearing his throat. Gilman put down the mug and they walked as if on signal toward the front door. "Perhaps Locke-Ober's at one?"

"No. I don't think so." His father liked Cassie—everybody liked Cassie—but he'd never bothered to meet Nina and Donald Kerwin; why bother to explain? "In fact," Gilman added a little maliciously, "I expect I'll still be looking for the wayward son of a distinguished Harvard man. A literature professor named Martin Spurling."

His father stopped the door in midpull and closed it firmly again.

"I know Martin Spurling."

Gilman frowned at the seriousness of his tone.

"I *knew* Martin Spurling, that is, forty years ago at the end of the war, when I was assigned to the same OSS unit in Washington. I knew him for two months, the way you knew people then. I haven't seen him since, except on television. I didn't know he had a son."

"Why is a professor of classics on television?" Gilman asked. His ears whistled like falling bombs. It was his father's turn to frown.

"You don't keep up with a damn thing, do you? Don't you know Martin Spurling is a great champion of Stefan Anders? He organized the American committee to support him; he held a press conference last week with the secretary of state. And Stefan Anders is coming *here,* to Boston, in two days to speak at Harvard."

Gilman reached for the door and grasped the handle. There were street conservatives like himself, like all cops, who might have started out as idealists but saw human nature at its worst day in and day out; there were polyester conservatives, who saw life through the lens of a television camera. His father was a Boston conservative, a Brahmin who distrusted the Kennedys and all Irish, who supported an Anglo establishment as automatically as he breathed. In Gilman's radical days they had quarreled over and over about the Vietnam War. His father's passion amazed him now.

"You don't admire Stefan Anders?" his father persisted. "You don't think he's a great man?"

"He's a politician."

"Rubbish. You make him sound like a ward boss in Chelsea. We're not talking about spoiled college boys protesting the system with one hand and clipping their trust fund bonds with the other. Stefan Anders is a true Jeffersonian, the right kind of rebel. He's a great symbol of what a man will still risk in the name of freedom. The whole Russian army is poised at the Polish border to smash him and he keeps on speaking out. You used to march in the street in support of what Stefan Anders stands for."

"Cassie's the marcher now." Gilman's face was flushed, his hands trembling. How could his father turn everything upside down? He pulled the door hard and felt the cold air hit his cheeks.

"Cassie's right," his father said angrily. "You should get up and look at the world around you. My god!" Gilman started down the steps without looking back.

"Look at yourself!" his father shouted from the door. "You're the old man, not me!"

20 ▉▉▉▉▉▉▉▉▉▉▉▉▉▉▉

"The law," Fahey announced, "is like sculpting with bullshit."

"Come on," Gilman said. When he had walked in the door of the Ritz bar he had intended to tell Fahey right away about the FBI, then changed his mind on impulse. Why make him skittish? Why scare off the one person who seemed likely to help him find Nina?

Why trust him? he had suddenly thought.

"Wake up, Gilman." Fahey shifted in irritation on his chair. "You're supposed to ask me how come it's like sculpting with bull-shit."

Gilman forced a smile and sipped the coffee he had persuaded the waitress to bring into the bar from the restaurant upstairs. To hell with old men's pronouncements. He was sick of old men's pronouncements.

"Because you can come up with any shape you want," Fahey said, *"but you can't hide what it is."*

Gilman drummed his fingers on the table.

"Listen," Fahey said, scooting his chair closer. "This lawyer swells up like a goddam tick and—here's Darlene bringing me another beer an' a bump. Good girl. Now you wanna bring my uncle here another cuppa?"

The waitress stopped at their table and handed out the new beer bottle and shot glass, balancing her tray with one hand while she did a little dip to pour the beer.

"Your mouth, Lieutenant Fahey," she said. "And your brother a monsignor too." A long-faced, beaver-toothed girl in her middle twenties, uncomfortably bony in a white apron and dark green dress that had "Ritz Hotel" stitched in script over her left breast.

"I hear Darlene gives good cork," Fahey said with a wink.

Darlene blushed and grinned in spite of herself and walked away with a flounce.

Fahey waved his hand over his vest in a gesture Gilman was beginning to recognize: a fat man brushing away crumbs. "Listen." Gilman bent over his coffee and heard the whine in both his ears, louder than ever in the hard December air, mosquitoes in a dark room, mosquitoes the size of Piper Cubs.

"Listen, I wanna tell you about this lawyer," Fahey said. "I'm there at his office about eight-fifteen, eight-thirty and the girl at the desk tells me, oh no, he's about to leave for court, can't see anybody. Now there hasn't been a court in Boston open before ten o'clock since the sons of Erin took over this town, so I go right in anyway flashing the shield, and this Yankee lawyer with the soft little bow tie and the soft little crewcut, like they all gotta be Archibald Cox now, he huffs and puffs his bullshit about the law and confidentiality and finally he remembers as a matter of fact he did happen to talk to a woman of that description a few days ago. She wanted his recommendation for a private investigator, she had a list of five from the phone book, she wanted to choose."

Gilman was already pulling his notebook and pen from his jacket, pushing the cup out of the way.

"What's the hotel?" The ballpoint was in his fingers, ready to end this, ready to write himself back to California, but Fahey was shaking his head hard enough to make his chins quiver and reaching out one small white hand to stop the pen.

"Now we go into hyperbullshit," Fahey said. "He's not talking. We get that far and all of a sudden he's backing up behind the desk with his two hands in the air and saying sorry, that's as far as he can go, but the law is like that, confidential of rights."

"He gave you the list of PIs," Gilman said. He had jerked the pen upright again, poised to reduce everything to a list, a little footwork, a trip home. For half an instant his eyes flashed past Fahey's white hair to the leaves falling on the grass of the Public Garden, the gray trees shriveled up for winter: I'm home already.

"Not even that," Fahey said. "But listen." He was unwilling to let his lesson in police work pass. He scooped a fistful of peanuts from the cut-glass bowl and ate from his palm, like a man lapping water.

"I want to tell you how I found this guy in the first place. I thought about it some more last night, Gilman, after you called. I could waste all week calling up no-good private jamokes from the yellow pages. Half the time you just get a disconnected anyway. But her husband was a lawyer, you said. Only you don't tell me what firm. So first I go over to the turret."

"What's the turret?"

"Police communications center in district A, downtown, where they got phone books for the whole planet. I look up his name, his firm in the San Francisco yellow pages—Hinman, Ellis, Frankel, right?—then I call a lawyer I know down on Congress Street and ask which Boston lawyers are the most likely to do business with that one. In other words, whose name is your sister-in-law gonna have heard?"

He reached to the next table and hooked its bowl of peanuts.

"In little things, Gilman, people are generally predictable. That's how I found the lawyer. That's how I'm gonna find your sexy lady."

Gilman stared down at the blank notebook.

Darlene came past with the clear bubble of coffee and refilled his cup, a slightly distracted look pulling her skin tight as she cocked her head to hear something the bartender was saying. In the stretched skin, the hump of her shoulders, Gilman suddenly saw the middle-aged woman she would become. And in Fahey's face, turned now to the business of the last few peanuts, he saw the short fine hair, the knob-cheeked kid he must have been fifty years ago. Everybody is a missing person.

Fahey nodded toward Darlene's shoes. "Nothing more than toe cleavage in the Ritz," he said with a grin.

Nothing was funny to Gilman.

*　　*　　*

On the other side of the tall, heavily curtained windows, tinted to keep the bar dark, bundled-up pedestrians were hurrying up and down Arlington Street, on their way to Brooks or Bonwit's, on their way to Lord and Taylor or Firestone and Parson's or Shreve, Crump and Lowe. Nina's world. Gilman scanned the women's faces as if she would turn up on the spot, cheerfully shopping. Fahey had the regular cop's disdain for people who couldn't make it onto the police force. He had drawn up his own list of private jamokes to call on personally, starting that morning with an ex-MP and a disbarred lawyer, both of whom rented office space near Washington Street, in the Combat Zone.

"Meantime, you thought any more about the 7-Eleven?"

Gilman shook his head. "It was just there, a place we stopped at near the condominium he'd rented."

"Kerwin was a civil lawyer, right? He didn't go around prosecuting Harvard kids for demonstrating their ignorance?"

"He worked as a special counsel for the Department of Defense in Washington until a year ago. A government lawyer." Doing what? "Then he quit his job and moved west."

"And he didn't have any disgruntled clients mad enough to follow him up the mountain?"

Gilman closed his eyes and saw Goddard's pinched, empty face again. In an hour, no later than that, he would call San Francisco and see if anybody in his squadroom had talked to the FBI.

"All right," Fahey sighed. "I start running my list. You go roust the old man in Harvard Yard."

"There's no point in that," Gilman objected, not sure why. He groped for a reason. "His mother told me the kid never sees his father. He wouldn't even change his name back."

"Listen," Fahey said, holding on to Gilman's upper arm and bumping the table with his belly as he stood up. "Listen. Forget what the mother tells you. The kid's a punk because of his father, right? Trust me. He's gonna show up once in a while to rub the old man's nose in it."

At the street he stopped and belched and gripped Gilman's arm again. "Ex-wife, OK," he said. "Ex-father, never."

Gilman walked fast through the Public Garden, over the footbridge that led to Charles Street and the top of the Common. Where was Goddard right now? Pistol-whipping a swan boat? Why go to Harvard, he thought, and track down Victor Turelli's father if the FBI were going to get there first? Perversely, he increased his pace. He disliked going to Harvard for any reason, but he disliked bureaucrats and bullies more, disliked sociopath cops absolutely, whether they worked for the FBI or not. Where the hell was Nina? He wanted to be looking for Nina.

At Charles Street he crossed by the entrance to the underground garage and strode uphill. On the left, under the intense blue winter sky, sat Beacon Hill and a row of Georgian buildings the color of old port. The Atheneum. Then the State House, where they had gone on boring raucous tours as schoolchildren to see its gold dome and the Sacred Cod. His father's last shouted words stuck in his mind like burrs. Stefan Anders wasn't going to save the world. Gilman could almost sympathize with Victor Turelli, overmatched by a self-righteous, judgmental father. I still have my heroes, he thought defiantly. My ideals are still there, under a thick slab of reality, tough green city plants pushing up through concrete.

Why can't Cassie see that?

The swinging doors of the Park Street subway station sent out a grandfather's bad breath of familiar odors—heat, cigarettes, sweat trapped underground for generations. Gilman turned and looked downhill toward the bottom of the Common. Hundreds of people of all ages and shapes were walking uphill toward him, and every one of them was the ghost of a person he could have become.

"If you're another reporter . . . ." Martin Spurling's secretary stood up behind her desk and swept her hand toward the rest of the crowded office: students pushing between other desks on their way to faculty studies, secretaries, jangling phones, morose-looking men dangling video cameras and tape machines.

"I have had it," she said, looking distinctly pleased with the confusion. "Since eight o'clock this morning people have been coming in here looking for him."

Gilman drummed the fingers of his left hand on the edge of the desk.

"You didn't see the papers today?" she asked.

He shook his head, still holding the ID wallet ready to show her.

"Look!" The *Boston Globe* had a picture of Stefan Anders and a headline in seventy-point type. The *Times* had a similar picture but smaller type. A sidebar named Martin Spurling as Harvard's official spokesman.

"His telephone's been going *crazy*—I talked to *Time* magazine. And *Newsweek*. And James Reston's assistant called. Those men over there are from UPI. The State Department called twice."

"For Professor Spurling?"

"Professor Spurling's introducing Stefan Anders on Saturday. It's right here in the paper, and it's on Saturday. You really didn't know? You're not a reporter?"

"I don't have a thing to do with Stefan Anders." Gilman handed her the ID wallet. She lowered her reading glasses from her nest of hair to inspect it, then frowned. Her tongue poked like a pink mouse between the wire of her dental braces.

"You're not here about the speech?"

Gilman shook his head. "I'm here on a personal matter," he said, and when she looked doubtful he added firmly, "police business. I came all the way from San Francisco to see him."

"Oh. He's not here," she said in a smaller voice. "Really. He left about ten to go to class. After that, he won't be back for the day."

And he had no listed home phone, home address, or schedule, not that she was allowed to tell him. Tomorrow afternoon at the soonest he would be back for his mail, maybe. Harvard professors don't keep a nine-to-five day, she said reproachfully, regretfully.

Outside, Gilman walked around the steps of Widener Library, crossed the Yard impatiently and stopped in front of Memorial Church to look back. It was like a movie setting for a New England university, he thought, too goddam perfect. Church and library face to face across an open field of grass and trees, the red-brick colonial church dwarfed by the gigantic library with the facade of a Greek temple, the body of a railway station.

He jerked up the collar of his raincoat. The elms and sycamores were dropping their last leaves now, golden semaphores, and peace-loving students in their army surplus jackets were strolling indifferently through them. His father had always refused to go driving into New Hampshire and Vermont to see the fall colors. A lot of dead things, he would grumble. Who goes on a trip to see dead leaves?

Gilman paced down the left side of the library. He could go to the university police, he thought, and flash his badge and drink their coffee and eventually get Spurling's telephones and addresses. But he was tired of calling on cops for help. He glanced at his watch and thought of Goddard. *Wary* of calling on cops for help.

At Massachusetts Avenue he found a huge iron gate to the street and a tiny back door to Widener Library. He hadn't been around universities often, but any professor senior enough to be named an official spokesman was bound to have two offices, he guessed, one for seeing students, one for doing his research.

Just inside the tiny door an attendant behind a raised desk seemed to be checking a steady stream of people in and out of the library stacks. When Gilman brought out his ID wallet and asked for Professor Spurling, the little man hardly bothered to glance. "Four thirty-eight, up the stairs, down the hall." He snapped a button, pulled open the door behind him, and waved Gilman in.

But they were catwalks more than stairs, aisles more than halls; and the catwalks were surrounded by thousands of books, stretching in every direction like cells in a body, over him, beneath him, through the spaces below the catwalks, above in darkened, shadowy levels. He felt suspended in a cave of books. His ears filled with sound, hissing. Donald Kerwin country, he thought, not his. His father's world, not his.

He pushed ahead, toward brighter light, and the stacks of books came to an end at a floor-to-ceiling grill of painted wire that separated the library area from a row of office doors and a normal-sized corridor. Gilman walked to his right until he found a door, figured out the one-way lock, and stepped into the corridor. Two doors away, at 438, a young woman stood just outside the threshold, hugging a set of books to her chest. "I'm sorry," she was saying. "I know I shouldn't complain. I know I'm lucky to be in your class at all."

She backed another step or two into the hall and a tall shadow filled the door. From his angle Gilman could see only dark cloth, pale blue and dark blue, one long white hand with an elegant gold ring.

"I just don't feel comfortable having my papers read out loud in class," she said. "I'm sorry."

The tall shadow nodded judiciously, a gesture of comprehension but not of sympathy, and stepped farther into the light.

"Where does it say you have to be comfortable, Miss Lehman?"

The woman stared up at him. His tone had been as cool, as polite, as indifferently neutral as if he had been speaking to the wall. When he said nothing else, she bit her lower lip, nodded once, almost in tears and walked away.

The man had already gone back into his office, the red-eyed woman had retreated into the stacks, when Gilman reached the closing door and knocked once, hard, his cop's knock that frightened bad guys and brought bullies to attention. Martin Spurling was backlit by the bright sunshine from his window, just as the porchlight had disguised his wife: two brilliant, dazzling shadows. But everything here was clearer and sharper than it had been in Framingham, every book, every piece of sharp-edged paper, every diploma and citation up and down the walls, everything in its place, disciplined to stand still and wait, to be not comfortable while its owner went about his business. When Martin Spurling asked his name, Gilman felt a sensation of ice in his throat. When he repeated the question and stepped out of the glare, a tall, handsome man with a face as distant as if it were pressed behind glass, the long-dead face of a Renaissance prince, Gilman felt for a moment as if he had just been challenged to a duel.

21 ▬▬▬▬▬▬▬▬▬▬▬▬▬▬

"I have nothing whatever to say to the police."

Nonetheless Martin Spurling sat down behind his desk and allowed Gilman, uninvited, to enter the room.

"So if you have no other business, Inspector Gilman," Spurling said.

Gilman pinched the bridge of his nose and walked across the rug to the window. The inner courtyard of Widener Library was a complex pattern of bricks, windows, criss-crossing beams. He had never met a man who sent out such coldness. Closed down, blocked out; a human iceberg. Instinctively, Gilman folded his arms across his chest. The idea of asking Spurling about the FBI's visit had died almost at once—let Goddard have a shootout with the iceberg—he just wanted to get back on the subway and start looking for Nina.

But when Gilman turned around finally to face the desk, he felt fascinated as well as repelled. "You do understand what I'm telling you, Professor Spurling?"

"Don't patronize me, Inspector."

"My sister-in-law's in a volatile state of mind, professor. I'm trying to find her before she finds your son."

"And I haven't the slightest idea where he is."

"In her own mind," Gilman said, "she's desperate enough to do anything." His ears screamed with pain. He was talking to drown their sounds, talking to hear himself talk, talking to push the professor someplace where the ice would melt. "In San Francisco she sounded as if she would try to hire somebody to find him, or even to hurt him. There are people like that in Boston, professor." Gilman moved his head without looking back, indicating the city beyond the library, beyond the civilized gates of Harvard Yard.

"You amaze me, Inspector. Such a world."

The sarcasm was so sharp, so mockingly hard that Gilman snapped his head up and stared. Martin Spurling leaned back in his swivel chair, apparently amused. In this light, from the window, the black-and-white photographs seemed to float above his head. One showed a young man in baggy trousers and dirty shirt, standing beside the fender of a battered French car, a Citroën with an odd hump-shaped gadget over the hood. In the background were evergreens, clouds, strange grainy cliffs that rose over the trees like the brow of a skull.

"Not every scholar lives in an ivory tower, Inspector."

Gilman rocked back against the window sill. His mind worked slowly around Spurling's sentence, excavating. "I apologize," he said, and heard with surprise that Spurling's sarcasm had crept into his own voice. "Your ex-wife told me you were a war hero. I forgot."

"Ah." Spurling came to his feet. "My ex-wife. An unlisted number and address in darkest Framingham. My own private unlisted study. You are a resourceful man, Inspector. Now I think it's time for you to be resourceful somewhere else."

"Have you seen your son since he came back from California?" Gilman stayed stubbornly where he was.

"I don't see my son at all, Inspector."

"You don't communicate? You don't give him money, talk?"

"If you spoke to my ex-wife," Spurling said, "you know that my son washed his hands of me completely the day he flunked out of Harvard College. Which he had entered only because of my position here. So he thought. So she thought. There was estrangement for many years before that. My ex-wife's psychoanalytical theory has to do with sons who fail to live up to their father's standards."

"Or vice versa," Gilman said.

Spurling smiled a small, wintry smile. Side by side, they were roughly equal in height, but in contrast to Gilman's habitual bearlike slouch, Spurling's erect posture made him seem the taller of the two.

"I like policemen," Spurling said with clipped irony. Irony, Gilman thought, is saying one thing and meaning another. How was this frost-man connected with somebody like Stefan Anders? "I once gave a lecture on my career in the OSS to the Boston patrolmen's association, and afterward two great burly cops, bigger even than you, Inspector Gilman, came forward rather shyly and asked what I thought of Jane Austen."

Gilman heard the contempt floating through the patrician irony, but he held his ground, drawing on reserves of anger. His father had known Spurling in the war. They both talked down from the same Bostonian heights.

"Wonderful. Jane Austen. Why not call me if your son gets in touch to talk about Jane goddam Austen?"

Gilman scribbled "Lenox Hotel" on the back of his card and flipped it onto the desk. In front of him, at eye level, a second photograph showed an older man, extraordinarily handsome, peering out from beneath the brim of a 1940s fedora and raising a thick cigarette to his lips.

When Gilman straightened, Spurling was standing by the open door, unmistakably dismissing him. There was absolutely nothing of his features in the mug shots of Victor Turelli, Gilman thought. A son would look at a father and see nothing of himself there, a stranger. And vice versa.

"I may be back," Gilman said at the door.

"I expect you will," Spurling said, drawing the same ironic smile from the same cold scabbard.

At the Harvard Coop bookstore, on impulse, Gilman stopped and bought copies of each of Martin Spurling's books.

22

"What do you call this?" Fahey asked in disgust.

He waved his cane at a porno poster on the brick wall in front of them, a four-color photograph of a blonde wrapped from breasts to ankles in chains so tight and hard that her flesh bulged over the links and her mouth made a surprised O, as if it had been squeezed open.

"Sexual freedom," Gilman said, but he thought of Nina and shuddered.

A day wasted. A day gone when he might have been checking hotels, checking cabbies, doing something instead of riding the subway to Cambridge and back. Nobody in San Francisco had been called by the FBI—he had at least managed to check that. In the Boston homicide squad Vico had never even heard of Hastings or Goddard. And now he was wasting his time in the Combat Zone with a garrulous old cop who couldn't find Nina if she drove up and shook his hand.

The Combat Zone, for godsake.

Gilman took a deep breath and started walking again. When he had met him on Tremont Street after seeing Martin Spurling, Fahey had said she had come down to the Combat Zone yesterday—his snitch swore to it. Gilman couldn't believe it, couldn't picture her here—the Combat Zone was the bottom of Boston, five or six grim blocks of adult movie theaters and striptease bars along Washington Street, punctuated by boarded-up windows and doors, porno shops, pawnshops, Chinese restaurants the width of a chopstick. Under the night sky the pavement was black and gritty. A few leering, emaciated hookers drifted down the sidewalks. Junkies in windbreakers and raincoats weaved in and out of neon lights. At the mouth of an alley across the street a middle-aged man fumbled with his zipper while a woman in a red wig like a fishnet crowded her pelvis against him and looked back over her shoulder.

"Herpes triangle," Fahey said, puffing to keep up with him. "The great unlaid."

The world that Cassie didn't know about, Gilman thought, or his father, for that matter. The Combat Zone was a place where you got a cop's-eye view of life, a place where idealism ran out of gas and heroes turned into pimps and hookers. How was Stefan Anders going to change the world down here?

"One more block," Fahey said.

Gilman walked even faster. He couldn't picture Nina here because Nina was too placid, too proper ever to come to a place like this. There was no such thing as sexual freedom, he thought. His mind was chained to images: Nina's face before Donald had died, Nina's small-boned porcelain wrists as she poured drinks, Nina's breasts. "I know how you feel about Nina's figure," Cassie had snapped—he was following her across the goddam continent—what the hell was Nina about?

"Right here," Fahey said, and Gilman stumbled to a halt, trying to pull back his last thought before it was gone. Fahey banged his cane on the sidewalk. Gilman took a deep breath and looked around.

"This guy said he would definitely show?"

"This guy said he would be here, corner of Washington and Stuart, at seven o'clock."

"And he saw Nina?"

"Two of them saw Nina. The first one, the ex-MP, told me he thought she was a class woman but he couldn't figure out what the hell she really wanted, she was just raving about finding this punk Turelli that shot her husband."

"He wouldn't take her?"

"He wouldn't touch her. He turned her down on the spot. This is one private jamoke with his license halfway in the toilet already. He said she should go home and forget it."

"And the other guy?"

"He took it."

Gilman looked up Washington Street toward the looming hulk of Jordan Marsh's, Filene's, the respectable commercial section of downtown. *Adults Only. Private Booths. Talk To A Naked Woman.* A wino passed them on the sidewalk, with his gray chin, his eyes like rotten apples.

"He took it. He said, give him a little time, he could get hold of her. He said he even knows who the guy is she's chasing, Turelli."

"Then where the hell is he?" Gilman said, punching his hands into his raincoat pockets, glaring. Fahey turned his round, pale face toward him, an Irish moon. Started to say something, changed his mind, crooked his elbow, to hold up his watch.

"Give him five more minutes, Gilman."

Fahey hiked his overcoat higher and they both stood in the middle of the sidewalk, letting the pedestrians flow around them.

"The Basin Street," Fahey said, pointing his cane, "used to be a mob joint. When you went in, you're supposed to head to the men's room first, where they put in a fake water tank over the john. A chain-pull gadget. The rule was, drop your weapon in the dry tank, then you go over to the bar. Very well-run dump. They only sell beer in a can, no bottles. Nobody sits at the bar with a piece; you pick it up from the john when you leave. They still had two, three homicides a year."

"I don't understand why she wouldn't tell him her hotel."

"This very spot," Fahey said, "where they put in this wino bench and the little brick patio, this used to be a parking lot with a parked trailer for an office and then an alley. Maybe fifteen years ago I was temporarily with narcotics, doing undercover work. They had me running an informer for them, a black guy that they caught dealing high-quality heroin over in Roxbury. But they weren't that interested in *him*, see—what they wanted was the guy who was supplying him, the big supplier. Three months I keep after my pigeon to set me up with this guy. I buy stuff all over Boston, up and down the north shore. I spend five thousand dollars of city money. Finally, I got to lean hard on the black guy, either set it up or start packing his bags for five-to-seven in Walpole."

He paused to turn slowly around on his cane, searching the street, a whale pirouetting on a stick.

"So he sets up a meeting on this very corner, this spot, where the alley used to be. And we come waltzing up about this time of night too, this kind of weather, cold enough to put cracks in your face. It's even sleeting a little, so the air is full of ice, the way it gets in Boston. There's almost nobody out, not even the junkies. And we walk into this alley. Now I'm out of sight of my backup car, you understand; out of sight of everybody, no gun, just a tape recorder and a hidden mike and this black informer who set me up, and suddenly out from behind the trailer three big guys, big as you, Gilman, they just kind of materialize and make a tight little circle around us. From the street you wouldn't know what the hell was happening. You'd think, guys talking, guys sharing a bottle. And we just stand there waiting and waiting for the big guy to show up. Waiting just like we are now."

A car alarm was going off somewhere down the block, and Gilman's ears were screaming in reaction, high-pitched sounds that seemed to dive in and out of his skull like shrieking birds. They said people went crazy sometimes from tinnitus. There were actual cases of suicide when people couldn't stand the invasion of sound any longer. He clenched his hands around the earplugs as if he would rip them loose in one blind, violent motion.

Fahey limped a few steps closer to the spot where the alley had been.

"All of a sudden," he said, "the guy shows up, the one I'm after for all these months. The enchilada. He's pushing two, three kilos of heroin a week out on the streets; he runs maybe fifty junkies like my informer there. He's a middle-sized guy in a camel hair overcoat, a gold collar pin. He's got a face like a piece of bone."

Fahey held Gilman's arm with a ferocious grip, as if they were both about to fall.

"He's also a guy that used to live three houses down from my own father's house in South Boston."

Gilman lowered his hands. The alarm kept ringing, his ears were exploding.

"If you've never done undercover work," Fahey said, "you don't know what fear is. It's like being a spy in the war, the old Resistance movies. You're alone, the only guy in the world, chin to chin with somebody who's seen you a hundred times walking in and out of this house in your blues, a guy with three hoods crowded so close around you they could each put a knife through your jacket, north, south, east, nobody'd ever notice. And he makes you. He knows exactly who you are. You're not fooling anybody anymore, undercover. And he opens his mouth, he's got a smile like he's opened a goddam grand piano, and he says, 'Hello, Mikey, how ya doin'?' "

"What the hell did you do?"

"I leaned over and pulled his ear down to my mouth and I said, *'I'm after the nigger!'* "

"Jesus."

"It's like a war, Gilman. Sometimes you got to use the other guy."

Gilman slowly turned toward the street. Old Resistance movies. His memory lifted, tugged. But who would use a punk like Victor Turelli? For an instant Goddard's face flashed through his mind. *Who else?* Then he shook his watch free of his sleeve. "Where's this guy's office?"

"It's a hole in the wall." Fahey drew an invisible map on the sidewalk with his cane. "He rents space in a room down on Summer Street, maybe ten minutes from here. Same kind of roach-pit neighborhood. He said I found him one of the two days a week he gets to use it all by himself."

"Let's go."

A junkie, shaking in his thin clothes, edged closer to them, sniffing excitement.

Fahey hesitated a long appraising moment. Then he limped two steps toward the curb and waved his cane at a passing Checker cab.

* * *

The office was on the fourth floor of a shabby nineteenth-century building, bounded by an alley on one side and a parking garage on the other. The elevator didn't work, and the sign on the office door said "Star of Orient Import-Export" instead of "Vincent Miskimin," but there was a light smeared behind one of the frosted windows, and when Fahey knocked the third time with his fist they could hear chair springs grind and shoes hitting wood.

A man opened the door and blinked at them in nonrecognition.

"You forget about us, Vincent?" Fahey growled.

Miskimin rolled his shoulders and lifted his chin defiantly, but he seemed to weave a few uncertain steps even in the doorway.

"Fahey. The roundest cop. The cop that swallowed Cincinnati." He turned his face toward Gilman, frowning, and in the dim light from the office Gilman could see that his pupils were dilated into black hollows and his skin had the texture of damp gray cardboard.

"Coked to the gills," Fahey said.

"I told you I'd meet you. I was just coming to meet you."

"It's seven goddam thirty," Fahey said, backing him into the office. "We waited knee-deep in hookers for you, Vincent, up at Washington and Stuart, like you said."

"Yeah, yeah, Fahey, sit down."

Miskimin waved one hand vaguely at two wooden chairs along a wall divider and walked carefully himself around a metal desk to a padded swivel chair. The plate on the desk said "Arnold Soo," and the office itself was crammed with battered file cabinets, stacks of small wooden crates, samples of brightly colored paper fans with scenes of Boston on them, and plastic bracelets in styrofoam display cases. Miskimin's name appeared only on one drawer of a file cabinet and on the framed investigator's license hanging on the wall beside a calendar.

"Gilman, right?" he said brusquely, without looking at either of them. He was a man about Gilman's age, thin through his upper torso but rounding like a pear at the hips. He jerked his necktie higher and fumbled to clear one side of the desk where he had left a coffee mug of something not coffee, a small plastic sandwich bag rolled tight and secured with rubber bands, and a pencil with a white tip.

"Vincent here used to be a lawyer," Fahey said, still standing. "Before he went and put his business up his nose."

"Fahey here used to be a son of a bitch," Miskimin said, "before he turned into a boil on a prick. You the guy looking for his wife?"

"Sister-in-law," Gilman said.

Miskimin leaned back in the chair and managed a lopsided, unpleasant leer. "Whatever," he said. "Class baggage, my friend. Nice little figure, nice little tits. Out of her fucking mind." He leaned too far back in the swivel chair and grabbed the edge of the desk with one hand for balance. Fahey looked at Gilman and shrugged.

"You told Fahey this morning you didn't know what hotel she's staying at."

"That's right. Secret. Secretive woman. She was going to hire me, then she changed her mind and said just to call a downtown lawyer she had if I saw this Turelli punk. She didn't like my office too much."

"But you told Fahey you could find out the hotel."

Miskimin put both elbows on the desk and cocked his head at Gilman. His pupils moved leftward, toward the coffee mug and plastic bag.

"Yeah, I found out. I spent all day on it."

"What is it?" Fahey asked.

"I get two hundred a day for my time," Miskimin said, looking at Gilman.

Fahey sighed. Gilman put two twenties and a ten on the desk.

Miskimin stared at the bills, then raised his head as if he were going to spit. "I said two fucking hundred a day."

When neither Fahey nor Gilman spoke, he sneered at each in turn. After a moment he took the money and stuffed it into his shirt pocket. "The Parker House," he said, standing up. "Down on School Street. Now get the fuck out of here."

"What's the room number?" Gilman asked.

Miskimin rolled his shoulders and made a motion to go around the desk. "You got fifty bucks' worth right there. Get him out, Fahey."

Gilman held up a warning palm. Fahey nodded, and with his cane hand flipped the telephone on the desk around; with the other hand he opened the Boston telephone directory tied to it by a length of string. Miskimin stopped an inch short of Fahey's chest, unable to get past, and watched while he dialed quickly and held the telephone out to Gilman.

"Parker House Hotel."

"I'd like to speak to a guest in the hotel. Mrs. Donald Kerwin, please."

The clerk left the line for a moment. "No Kerwin registered, sorry."

"Has she been there at all this week? I'm a relative trying to reach her."

"No Kerwin at all."

Miskimin raised both hands to shove Fahey aside and the cane came up and around with a crack, staggering him backwards.

"Cokehead," Fahey said and brought the cane down again on his neck, like a man beating a rug, and Miskimin turned, stumbled over the chair, and fell.

Fahey stooped and grabbed his collar with one small hand and yanked him to a sitting position.

"I feel bad," Miskimin whispered, holding cupped fingers under his mouth.

"You feel like a turd that won't flush," Fahey said. He reached for the money in the shirt pocket, and Miskimin gripped his hand convulsively.

"Don't take it back." His face was pure white now, dead cheesy flesh except for a pink welt the cane had raised from jawbone to ear.

"Give the man something for his money."

"I *need* the fucking money," Miskimin said and twisted his head toward Gilman.

Fahey started to pull and Miskimin clutched his wrist with both hands.

"Turelli," he said and stopped to swallow. "Turelli is a weird kid. You see him on the streets every day, then sometimes for weeks he's just not there anymore. He dresses like he's . . ." Miskimin stopped again to lick bits of skin from his lips. "I told your girlfriend she shouldn't mess with a head case like Turelli."

Fahey jerked his fist upward and Miskimin clung harder. A film of sweat covered his face.

Sometimes you have to use the other guy, Gilman thought. He wanted to turn on his heel and walk out. He imagined Nina coming into a room like this and stopping in horror, Nina accustomed to Donald Kerwin's world, unprepared for Gilman's. How long could she really stick looking for Victor Turelli before she turned and ran for California?

"Let him go."

Fahey released his shirt with a grunt and Miskimin sank back into the chair, hands over heart.

"She didn't hire you," Gilman said. Miskimin nodded. "But you'd bust your ass to make money out of her anyway, wouldn't you?" Miskimin's eyes sought the plastic bag; Gilman pushed it away. "Who'd you go see?"

"Nobody."

"You went to see Turelli."

"No."

"You told him you knew somebody who was looking for him. You'd tell him that for money."

"No."

Junkies are frail, soft people. You can crush a junkie like a paper cup. Gilman bent over him and brought his fists up, knowing his size alone would terrify Miskimin, thinking of Goddard and hating hard guys, all hard guys right or wrong.

"Turelli's not around," Miskimin whispered. "Nobody's seen him." Gilman moved his fists slowly higher. "You could try a little Vietnamese bitch he talks to sometimes. She works nights, the phone place on Stuart." He tilted his head toward Fahey. "*He* knows. Phone sex, whatever it's called. Her name's Janice. Janice Nhu."

Gilman straightened and stood back. "Sleep it off," Fahey said. "Go down to detox and shape up for crissake, Vincent."

Gilman put another twenty on the desk, sliding it under a can of ballpoint pens, and turned to go. Miskimin stared at the money, then wiped his face with one hand, still pressing his shirt pocket with the other. As Fahey reached the door to the hall and pulled it open, he cleared his throat painfully.

"I see more than you think, Fahey. I still see things," he said. "Your little debutante had a .22 pistol in her goddam purse. She finds Vic Turelli, she's going to kill him."

Janice Nhu had nothing to say to them.

When they banged open the door to her cubicle at P-K Productions on Stuart Street, two floors over a topless bar called The Club Thunderbird, she was leaning against a child-sized particleboard desk, speaking French into a telephone.

"This is legal business," the Chinese woman beside Fahey said, still trying to push him away from the threshold. "This place is clean."

"It's beautiful," Fahey said. "It's what Thomas Jefferson dreamed about, he was writing the First Amendment. Tell her to get off the phone and speak English."

Janice Nhu raised her middle finger and glowered.

"Let her finish her call, for fuck's sake," the woman said and succeeded finally in pulling the door closed.

"You got *that* right," Fahey told her. He lit a new cigarette with his Zippo lighter and grinned at the angry woman. "I don't know about San Francisco, Gilman. In Boston this is for guys who can't get on the winning end of a blowjob. The racket is they take your credit card number and they call you back collect. Then some bimbo like Janice in there talks dirty to you or reads out loud from *The Wall Street Journal*, whatever turns you on."

Gilman looked at his watch. "I give her one more minute."

"You got to watch out for premature disconnection," Fahey told the woman. "All these young studs hang up too soon." She set her face and slipped into Janice Nhu's cubicle, closing the door behind her. Fahey leaned his bulk against the plasterboard partition and pushed the next door open with his shoe. Inside at another under-sized desk, looking up with a surprised expression, a woman in Levis and a dirty blue sweatshirt was also speaking into a phone.

"I'm five feet six," she said softly. With her free hand she motioned them frantically away. "I'm, like, thirty-six twenty-four thirty-five, brown eyes, long black hair." Her figure was hidden under the sweatshirt, but her hair was bright yellow and cropped close, in punk fashion, with a luminous green strip running across the top.

"Her hair looks like she jump-started it with a battery," Fahey said loudly, and the woman rose from her chair. "And I'm in the mood," she said into the phone, slamming the door.

"You got a warrant?" Janice Nhu asked behind them.

Fahey looked at Gilman and inhaled smoke.

"That's what I asked them, too, they come barging in waving a badge, they own the fucking world."

"Can you tell me if you've seen this woman?" Gilman extended the photograph of Nina Kerwin that he had brought from San Francisco.

Janice Nhu raised her lip in a short, scornful laugh. "Try a ladies' tea club."

"This one?" He held out the mug shot.

"That's Vic Turelli," Janice Nhu said without touching it. She lifted one foot and adjusted the bright red plastic rainboot she was wearing. Her voice was lightly accented; her face was small and heart shaped and cemented shut with makeup. "Victor Turelli. I don't know where he is, man."

"When was the last time you saw him?"

"Hey, I don't keep a diary. He travels. He might be in Europe now, for all I know. He goes to Europe, California."

"You know where to find him when he's in Boston?"

She glanced at Fahey, then back to Gilman. "You gotta be crazy, man. Come in here wired up like that, both ears, you think I'm gonna talk about my friends to a cop?"

"It's a personal matter," Gilman said. "I want to talk with him, that's all."

"It's a personal matter, you can go fuck yourself. You creeps costing me money," she said, walking back into the cubicle.

"Right. Welcome to Boston," Fahey said. "Whadaya want to do now, Gilman—go see the topless librarians at the Atheneum?"

"She's lying," Gilman said.

"She lies in her prayers, Gilman. She's a hooker."

"Why speak French?" he asked stubbornly. At the other end of the room the Chinese madam was standing by a phone and watching. "Why do the phone talk routine in French, in Boston?"

Fahey pulled open the door to the stairs. "Canada. They probably get a lot of calls from horny lumberjacks in Canada. All the Vietnamese girlies speak French. I'm going home, Gilman; you wore me out."

"I'm staying," Gilman said. She was lying, he thought savagely. Everybody was lying. Nobody had heard of Hastings and Goddard, but they were real, they were there—what the hell had Nina stumbled into? He pictured her in cubicles like this, streets like this; his mouth was dry with fear. How could he rescue somebody he couldn't find?

Fahey shrugged and started down the stairs. "Call me in the morning," he said over his shoulder, "you want to try something else."

Gilman stared for a moment longer at the cubicle doors, then slowly followed him down.

Twenty minutes later Janice Nhu hurried out the front door of her building and started walking fast to her left. Gilman waited for a count of three before he stepped out of the shadows in the service alley where he had been standing.

Fifty yards past him, at the doorway of a darkened smoke shop called The Owl, she paused, looking for someone.

"Janice."

She spun and dodged, but Gilman's bulk filled the little doorway.

"Let me go, man!"

"Who are you looking for, Janice? I'm not going to touch you."

She said something in Vietnamese and slapped both palms flat into Gilman's chest, pushing him backward a step, but he still blocked the doorway, the cruising cars and pedestrians saw only a man's back, a hooker's polished face.

"You saw the white woman."

"I never saw her."

"You know where she is right now, that's where you were going."

"I don't know nothing."

"Does Turelli have her?" His hands shook. He squeezed his eyes shut for an instant against the sudden vision of Nina, Turelli, whatever might happen in the Combat Zone. *"I want to know why you were speaking French."*

The small face lifted in a triumphant sneer and he felt the hard point of a knife against his back.

"Be cool, guy," a voice said in his ear. "This thing come right out your belly button."

"He's a cop," Janice Nhu said.

Gilman twisted his head to see two men crowding his back: sleek black hair, windbreakers. A car jammed with teenagers cruised by, radio blaring, somebody leaning out a window and whooping into the night. Gilman turned on his heel, slamming the blade away with his left elbow, and one of the Vietnamese men swung and punched him wildly on the shoulder while the other yelped and scrambled after the knife.

"Gilman!" Somebody that looked like Goddard was shouting his name two blocks away.

The first man punched his neck, lunging, and then both of them were running, jackets flapping, heading down Washington Street toward brighter lights, and when Gilman turned back to the doorway Janice Nhu was gone.

In thirty seconds he spotted her again, looking over her shoulder and ducking behind the signboard of a pizza parlor. A middle-aged man grabbed drunkenly for her arm and she shook him away, whatever she said cut off by wind and sounds of traffic. The red boots flashed, then disappeared.

At the corner of Washington and Winter Streets he spotted her once more, silhouetted for a heartbeat under a streetlamp. Between them, up and down Washington Street, big-finned cars slid past in pools of light. She turned and ran.

A signal changed half a block away and Gilman was twice driven back by horns and fenders as he tried to cross. When he finally sprinted between two trucks and reached the streetlamp, the sidewalk was clear all the way to the corner: no Goddard, no Janice. At the end of the block, panting, he looked up and saw a dead neon

sign over a double door: Avery Hotel. The hand-lettered sign underneath it said "Closed for Good. No Trespassing." Sheets of plywood
covered the first-floor windows, on each one a stapled notice said the
Avery Hotel was condemned by the board of health, an unsafe building.

Gilman retraced his steps at a trot and found a dark, narrow
alley lined with dumpsters, their great rusty jaws overflowing with
trash.

Where was she?

Every instinct he had as a cop told him something was wrong.
She was lying about Turelli; he could taste it. Was she lying about
Nina too? Was Nina here?

He kicked through the trash from the filthy dumpsters and
found himself in a faint circle of light. Twenty feet in front of him
was a delivery door covered with board-of-health signs and spray-
can graffiti. There were no lights behind the door, no sounds.
Gilman tried the handle and pulled it open.

Cold, black, a sensation of falling: in the murky light, beams of
lumber, door frames, nameless vertical objects rose from the floor.
Fixtures hung down from the ceiling like roots. Farther on he could
see only pale wormy lines of blue and gray that crept over the tops of
plywood barriers, or scuttled under their edges.

Corridor. Kitchen. Hallway. By the time he reached the lobby
his eyes had adjusted enough to let him pick out shapes, his feet had
developed their own shuffling rhythm over the invisible floor. Janice
Nhu would have had a flashlight ready, to move so fast.

He paused. A railing, stairs. When he squinted hard and looked
sideways he could see what must have been the registration desk in
the lobby, a glint of light on metal hooks.

On the second floor there was no more plywood over the windows. Yellow stripes from moving headlights writhed up the walls
and over the ceiling like snakes.

Gilman started down the corridor. Some of the doors to the
rooms were open, allowing light to filter through. The closed doors
yielded to his touch. He stepped inside each room, sniffed, waited to
focus. His imagination filled them all with faces—she could be in
any one of them. Janice. Or Nina. Or both.

On the third floor he peered from the window of a corner room.

In the distance, small and sharply lit, he could see the street-lamps in the Public Garden. Along the sidewalk pedestrians were leaving a Boylston Street theater; in the street cars wove in and out, noiselessly signaling. He stepped back and hurried through the empty room, stripped of all furniture.

When he reached the main corridor again even the faint noises of the street faded away, leaving him only the hiss of his ears. His thoughts made audible. His head was a bowl of breaking waves, an antenna pulling sound from the air. He drew the pistol from its holster and walked along the center of the musty, spongelike carpet.

Sixteen rooms to a side. Elevator doors in the center. Maids' closet. One short dogleg corridor. At the elevator doors he stopped again, listening. Far below, in the cave's belly, cables creaked and twisted. Metal retreated from the cold New England night, groaning. He passed on, to the darkest stretch.

How could he be alone? His ears were filled with voices. His skin was like iron, his blood drummed against it. He stopped and picked out the single open door on his left where the shadows seemed to be moving.

Empty.

He gripped his pistol regulation-fashion so that the muzzle pointed at the ceiling, and he took a step forward just as the first shot blasted the air apart and set off a bomb in his ears.

"You!"

High-pitched, furious, out of the darkness.

Gilman rolled over the carpet, tumbling, dodging. The face above him floated, fired again, too high, and Gilman himself sat up and fired once, twice, and Victor Turelli vanished.

23 ▬▬▬▬▬▬▬▬▬▬

"Five pictures taped on the wall," Gilman said.

He slipped them across the table to Fahey one by one.

"They're all from newspapers. The last one came out of today's *Globe*."

Fahey smoothed it onto the table beside his beer glass. Like the others it had been ripped rather than scissored from the page. The caption was missing, but the face was instantly recognizable as that of Stefan Anders.

"I don't get it," Fahey said, after a moment.

That's because you don't live in Cassie's world, Gilman thought, and heard her voice rising, lecturing, joining his father's voice in a chorus. The world is coming apart at the seams because of political violence, political indifference. Lawless, fanatical men in power, a new generation of spoiled kids stoned out of their ideals on ignorance and entertainment. What we need to save us is a hero.

Be a hero.

"I don't get it either," Gilman said emphatically. "But that wasn't all. I went over the rest of the room. No more pictures of Stefan Anders, but here's something else—the kid turns out to be a Resistance freak. His father fought in the OSS, remember. On the

floor he had fifty, sixty books on the French Resistance and the OSS,
most of them stolen from libraries."

"Nothing else political?"

"Nothing." Gilman had emptied his pistol into the darkness of
the Avery Hotel, but after the single glimpse of Victor Turelli's face,
he had found no other trace of the boy himself, or Janice Nhu, or
Nina—only a room furnished with mattresses, a camp stove and
some utensils, a sleeping bag, a battery lamp.

"And he had war posters, all that stuff in his room at home too,
out in Framingham?"

"All of that." Gilman finished his beer. A passing waiter
grabbed the empty bottle by the neck and hovered expectantly until
Fahey rotated his big head and held up two fingers. When Gilman
had called, he had rumbled ominously about California time and
favors after midnight, but when Gilman had reached the Blue Grill
Fahey was already there, seated in the booth, dressed in his gray
three-piece suit and drinking beer.

"He kept a diary," Gilman added. "I looked through it. Before
he went to California, Turelli made a trip to France to see where his
father had fought in the war. In Paris he spent all his time looking up
people his father knew. Janice Nhu helped with his French."

Fahey smirked.

"He found one of his father's old Resistance comrades, a
woman, and wrote down everything she told him. Look."

Gilman pushed a red and black school notebook across the table
and Fahey picked it up with a sceptical expression on his face. He
licked his thumb and raised the corner of a page.

July 30. To be in the Resistance required *sacrifice*, she
said. Nobody knew how much. What you did, you did *in
secret*. You led two lives, you lived a *lie*.

Scrawled sideways along the margin:

I'm three years old and already afraid of him. I take down
one of his precious books from a shelf and start to color all

the pages with a crayon and I look up and he's coming toward me yelling he has a face like a comet.

Fahey looked up from the notebook and grimaced. "Garbage in, garbage out. What's this supposed to prove, Gilman?"

"I don't know." Gilman was weary, sore; his ears made high-pitched painful whistles. "There's something *wrong* here. The kid talks about his father on every page; he hates him, but he's obsessed with him."

"And you're starting to sound the same way, Gilman. It's one o'clock in the goddam morning. How's this gonna find your sister-in-law?"

"He had this picture folded inside the diary."

Fahey took the photograph he handed him and held it to the light. "It says *Jules Chabot. 'Colonel Verlaine.'* So?"

"Turelli's father wrote a book mostly about him. That's where that picture comes from. His father fought with Colonel Verlaine in the Resistance until Verlaine was killed by the Germans."

Fahey lowered the photograph to the table and studied it for another moment. Then he mashed out his cigarette in a tin ashtray shaped like a trivet, already overflowing with butts and ashes.

"In nineteen forty-four," he said slowly. "Yeah. You wouldn't know squat about that, would you? Ancient history. You were what—two, three years old? I was twenty-four. I came over in the third day at Omaha Beach, with the Seventh Armored. Twelfth U.S. Army, Seventh Armored. I remember about Colonel Verlaine. He was down south somewhere. The French went crazy when the Germans shot him, and the Germans went crazy right back; they spent days down there massacring civilians when they should have been moving their tanks up to Normandy. They burned a church full of women and children in one town. They hung a hundred Resistance guys from the lampposts. If they'd moved their tanks up right away, nobody knows what would have happened; they would probably have shoved our asses right back in the ocean. Everybody forgets how close the goddam war really was."

"I don't know."

"Believe it," Fahey said. He pulled another cigarette from his pack and rolled it between two fingers like a cigar. "I called down to the turret. Nobody reported any shots tonight in the Combat Zone—big surprise, you got to set off an atom bomb to get their attention down there anyway—no hospitals report a white male gunshot victim in his twenties."

"There was blood smeared shoulder high in the hall," Gilman said.

"All right. You're Deadeye Dick in the dark. A place like the old Avery, that could just be from roaches you hit by accident. Or the Avery's got rats the size of Volkswagens running up and down the hall, for crissake. Or you hit him, but you didn't hurt him? You don't want to report it?"

"Would it do any good?"

"Not a bit."

Fahey put the cigarette back in the pack and rubbed his face hard with the palm of one hand, twisting his jowls as if they were sacks of soft white pudding. The waiter returned with two more beers, and Gilman spread a five dollar bill on the table.

Fahey wiped the lip of the beer bottle with the side of his hand and took a swallow. "His father teaches at Harvard, right? The professor you went over to see?"

He was thinking out loud, not expecting an answer. Gilman looked down at the open notebook. History kept punching into the present, he thought, like a fist through a sheet of paper.

He turned a page without actually seeing it and for an instant memory surged back over the noise in his ears: *a wonderful book about Verlaine by a man named Martin Spurling.* Donald Kerwin's voice in the 7-Eleven before he died.

Gilman jerked his head up, blinking suddenly. Then revelation fell slowly away. His shoulders slumped and a sour bile of disappointment filled his mouth. Donald Kerwin read a book a day. He had read Spurling's book; a million other people had too. So what?

He ignored Fahey's stare, looked down again, and turned another page of the notebook.

July 31. Every unit had execution squads. Leader would choose collaborators, Milice officers, even traitors within the Resistance to be shot. *No one admits now they did this*.

She told me in English, she wanted to be sure I understood.

There were two kinds of targets. The first kind you simply set up for and aimed at directly. The second kind was called a target of opportunity. One you took when you could, when it popped up.

She brought me to see an old Frenchman who was dying of cancer who had fought in the Dordogne. "Your father reminded me of clay from the river," he said. "Moist, soft, excellent for potters. Once exposed to air it begins to harden."

The rest of the page was torn off. Fahey was running his fingers through his thin white hair. He glanced at the television over the bar and waved a vague hand at somebody he knew. Executions. They had traced the man who tried to kill the Pope back to the Russian KGB and the Bulgarian government. Cassie's obsessions; paranoia. Why did the pictures all feel like pieces in a puzzle? He looked up. He wanted Fahey to calm him, soothe him, be reasonable.

"What you got, I think," Fahey said, "is a kid living a double life."

"A crazy."

"A crazy kid who has a place in the suburbs, takes college credits in basket-weaving or whatever, a trust fund that lets him go hopping all over the country to ski resorts. A doctor mother, a professor father. And all the time he's set up a crash pad in the Combat Zone, he's got a goddam library of 1944. He's living like some underground fighter in the war."

"He's living the way his father used to live?"

Fahey stopped the beer bottle halfway to his mouth and gave Gilman a curious look.

"Your old man went to Harvard, didn't he, Gilman?"

Gilman drank and said nothing.

"I got the unlisted number you wanted," Fahey said. "I also called a guy I know in the San Francisco PD." He yanked out the cigarette again and lit it with surprising quickness. "I asked all about you out there. They think you're a good cop, but you dress like a Goodwill truck, and you argue with lawyers. Your old man went to Harvard and Harvard Law, you never went to college at all."

His face was a broad white moon emerging from a wreath of smoke.

"You got no kids, right?"

Gilman drank beer. He would buy a huge button that said he had no children and wear it to show to strangers.

"I got six, all grown. There's only two ways to punish your parents, Gilman," Fahey said. "Be different from them. Or be like them."

On impulse Gilman stopped the car and walked to the telephone booth, stepping across ceramic black puddles of rain from a brief shower that had fallen while he was in the Blue Grill. He punched coins into the slot and dialed the unlisted number Fahey had gotten for him.

Martin Spurling answered at the second ring.

"This is Gilman, Professor Spurling."

"You obviously know what time it is, Gilman. You're calling on an emergency, yes or no?"

"Yeah." He was obsessed with Martin Spurling too—he admitted it. He knew exactly how Victor Turelli felt. "I got a look at your son tonight for a minute."

Spurling hung up without a word.

Gilman took a breath and stared past the edge of the telephone booth, toward the curve of sand and lapping water on the other side of the road. The parks commission sign on his right said "Malibu Beach," a place he had forgotten was in Boston first, long before California. They wore wooden stocks in Boston, bikinis in Malibu.

He took out more coins and dialed again and Cassie answered instantly, as if she had been holding the telephone in her hand. In San Francisco it was only ten-thirty, a continent away.

"Me."

"Did you find her yet? I've been so worried."

"Still looking. She hasn't called?"

"Nothing, not even a call for the girls."

Gilman listened, answered her questions mechanically. He pictured her in their bedroom, sitting on the big bed with magazines and books heaped around her. The marital bed. "Marital-martial": cousin words. Victor Turelli had gone to France to learn about his father in the war. He was obsessed with learning about his father. So why had he gone to Tahoe City?

"If you're still there on Saturday, you could go hear Stefan Anders," Cassie said, and Gilman bristled at the note of challenge in her voice. The world was coming apart, as usual; he should save it. Political violence was Cassie's version of the Combat Zone, he thought. But naive, abstract; an intellectual's idea of evil. He listened with a grim face.

Except, what the hell had Donald Kerwin done to bring the FBI down on him?

"I love you," Cassie said softly.

After he had hung up, he stood stiffly in the booth for another moment, left hand still gripping the telephone tight. The war was over, it was over forty years ago. But it was still going on somehow for Victor Turelli. For who else? He felt time flowing through the night and around him, like a stream, spreading out and into the black open spaces of Boston.

When he started toward the car, the stars in the New England sky had dried to a thin, lacy crust.

24 ▬▬▬▬▬▬▬▬▬▬▬▬▬▬

The first tick sounded like snowflakes hitting a window.

Spurling was awake in an instant.

The second tick came from the ground floor, wood pulling away from wood and catching. He reached carefully and slid the drawer of the nightstand open without a sound. His feet felt for slippers under the bed.

At the landing he paused and extended the pistol until its blue barrel glinted. He lived on Francis Avenue, one of Harvard's faculty rows. Enormous Victorian houses were set back under stately oaks and sycamores, fenced, patrolled, a peninsula of affluence on the borders of unprosperous, unfashionable Somerville. Not a house on it had escaped burglary. Not a liberal professor on it without his electronic alarm system, his dogs, or his unacknowledged handgun.

Spurling let his eyes flick for a moment toward the clock at the bottom of the stairs. Gilman had called less than half an hour ago. Would the policeman have the nerve to come to his house like a common burglar?

At the third step from the bottom he paused again.

The big house creaked and shifted its weight in the night. Spurling glanced toward the padded door on the left that led to the kitchen, hesitated, then decided. He leaned toward the source of the sound on the right, his study. His heart thundered as if he were twenty years old and back in the war. His hands moved even before his eyes picked out the shadow—left hand thumping the light switch, right hand lifting the pistol and aiming.

"Did you come to steal money?" he asked wearily. His heart shook and slowed. His thumbnail snagged the safety catch on the pistol and pushed it forward.

Victor Turelli slammed the desk drawer shut and straightened to his full height, blinking.

"I wouldn't take your goddam money!"

"Ah yes," Spurling drawled. One part of his mind noted critically that he had already vaulted back to the ramparts of irony. Irony was his self-defensive mechanism, automatic, unsleeping. He knew that outside the classroom he almost never spoke now without irony. "Grandmother's generous trust. Mother's medical practice: phobias cured, spells cast, for a hundred dollars an hour. In that drawer you'll find only my private correspondence, nothing else." He discovered that he had stepped backward as his son had come forward, and now stood six paces away from the door to the hallway and the stairs. He watched his hands as if they belonged to some other person. They deposited the pistol on a bookshelf, pointing sideways. They pulled open a cabinet of bottles and glasses standing beside the books.

"You could knock or call," he said. "You could even come in the daytime like other people." When Victor had been briefly a student at Harvard, he had worn the same kind of cast-off Army clothing he wore now—Spurling had watched in disgust as his son crossed the Yard. A jacket with the faded outlines of a sergeant's stripes. Dirty, unpolished combat boots. Blue Navy watch cap. In eighteenth-century London, troublemaking upper-class rowdies had dressed in the equivalent of Georgian combat fatigues to shock their parents' bourgeois sensibilities. *Plus ça change.*

His hands poured bourbon into a glass, then fumbled around the sides of a plastic ice bucket, but the ice cubes from early evening had long ago melted. He lifted the top of another small, empty bucket. He would do anything to avoid looking at his son.

"I've been traveling," Victor said in the high strained voice he always used with him. Whatever went wrong with people had gone wrong early with Victor, he thought. You could see it in his eyes; you could always see it in his eyes, from early childhood; something not quite right, something single-minded, angry, hopeless. It had been a mistake to marry. He was incapable of the tenderness his wife wanted, underneath her bluster. He had long ago rendered himself too obdurate for what she wanted, what their son wanted. If you looked for irony, the name Victor was a good start.

"You went to Lake Tahoe in California, didn't you?" Spurling forced himself finally to turn around and face him. "Your mother sent me my share of extraordinary legal bills, on the assumption apparently that I should somehow pay them."

Victor paced back and forth by the desk, always a child in motion. "Before that I went to Europe," he said.

"Ah."

Spurling drank the bourbon straight and looked at the pistol lying on the shelf. After the war he had kept a gun by his side for months, carried it illegally to classes at Harvard, into the library, restaurants, when he walked the streets at night. His view of human nature, he told himself, was eighteenth-century. Trust no one. Expect the worst. Man is animal *rationis capax*. An animal "capable" of reason, but not bloody likely to use it.

"My French was perfect," Victor said, "fucking perfect. I talked to everybody."

"Then your six months at Harvard weren't altogether wasted, were they?" Spurling murmured. Another voice inside him was riding over his irony, shouting caution. But his face betrayed nothing. His body was a shell. His face was a mask, with slits for his eyes to peer through.

Victor twisted his lower lip and stared at him with his half mad eyes. "I talked to *Brissac*!" he said suddenly.

Part of Spurling's mind watched with amazement as he turned calmly back to the liquor cabinet and poured more bourbon into the glass. But his hands, he noted, were unsteady now; his hands quivered as if he had been struck.

"What do you want, Victor? Why are you here?"

"Do you know a man named Goddard in the government?"

"What are you talking about?"

"Or Hastings? More secret than the CIA, both of them!"

"You're drunk; you're high on something."

"You've seen them—I've seen them too—they want me, they know I'm your son. *They know everything!*"

The glass rose unbidden to Spurling's mouth. In the clarity of his shock he noticed for the first time the lump under the left shoulder of the army jacket and the stiffness of Victor's movements.

"I've never heard of them."

"In the Resistance"—Victor said wildly, pleading—"they called you *un confrère.*"

Spurling looked at his son with no expression whatsoever, a face of ice.

"I've been hurt—I came to you for help."

"Get out, Victor," he said.

25 ▬▬▬▬▬▬▬▬▬▬

At eight o'clock the next morning, sitting in his bedroom in the Lenox Hotel, Gilman called the main offices of the FBI in Washington. For half an hour he sat by the phone while his call was kicked up a long ladder of receptionists, secretaries, supervisors—there were no agents named Hastings or Goddard in the Boston area, sir. If individuals in Boston identified themselves as agents, Gilman should certainly examine their credentials closely before cooperating. And if he would leave his name and number . . .

At five minutes to nine, Gilman pulled through Harvard Square and drove up Mount Auburn Street to Cronin's bar, where he turned sharply left out of traffic and sped down a narrow alley.

He remembered it from the days when his father would bring him over to watch Harvard football games—it was Cambridge's famous unmarked parking lot, where every student and professor in the know went to find a space and avoid a ticket. The alley led past Cronin's and a Dunfey's Motel into a huge stretch of potholed asphalt the city had never got around to improving. On the right stood a long line of empty MBTA buses and maintenance trucks. On the left were five or six metered rows, jammed with cars.

Gilman worked the Plymouth down the line of buses, scanning

impatiently for a place. Cars were double-parked, triple-parked, in typical infuriating Massachusetts chaos. When he reached the end of the last row, the asphalt gave way to a narrow strip of mud and gravel. Just beyond that stood a low stone wall, separating the cars from the slanting tracks of the MBTA tunnel below and the open space where the subway trains emerged, sunned themselves briefly, then reversed for the trip back to Boston.

A few other drivers had already risked parking in the soft mud. Gilman gunned the motor up the slight incline, got out, and saw Goddard.

Gilman slowly straightened, key still in his hand at the door lock.

Goddard walked two steps toward him and stopped. He was twenty yards away, dressed in the same black topcoat he had worn before. He opened the coat slowly and reached inside. Hastings stepped from behind a van, another twenty yards to Goddard's right.

Gilman moved to the back of his Plymouth and edged into the nearest metered row. There were people in the lot, one or two students late for class, but they were all far away by the motel, hurrying toward Harvard Square. Gilman went sideways behind parked cars. Goddard followed silently. Gilman ducked behind a pickup truck with a camper top, stooped, scrambled in a crabwalk past half a dozen cars. When he popped up again, Goddard was the same distance away, peering over a meter. Hastings was gone.

Not FBI, Gilman thought. Despite the chill air his face was slick with sweat. His ears pounded with blood. Not cops of any kind. Who runs them?

Hastings appeared at the fender of a car thirty feet away.

Gilman backed and circled away from him, to the right. Then it was Goddard's turn to disappear. Ten seconds later he surfaced in the same row, and Gilman, still backing away, could see the bullet chambers glinting in his revolver, the sluglike silencer on the barrel.

No second warnings. If they backed him against the train wall— squeezed him into a corner . . . He would take Hastings first, he thought. Hastings was closer, smaller; he would throw him up as a shield. Over the boom in his ears a new sound penetrated. Cat and mouse, shift to the right again. The motel lobby came into view.

Goddard stopped, bent slightly at the knees in a shooter's stance. Braced his elbow on a car roof.

An orange MBTA bus rolled abruptly out of the line by Cronin's and toward them. "Not in Service." Hastings twisted his head to see. Gilman sprinted to his right and stumbled past the last few meters, forcing a huge grin to his face, holding up his thumb in a hitchhiker's sign. Behind the windshield the driver grinned back, a kid of twenty in dirty mechanic's uniform, slowing the bus, pumping the door for a lark.

Gilman swung up just as Goddard lowered the pistol and started to run. When he looked into the driver's mirror a moment later, they were standing side by side, staring.

Professor Spurling's class had begun ten minutes ago, his secretary admitted.

Gilman stayed planted where he was in front of the desk, refusing to move.

She looked unhappily around the office. It was silly, she said, but she shouldn't give out university information. At the desk behind her, another secretary shrugged and resumed typing. A trio of students shifted their bookbags across their shoulders and made impatient faces. Gilman waited two seconds, then simply reached across her desk and picked up the mimeographed schedule she had consulted.

"Hey!"

Comparative Literature 161A. Mr. M. Spurling. Monday, Wednesday, Friday, 9–10 a.m. Sever 11.

Ignoring a bleat of protest, he moved to his left and ran a finger down a jumble of posters and announcements on the bulletin board until he came to a red and white map of Harvard University. Next to it the newest, biggest poster, six bright copies strung in a horizontal line, announced that Stefan Anders would speak on Saturday evening, in a place called Sanders Theatre.

Tomorrow.

Martin Spurling's name was printed just below Anders's.

Gilman set off across Harvard Yard with the torn map in his hand.

*   *   *

When he pushed open the door of the classroom, Spurling was just in the act of chalking a name on the blackboard.

At Gilman's entrance he turned, looked up, and broke off his lecture in midsentence.

In absolute silence Gilman walked slowly down the middle aisle. Students on the left and right began to raise their heads from their desks and crane to see him. Ignoring them, he chose a seat halfway along, in the middle of a semicircular row, and sat down. Spurling waited, hand motionless over the blackboard, gazing coldly up from his lecturer's platform at the base of the little wooden amphitheater. Then without acknowledging the interruption or Gilman's presence, he resumed.

It was the war again, Gilman realized at once. He leaned forward and rubbed the earplugs of his tinnitus masker, indifferent to the students' whispers. Spurling was lecturing on the war, the subject that obsessed his maniacal son. The names written on the board were Albert Camus, Simone de Beauvoir, Jean-Paul Sartre, Jules Chabot. He was describing to the students the literature of the French Resistance.

And he was good, Gilman thought as the class recovered its momentum. The bastard was terrific. He spoke without notes. He moved back and forth on the platform, sometimes raising a hand for emphasis or snapping his voice to make a point, occasionally pausing for long challenging silences, as if his thought would take a moment to cross the gulf to his audience, their reaction another moment to return. Once or twice he read in French from an open book on the lectern and the students laughed. Once he simply stood in front of the blackboard and recited in French, something mellifluous and melodramatic that ran up the classroom in waves of sound and thrilled Gilman like the sight of the ocean.

Five minutes from the end of the hour, Spurling closed the book crisply and looked far away, over their heads, to the top of the smudgy windows that opened out onto the great bulk of Widener Library at anchor in Harvard Yard.

"You will find in all their variety of form," he said, "in the plays and essays of Camus and Sartre, the fiction of Simone de

Beauvoir, the poetry of Jules Chabot—in all that rhetorical variety you will find a single powerful theme that unifies them as writers, as thinkers, as resistants.

"Freedom.

"But nothing so simple as mere freedom from the tyranny of the Nazi occupation, though that is the point at which the theme most often begins to emerge.

"The freedom these writers treat has to do with the choice a person makes, the choice each of us makes, at a crucial moment in our lives, which defines forever our essential, our *existential* character. For paradoxically, no one was ever more free to be himself than in the years of German occupation: that is, to be the person he decided to be, and to accept responsibility for his choice. Or to put it as Jules Chabot did, 'Colonel Verlaine' . . ."

He stopped and looked dramatically around the lecture hall. Every student was utterly still. None of them could be ignorant of Spurling's history, Gilman thought, not after the newspapers and television of the last week. He could feel the room hold its breath.

"As Colonel Verlaine said to me personally, when I was approximately your age, some forty years ago now, privileged to fight beside that great hero and writer, 'Freedom is never more intense than when it no longer exists.'"

On Spurling's face for a moment there was a look of pain, but he went on without hesitation.

"By that, he meant that with all the Nazis had taken away, one freedom had still been left to us, inevitably. Each of us was still free as never before to choose our own fate—to resist or to accept. For in ordinary times we tend to overlay our lives with a thousand amusements and distractions and evasions. We forget our absolute freedom to define our essential character. But under the German occupation there were no such evasions. Each day, at every beat of our pulse, we had to decide on what terms we would live, or die."

"We" and "us," Gilman thought. For some men the war would never be over. They thought of it every day of their lives; it colored their lives like a dye. His mind was moved, but whether with anger or envy, he couldn't tell.

"The questions the war posed," Spurling said, "were, What

will you give your absolute loyalty to—self or cause? And more cruelly still, If in this condition of purest freedom you discover your
essential self—the self you were meant to be—will you be willing to
sacrifice it then, or sacrifice others for it?

"The brightest among you will have already guessed that in
these books, as in the Resistance itself, the theme of freedom be-
comes inextricably entangled with the theme of betrayal."

Spurling halted abruptly, taking them all by surprise, his voice
dropping nearly to a whisper at the last word. With no further dis-
missal he took the closed book under his arm and bent to replace it in
his briefcase. One by one the students closed their own books and
notebooks. No one spoke. A few began to rise timidly from their
desks and to shrug on their coats and bookbags.

From the platform Spurling watched without speaking as the
classroom slowly emptied and noises grew louder in the corridors
outside. Then he came up the aisle toward Gilman.

"If you appear in my class again," he said, stopping opposite
Gilman's seat, "I shall have the university police throw you out."

Gilman got heavily to his feet, adjusting his tinnitus wires, and
squeezed out onto the aisle beside Spurling, blocking his way. What
was he like at twenty-two? Gilman wondered—these kids' age,
Fahey's age, his father's. Old men talked about the war incessantly,
and you knew nothing finally about it.

"My father says he served with you in the OSS."

Spurling's eyes were frigid and black. His face had the handsome sheen of a man who has always taken care of himself, Gilman
thought irrelevantly. Why the hell doesn't he wear glasses like everybody else in Harvard Yard? Why don't his ears ring and his hands
shake? From the corner of his eye he could see the second hand
tracking the circle of the classroom clock. Where was Nina?

"Your father was who?"

"William Gilman. A lawyer. He worked down the hall from you
in Washington, he says, when the OSS was going out of business
after the war."

"I have no memory whatever of your father."

Students were crowding into the lecture room now, taking seats for the next class. A woman wearing a blue business suit and yellow running shoes came hurrying in, smiled a greeting at Spurling, and set her own briefcase on the lecturer's platform.

"Yeah." Gilman didn't move. "I stayed up most of the night reading your book on the French Resistance," he said. "Then I went through some of the three thousand other books on the Resistance that your son had stolen."

For a long moment Spurling simply stood in the aisle facing him while the students streamed around them, choosing their seats. "Come outside," he said, and began walking toward the exit.

"Where did you get my son's books?" He stopped at the foot of an uphill path, in the shadow of Widener Library. His voice was controlled, contemptuous, but he stood waiting for an answer.

"He put slips of paper between pages he wanted to mark," Gilman said. "Wherever they talked about execution teams in the Resistance: people who secretly killed collaborators and traitors. You don't mention them in your book." He reached into his raincoat pocket and pulled out the paperback copy of *The Making of a Maquisard* that he had bought in the Harvard Coop. With a cold, indecipherable smile, Spurling took the book from him.

"There were teams like that, weren't there?" Gilman said.

Spurling looked at him for another long moment without speaking. "Sometimes a French civilian was accused of collaborating with the Germans. Yes."

"Your theme of betrayal," Gilman said.

Spurling opened the book to the title page and took a gold Cross pen from his pocket.

"He marked one page where you said that the OSS was afraid of what its agents might do when they got back to civilian life." Gilman had no idea what he was saying—he was floundering wildly, pushing in any direction. There was no point in asking a man like Spurling about Hastings and Goddard or anything else. He ought to be back on the street, searching for Nina. But at that instant he was uncontrollable, driven. More than find Nina, more than find Victor Turelli, he wanted to break Spurling's ice into pieces, he wanted to open up the professor. "They were afraid trained killers would keep on killing after the war," he said. His mind made a ghoulish, crazy image: open him up like a coffin.

Spurling wrote something in the book and handed it back to Gilman. "Dangerous persons like me," he said with withering irony. "Yes."

Gilman took the book and opened it to the page where Spurling had written. A small, neat handwriting, every letter clear and firm. The inscription was a single line of Latin followed by his signature: *Felix qui potuit rerum cognoscere causas. Martin Spurling.* Gilman shut the book crisply, just as Spurling had done in his lecture. He would be damned if he would ask what it meant.

"I found your son in the Combat Zone last night. He took a shot at me. He tried to kill me."

Spurling's face closed. "You're a sick man, Gilman. I don't believe you. You're obsessed with my son. You're obsessed with me. If I see you again, I'll have you arrested."

He had walked five steps up the knoll, toward a low, shabbily modern building where the words "Lamont Library" had been scraped away from a brow of ivy. There were libraries wherever you turned in Harvard, Gilman thought. The place was an elephants' graveyard of books, books came there to die.

"Just a minute!" Gilman shouted.

Thirty feet away, Spurling stopped and looked back, rigid, trim, outlined against the skeletal branches of a dying elm. At that distance, in the glare from the thin New England sun glancing off the library windows, his white hair appeared almost blonde again, metamorphosing back into the past.

"Do you have a question?" he said.

Gilman walked a step closer. Two men in overcoats came around a curve in the path, for a panicky instant looking like Hastings and Goddard. Did he have a question? Dozens. Why did your son kill Nina Kerwin's husband? What do you know about phony FBI men who follow me? Why did you care about Stefan Anders? Who do you love?

"Yeah." There was an unbearable rush of sound in his head. Gilman surprised himself with the question that finally emerged. "What did you really do in the war?"

26 ■■■■■■■■■■■■■■■■

"What the hell did he say?" Fahey asked.

"He said I was crazy."

Gilman stood up suddenly from the bench and walked three restless steps along the brown grass before turning back to Fahey. At the edge of the Boston Common, a hundred yards away, midday traffic honked and belched up and down Tremont Street. A mechanical cherry-picker extended its long neck and nodded like a bright green prehistoric beast while the workman inside repaired Christmas lights. There were people walking in every direction on the Common, but nobody was heading toward them, no two men.

"He said I was crazy. His war record was immaterial. His son was not obsessed with the war; there was no evidence those books and photographs belonged to him. I had nothing for proof. 'Nothing will come of nothing,' he said."

Fahey shifted his bulk uncomfortably on the bench and squinted toward the corner of Avery Street.

"You can't see a goddam thing from here," Gilman snapped. Frustration was coming up everywhere in geysers of anger. He tried for a moment to control it, then snapped again. "I asked you to watch Janice Nhu's door, dammit. I don't see why you aren't down there on Washington Street."

"I told you once, Gilman." Fahey's voice was patient, level. "I stand around Washington Street, I'm made. Half the winos in the Combat Zone are creeps I've busted one time or another. The other half are just naturally gonna notice a slim, good-looking guy like me. I'm spending three dollars an hour of your money. I got four hooky-playing kids posted where I want them. I promised twenty dollars bonus to the first one that sees Janice Nhu and comes busting his ass up to this bench to tell me. She's covered, don't worry."

"You really trust street kids to come and find you?" Gilman paced to the other end of the bench and watched a large group of men and women setting up some sort of exhibit or track on the open space between their little hillock and the fence of the Central Burial Ground by the Boylston Street MBTA station. Nina wouldn't go back to Miskimin's office, he was sure of that. It was the longest of long shots that she—or Victor Turelli—would come to Janice Nhu.

"Street kids in a place like the Combat Zone see everything that happens anyway," Fahey told him. "They're like the goddam Baker Street Irregulars."

The literary reference faintly surprised Gilman and made him look up. Fahey with a book in his huge lap, reading. Gilman didn't understand anybody now; all the people he knew were slipping loose, out of their categories and forms. He shoved his hands into the raincoat pockets and watched a stout woman march across the grass toward the exhibit, pulled like a ponderous boat by three small bobbing dogs on a leash.

"Dog trials," Fahey said from the bench behind him. "For the Jack Russell terriers." He bounced a menthol cigarette out of his crumpled pack and tapped the filter against his thumbnail. "They do it once a month on the Common or over at Olmstead Park by the Fenway." As he spoke, Gilman saw other owners and dogs converging on the open space. Next to the fence two more beefy women were setting out folding chairs and a card table.

He tugged viciously on the wires of his tinnitus masker and stalked away again. When he'd left Spurling in Harvard Yard, he had called Hertz from a pay phone and told them his Plymouth wouldn't start in Cambridge and they would have to pick it up. Then he had taken the subway to the Haymarket Station and rented another car from a different agency, using the desk at the Bostonian Hotel. Was he crazy?

Fahey lit the cigarette with his battered Zippo and clicked it shut. Then with a grunt he heaved himself up from the bench and walked closer to the path, observing the dogs. His breath was full of mint. From his armpits and cheeks there came the same smell of mint. He was a huge fat man, a great snow-covered house smelling of mint and smoke.

"You think the old man's hiding something, right, Gilman?"

"I think," Gilman said slowly and rubbed his face with both hands. He saw Spurling again, striding downhill toward him in Harvard Yard, hawk-faced, white-haired, ice and irony. His face had betrayed nothing at all when Gilman mentioned the Resistance, the execution squads. Stubbornly, irrationally, Gilman played the film again in his mind and this time saw Spurling flinch and turn away.

"What if he had a secret?" Gilman asked hoarsely, starting his sentence over. "What if maybe he did belong to an execution team in the war?" Below them people were arranging orange plastic cones in a fifty-foot rectangle, marking boundaries. "What if the kid went to France and somehow found out?"

"And the kid's a crazy. He hates his father, he says, but he wants to be just like him?"

Gilman nodded carefully, once.

"So why kill your brother-in-law, Gilman? He wants to execute collaborators the way his old man did in the war, why go all the way to California, shoot a perfect stranger?"

"The FBI," Gilman said and stopped.

"No. You checked with Washington—what do you want? Nobody can just call up the FBI and turn them loose on a guy, Gilman. They don't deliver like pizzas. I can't do it, you can't do it. The chief of Boston PD probably can't do it. No Harvard professor's gonna do it, war hero or not."

One of the women below them was carrying a clipboard and clearing a space through the crowd, while owners were kneeling at the far end of the rectangle and stroking their dogs. "Those are burrowing dogs," Fahey said. "I got a Jack Russell myself. They started out breeding them in England to go down holes after foxes. The big hounds would chase the fox until it went down in a hole, and the hunters would come riding up, pull their Jack Russell out of a pouch on the saddle, and tell him to dig the bastard out."

"Go to the Ground," someone announced in a booming voice. The crowd was now well over a hundred milling people, many with dogs, others simply standing and watching. The voice grew even louder. "'Go to the Ground' is the underground maze trial."

"What happens," Fahey said, "is the dogs start down at one end and run through those cones. The dog club people dig a little maze under the ground at the other end, about ten, fifteen feet long; then they cover it over with dirt and grass. Usually they put a rat in a cage at the end, because your Jack Russell dogs hate rats. So everybody does what they're supposed to. The dog goes through the maze as fast as he can, he finds the rat, he barks his goddam head off."

"The winner last month," the voice shouted, "was William Butler Yeats, in a time of forty-eight seconds. Everyone wait right here."

"The kennel club won't say so, but half the time the dogs kill the rats, even in the cage."

"You think I'm imagining it," Gilman said.

Fahey gave him a curious look. Nearby a woman hurried past carrying a Jack Russell under one arm and an infant under the other. "They told me back in San Francisco you're divorcing your wife, Gilman."

"No." Gilman spoke instantly, without thinking. He wasn't sure whether he was shocked or not.

"I don't know, Gilman. You're under a lot of strain." Fahey braced his weight on his cane and flexed his bad leg. In the red anorak he had worn today instead of his overcoat, Gilman thought irrelevantly, Fahey looked like a barn door with legs. "Your wife, your sister-in-law, whatever's going on there. You tell me stories, but nobody else has ever seen these guys, the FBI's never heard of them. And you don't look like you've slept for two days. To tell the truth, you look like a sock full of shit right now. Go lie down at your hotel for two or three hours, then come back here. I'll call you if something happens."

Gilman started to shake his head and object.

Fifty feet away the woman with the clipboard had reappeared holding a small metal cage with a brown rat in it, and as every dog in sight began to bark and leap and howl, Gilman clapped his hands to his ears, as if his head were about to explode like a bomb.

When the telephone rang, Gilman woke groggily and ran his hands through his hair. The telephone rang again. He blinked and shook his head. He had sprawled on the bed fully dressed, and now he sat up slowly, still half asleep, frowning at the muddy streaks his shoes had left on the cover. At the next ring he reached vaguely forward, through a tangle of tinnitus masker wires, and picked up the receiver.

Her voice so surprised him that for ten seconds at least he made no answer.

"Are you there?"

"Nina?"

"Did you hear what I said?"

"Nina, where are you?" Somehow he was standing and pulling the telephone toward the door.

". . . whatever. Cassie was going to tell you, didn't she tell you?"

Gilman's eyes turned toward the wad of pink message sheets he had picked up from the desk on the way in—all from Cassie: "Please call." He had parked on the street four blocks from the Lenox and walked down Exeter Street in the center of a crowd, scanning for Hastings and Goddard. He had entered his room with his hand on his gun. He had thrown the message sheets down in a ball on the floor.

"Go home!" Nina shouted into the phone.

"Tell me where you are."

"I've found him," she said, quavering. "That's all you need to know. I've found the son of a bitch that killed Donald. I found him by myself. I called Cassie to tell you both."

Gilman's ears tuned in and out as she spoke; his mind raced. There was all the fiercely wound tension in her voice that he remembered from San Francisco, all the slurred words and choppy rhythm. But something else too, softer, more hesitant under the fierceness, more like the Nina he knew. Through the sound of her voice telling him again that she had called Cassie, he heard automobiles, engines, the faint squeal of tires starting to roll. Why call Cassie?

"Go home *now*," Nina said. "Let me do what I have to do—"

"Nina—"

"He was the best husband," she said, beginning to cry.

She wants me to stop her.

"Nina—" He heard metallic rattles in the background, a bell ring once. Where was she? Where had she found Victor Turelli?

"You don't know what it's like," she said. "There's just one picture fixed in my mind. No matter which way I look. No matter if I close my eyes, talk, drink—I see Donald's face in the coffin—I see his face, his hands, his legs—*and they never move*."

"Nina, tell me—"

Another bell rang. The line went dead with a click.

Gilman swung his bulk around in the narrow room and slammed the telephone down, cursing. A moment later he was juggling it together again, flipping through his tiny notebook for a number, and starting to dial.

There was nobody waiting on Exeter Street, no men with guns, no kids in the French Resistance. Gilman forced himself to slow down and pause for a beat on the hotel steps, glancing each way, up and down the sidewalk. In another minute he was sliding into the driver's seat of his car and beginning to fumble for a map.

Angela Freeling hadn't answered. He had dialed the number twice from his room and both times got only a machine. Gilman found the turnpike on the map and moved his finger toward the nearest entrance. With his eyes closed, over the steady whistle of his ears, he could hear the bell sound in the background again, tires move. If he had winged Victor Turelli with his gun, sooner or later the kid would find a doctor. If his wrecked ears hadn't betrayed him, the sound of the bell and cars came from a toll stop out on the turnpike, coins flying into the plastic funnel. Gilman punched the car into reverse, made a U-turn on Exeter Street and began to look for signs for Framingham.

Newton first, he thought. Then Newton Center. Weston, Wayland. He tried to run the exits through his memory. Cochituate. Natick. Past Boston University and Cambridge Street the railroad tracks raced alongside the turnpike, bright and polished as nerves. Past Newton there were blue-tinged hills rising abruptly out of the horizon like humpbacked whales. Glassy, brittle ponds stiffening for winter. Gilman slowed for the toll booth at the Natick exit, looking for Nina, then sped up again and headed west on Cochituate Road.

At the junction of Concord Street, he turned left, past Framingham Center, leaned into a curve, and passed a delivery van whose driver raised one hand in protest, a white spot spinning away in the mirror. Learned Pond. Farm Pond. The whole countryside was ponds and fields and spidery black trees, the landscape of his childhood, as unlike California as it could possibly be—who goes to see dying things? his father had asked.

How could you be loyal to a landscape?

Leaves swirled into the air on gusts of wind, rising suddenly from the curbs like flocks of red and golden birds.

No one answered Gilman's knock.

He waited three more minutes by his watch, then backed off the porch steps and looked to his left, over a border of ornamental stone and flowerpots. Where the hell was Angela Freeling? Where the hell were her prehistoric dogs?

At the corner of the house the brown lawn dropped steeply away in the pale afternoon light, toward thick woods and what seemed to be one end of yet another pond. On impulse he crossed behind the garage and stopped to rub grit from a window pane. There were two cars parked inside. He walked to the next window and rubbed again.

"Did you need something?"

Gilman spun to face a middle-aged woman carrying a cardboard box of Christmas decorations.

"My watch must be slow," he said, straightening, smiling, making a gesture with his wrist.

She shifted the box in her arms.

"Our appointment was for three," Gilman said. "I was afraid Doctor Freeling had already left."

"She did. She left over an hour ago, easily."

Gilman smiled ruefully and tried to make silent calculations. He had lost at least fifteen minutes following a poorly marked road into an endless new development of houses. If Nina had called from anywhere in Boston, she could have been in Framingham long, long before.

"Is anybody else around? I didn't get an answer at the door."

"People are in and out all day," the woman said shortly. "Patients."

"It was actually her son I wanted . . ." Gilman let the sentence trail away. Nina could be somewhere else entirely, his guess entirely wrong.

She tucked a loop of colored lights back into the box with one hand and tilted her head in the direction of the woods. "I haven't seen him. You could try the boathouse, I suppose. He spends a lot of time there when he's home. It's locked this time of year, to keep the high school kids out, but he has a key."

When she said nothing else, Gilman looked at his watch again, thanked her, and started down the sloping back lawn. Just before the first line of trees, he turned to look back and saw her, standing now beside her own garage, still watching him.

The lawn turned to mud at the bottom of the hill, a wide brown hemline littered with cans and paper and crumpled food cartons. At the far end Gilman stepped over a narrow creek that led toward the pond. From there the row of houses on Angela Freeling's street was completely out of view. The woods extended north and south in an unbroken stretch. He paused to glance up. The sky was murky with low white clouds, and the leafless branches of the trees stood out against it like veins in an eye. His ears bubbled like cauldrons.

In another hundred yards he had reached the pallid crescent of beach and stopped, standing well back in the shadows, conscious of the gun in the holster under his armpit, the Avery Hotel. On the left-hand side of the pond stretched a shaggy promontory of evergreens, and a quarter of a mile beyond it, parallel to it, a long white wooden boathouse extended out of the shadows into the water. No houses, no people. Deserted.

Gilman pulled up the collar of his raincoat, against the chill. In half an hour more the sun would drop below the hills, the woods

would blaze for a moment and go dark. Warily, he started left, skirt-
ing the little creek, parting the bushes and low branches with his
hands as he worked down and over, toward the boathouse. His breath
filled his throat with hard balls of cold air. He came to the edge of the
promontory and looked left and right, all across the empty pond.
And when he stepped into a clearing, the evergreens overhead flew
suddenly apart and Victor Turelli dropped onto his back like a claw-
ing cat.

"Bastard!"

The impact knocked Gilman sideways, staggering him to one
knee. Turelli's boot caught his arm as he was rising and he fell backward and rolled over twice on the path and landed facedown.

By the time Turelli reached him again, Gilman had arched on
his hands and knees and was fumbling for the gun under his coat,
where the wires of the tinnitus masker had tangled. Turelli kicked for
his head, but Gilman was rolling again before it landed and he felt
only the toe of the boot slamming into his ribs like the end of a board.

And then he was up and they were facing each other, circling.
His gun had disappeared, somewhere under the dark leaves, in the
lake—the wires bunched out of his shirt as if he were made of metal,
a tin man losing his stuffing. Over the whine of his ears he could hear
his breath sawing its way out of his throat. His heart pounded against
his ribs like a fist.

"Where's Nina?"

How could the kid understand him? His voice was lost in the
whistles and thumps of his body, the kid was lost in a world of his
own.

Turelli charged once, a feint, three or four steps, prancing on
his black boots, and Gilman staggered away, uphill and backward.
Turelli stamped forward again, lunging.

He wore black boots, black leather gloves, a lumberjack's shirt
and Levis. The left shoulder rose in a bumpy swell, just as it would if
there were a bandage under it.

"Where's Nina Kerwin?"

Turelli came closer, kicking his feet, driving Gilman backward
in a crabwalk to the top of the ridge that formed the promontory.
Shorter than his father, thinner. Up close his eyes had a glasslike

hardness. They were astigmatic, crossed—something about them was wrong. Gilman stopped, balancing his hand on a bushy limb. But the boy moved with concentration. He looked rational, determined, dangerous.

"You're a cop," he said distinctly. "They warned me you were coming." From a sheath on the Levis he pulled a long-bladed knife.

Gilman straightened and took an automatic step back. Mud gave way under his heel. Turelli walked uphill slowly, holding the knife extended in his right hand and moving it in tight hypnotic circles.

"Give it up," Gilman said. His voice was hoarse. He was forty years old and out of breath.

"They told me you were coming," Turelli said and pecked the knife at his face. "A disabled cop, they said. You want to stop me, but you can't."

Gilman retreated another step, risked a glance over his shoulder, and Turelli stalked closer, feinting with the knife toward his groin.

"Who told you?" Gilman said.

"You followed me into the Zone. You went to see my father."

Gilman doubled into a crouch, instinctively raising his hands.

The blade flashed out of the sky and he dove to his right and started to tumble, over and over, crashing downhill, coming apart. His raincoat snagged on a log, ripped away in strips. Coins and pens spilled out of his pockets. One shoe flew end over end into the air. He was still rolling when he hit the water and still struggling to his feet, five yards from shore, when Victor Turelli began to wade toward him.

The knife sliced again, on an upward curve, a bright fish leaping, and Gilman dodged as it passed millimeters behind his neck. They butted skulls, fell apart gasping in a flurry of hands and spray. The knife slithered away. Turelli grabbed Gilman's throat with both hands and forced his head under, while Gilman went for the bandaged shoulder, hammering it with his fist until the kid toppled back screaming in pain and Gilman sat up, waist deep in the pond, gagging. When he shook his head clear, Turelli was running unsteadily along the beach, toward the boathouse, splashing in and out of the water, and then Gilman was on his feet somehow and somehow running through the shadows.

He caught up with Turelli ten yards from the boathouse door, tackling him at the waist and sending them both sprawling onto the sand. But by the time he got to his knees again, Turelli had sprinted away, head down, toward an overturned canoe by the door. He was pulling a broken paddle from it when Nina Kerwin stepped out of the trees holding a gun and everything halted—clouds, feet, breath, sky, everything came to a stop; the three of them stood in tableau, frozen.

"I'll kill you if you move," she said in a high, uncertain voice.

In slow motion Turelli turned his head to check Gilman's position. Gilman could see his chest heaving. Behind Nina in the dark woods light flickered. He staggered to his feet. Turelli took a step.

"I will." She raised the gun to keep it level with Turelli's chest. "I will."

Cassie would have shot, Gilman thought. If she had gone this far, Cassie would have shot him by now.

Turelli swung the paddle hard and the gun flew out of her hand.

Nina screamed and fell. The flat yellow wood bounced off her shoulder and then Gilman was on top of him, swinging his fists together and down like a club.

Momentum carried them slipping and rolling into the boathouse door. The paddle came flailing down on his ribs, his ears. His head burst apart in pain. He punched, rolled and punched again. Abruptly, Turelli's face was under him, a deep oval of blood, his hair smeared with it, his wrists like stalks of straw under Gilman's heavy knees, and Gilman was swinging his fists back and forth in a rhythm of savage anger.

"Over, kid, all over," Gilman said. His voice came from far away, scraped raw from the sides of his throat, unrecognizable, and he saw with detached surprise that he was still slapping the kid's face, splattering flecks of red across his own hands and sleeves.

"You're not in the army anymore, kid," he said, slowing his hands with an effort of will.

"I am, I am," the kid panted.

"What are you going to do in the war, you son of a bitch?"

"*Les confrères* know! Ask them."

"You're crazy," Gilman said, but the kid didn't look crazy, his voice had a rising note of triumph. Gilman jerked his belt loose from his trousers and started to tie the two wrists together. His mind was floating up from the scene like a balloon. From farther and farther away he saw Nina, sobbing and huddled against the coarse white sand. Saw his own hands slippery with blood and saliva looping the belt and tightening. In the distance a new whine was beginning to block out the other sounds in his head.

"What do they know, kid?" Gilman maneuvered the belt. He would hang Turelli from a strut in the boathouse like a carcass of meat and beat him back into sanity before he killed him for killing Donald Kerwin. His mind snagged on a question.

"I went to Paris," Turelli gasped. "Didn't I?" Pain made his voice sharper, more reasonable with every word. "Didn't I see the old woman who knew my father?"

"Who the hell are *confrères*?" Gilman's hands were as cratered and cold as the moon.

"Watch!" Turelli cried, an instant before Martin Spurling's silhouette appeared on the promontory ridge, flanked by a pack of shouting cops.

27

"Sheer coincidence," Gilman said to Nina.

The certainty in his own voice startled him, and he heaved himself from the chair to pace halfway across the room and back. At the huge tray of bottles that the Park Plaza room service had sent up he stopped to pour brandy into a water glass, then carried it over to a window.

"The neighbor lady called the cops," he said. "She saw the pistol under my coat. Spurling just happened to pick that moment to show up looking for his wife. Ex-wife. An impromptu conference."

Nina nodded solemnly from where she sat cross-legged on the end of the bed, wrapped in a nightgown of her own and a white terrycloth robe that the hotel had given her. But Gilman frowned at his reflection in the window and pulled hard at the brandy, vaguely unsatisfied with his explanation. "Incompletely happy," in one of his father's dry phrases. Spurling had never taken his eyes off him, not even for an instant, not even to look at his son. When the cops had dragged Gilman up from the wildly struggling boy, he and Spurling had suddenly stood face to face, inches apart, and Gilman had felt the coldness cut into him as never before—less hatred or anger than absolute coldness, a complete withdrawal of warmth, of life. In the war he could have killed millions.

"I had no idea who he was," Nina murmured. "I hadn't heard of him."

Gilman nodded and drank.

Nina's eyes swam helplessly in tears.

"With a little luck you would never have met him," Gilman said, clearing his throat, talking simply to give her time to recover her poise. She was still on a roller coaster of emotion, he thought, one moment apparently calm, in total control, the next moment shaking as if she would break into pieces. She sniffed and blew her nose on a tissue.

"I couldn't face dealing with private eyes and bars," she said. "I tried; I tried for two days. Then I went over to Cambridge and asked in the Harvard admissions office for Victor Turelli's home address, but they don't give out information like that—*nobody* gives out information there—-and I finally thought of going to one of Donald's old teachers at the law school who remembered him, and *he* made all the calls for me and finally pried it loose."

Gilman poured more brandy. In most things people are predictable, Fahey had said. It was in character for Nina to turn to lawyers for help. He should have thought of Harvard Law himself.

"Even then I sat in the car outside his mother's house for half an hour, till people stared at me," she said. "I couldn't bring myself to shoot, even then."

Gilman paced in front of the window, baffled by his own jittery restlessness. It was in character for her not to shoot, too. Unlike Cassie, he thought, despite everything that had happened Nina didn't really believe in the violent world that existed outside Marin County, outside lawyers' comfortable offices.

To the left as he turned he saw the spire of the Arlington Street Church, modeled after St. Martin-in-the-Fields in London, he remembered. A Civil War church. The whole thing rested on a thousand wooden piles driven into the boggy landfill of Back Bay. Beyond it he saw the facade of the Ritz-Carlton and the pathlights of the Public Garden, leading to the bottom of Beacon Hill and the nineteenth-century houses that would soon be turned into condominiums. The past sticks up everywhere out of the Boston landscape, he thought, like the ribs and timbers of a shipwreck.

Why the hell had Turelli killed Donald Kerwin?

"He's still out there," Nina said, shuddering, and he realized with surprise that she was standing beside him, shorter than Cassie, in her bare feet, not quite reaching his shoulder.

"By now he's in a holding cell in the Middlesex County jail," Gilman said, and pointed with his glass toward the window, the distant horizon of lights that would be Cambridge, just across the river. "After they booked him, the procedure would be to take him over there until the doctors can decide what tests they want to run. A cop named Fahey promised me he'd watch every minute."

"I've seen him twice in my life. I never want to see him again," Nina said, bobbing her head, veering toward the raspy, hysterical note she had been fighting back for hours. Gilman put his arm across her shoulder.

"We've got to stop meeting like this," he said lightly.

"To run off like that." She dug her fists into his shirt, twisting. "To leave the kids, and think I could be some kind of avenging fury for Donald. I must have been *crazy*."

She was a white reflection in the window. In separate squares of glass he could see her hair, washed now, blown dry, stylish; the gold glint of her wedding ring high on his shoulder; the pink curve of hip and belly where the terrycloth robe had parted. His own body was likewise broken into sections by the panes, distorted, as in a cubist painting. A head too long and angular. Sloped shoulders and back, stretching the blue fabric of his shirt. Big ham-colored hands separated, stroking her hair.

"And that detective Miskimin," she said with a nervous laugh that began too high. "I couldn't believe I was there in his terrible little office, and all those addicts and prostitutes on the street outside, staring at me when I went in."

She pushed away and padded across the room to the drinks tray. "Your kind of world, yes?" she said, her fingers chasing ice around the aluminum bucket. "Low life with a vengeance. The mean streets.

Donald always said you had the strongest kind of protective instinct, it was a shame you weren't a father. He said you became a policeman because that was the model of father you had—is that right?"

Gilman shrugged, barely hearing, wondering if he should try to replace the busted tinnitus masker. His eyes were still on her hip, her strong legs. He could recognize her walk anywhere, he realized, at any distance.

"He said you worked so well down in the Tenderloin with those people because you were so protective." She poured three inches of scotch into her glass and swallowed. "Works the same way with hysterical sisters-in-law, too. No?"

She showed him her face again, holding a faint little smile up for him to admire, automatically half-flirtatious. Distance softened the lines, Gilman thought, but the transformation that had started with Donald's death had gone on and deepened: the sharp-featured socialite looked ten years older now; without makeup her skin looked weathered by fatigue.

"You miss Donald too," she said. She had already finished the scotch and was refilling her glass with an unsteady hand. Gilman crossed the room and poured more brandy into his own glass.

"The last time I was in this hotel," he said, clearing his throat, "it was still called the Statler Hilton, and about half the senior class of my high school tried to pile into one little room, like the ship's crew in *A Night at the Opera*. Somebody had rented it with his father's business account number, and somebody else had bought a case of vodka over at a liquor store in Harvard Square where nobody ever asked your age, and the hotel manager finally threw us out at two in the morning for wrecking the room. When my father found out, he just said, 'Youth must be served, but preferably not boiled or stewed.'"

Nina managed a smile and perched on the edge of the bed. A very sexy lady, Fahey had said the first time he saw her picture. So no wonder you're chasing.

"He wasn't actually mad," Gilman said. "He told me later that a hangover is the closest modern man can come to a mystical experience."

"You and Cassie. Cassie was so good on the phone. She said not to worry about anything." She sniffed loudly and swallowed scotch. "She said as long as we were staying in separate hotels she was happy."

Gilman smiled wryly. Unbidden, a memory came into his head: when they had gone to Trader Vic's on their sixth-month dating anniversary—fifteen years ago? was it possible? After three Planter's Punches, Cassie had asked if the bartender could marry them, like the captain on a ship. They had made love under a tree in the garden and afterward she had grinned and said the yard moved. He was bound to Cassie by countless silken ties of marriage.

"Uxorious," Nina said. "Donald once said you were an uxorious man." She pronounced the word carefully, drunkenly. "Devoted to your wife." She drained the glass of scotch, put it back on the tray, and stretched out full length on the bed, facedown. "One of Donald's big words. I miss his big words."

Gilman sat down on the edge of the bed and rubbed the back of her neck with one hand. She murmured something into the pillow. Despite the drinks, the valiant efforts at lightness, the muscles of her neck were like steel cables. He drank more brandy. In ancient Rome, he remembered from somewhere, crimes committed while you were drunk received double punishment. He was, he thought, a kamikaze pilot in the war between the sexes.

"You miss him too," Nina said again. In the pane of glass his reflection was nodding, smiling sadly to match her smile. But his mind was rising, inching back to Martin Spurling.

"Donald probably knew about Nazis and the French Resistance," Nina said. She raised her head and shoulders and slipped the terrycloth robe down so that Gilman could squeeze her neck with both hands, her shoulders and upper back.

"He knew French," she said, slurring her words even more. "He was perfectly fluent. When he was at Oxford he studied French and Latin. My mother always said he should be a college professor instead of a government lawyer. That feels good."

"It should. I've got a black belt in massage."

Gilman slid his hands from her shoulder blades to her sides and back, watching the skin bunch under his fingers and ripple. Skin on skin. There is a difference between feelings and sensations. Hard knots of tension pressed back on either side of her indented spine, and Nina slipped the pink gown and terrycloth robe farther down until her back lay free, down to the rising curve of her buttocks.

"Donald took us all to that nude beach by Santa Cruz, you remember?" she asked. She had turned her head flat on the pillow, her eyes closed, her mouth open. "I didn't even want to take off my bra," she said. "He loved things like that. He was a lusty, sensual man. So funny." Gilman's hands reached the small of her back and slipped to each side of her waist. Smaller than Cassie, cool, silken skin. He remembered the beach. He remembered her slender torso, the small breasts like buds, Cassie's tart jokes. She raised onto her elbows, letting her breasts hang down against the cover of the bed, bells.

"When we got married," Nina said, her voice not quite a drunken giggle, "he wanted me to promise not to wear panties under my wedding gown."

She began to turn over on her back, her eyes coming to his, wide open, wet with tears.

In the Resistance, Spurling had written on the first page of his book, fear charged everything we did with an overpowering erotic energy—desire and fear were only two sides of the same blade. Sir, the whole of life is but the keeping away of the thought of death. His hand slid across her stomach, touching the curve of her right breast. Come back to Puritan Boston and break free, Gilman thought. The tips of his fingers were on fire. Her hand touched his, moved it higher. But Gilman is an uxorious man. She closed her eyes, taking a trembling breath. If you discover your essential self, what should you sacrifice to save it? or who? Her nipple was wine red, hard as glass. His heart shook, at the point of explosion. He had never had a war to set him free. He was unmanned by the wars he had missed. In his ears a great ocean of blood was crashing forward.

He closed the robe and tucked it under her chin.

He was already at the drinks tray, pouring more brandy into the water glass, when he heard her say behind him in a drugged, drowsy voice, "The last job he had in Washington for the Defense Department, Donald even gave a French name to it. Something French, I don't remember. He would come home speaking French and teasing the girls that they might have to move to France instead of California.

He was still talking to somebody in Washington about it the week before he died."

Gilman squinted at the lights on a bridge across the Charles, then shifted so that he could see Nina in the window again without actually facing her. *I went to Paris, didn't I?* They were avoiding each other's eyes, burying embarrassment under chatter. He drank the brandy in a gulp, feeling too drunk to think, too drunk to care about whatever was irritatingly wrong in her last sentence. By sheer force of cop's habit, he asked a question.

"Who did he talk to?"

"I don't know. Somebody hush-hush in the government. The man even flew out to see Don one day. Downtown, I guess. I never met him."

"You don't remember his name?"

"No. But it was the same name as a San Francisco men's store," Nina said sleepily. "I remember that."

Gilman turned.

"Hastings," she said.

28 ━━━━━━━━━━━━━━━━

Six hundred miles away, over the Atlantic, Stefan Anders dozed lightly in the first-class cabin of an Air France 747.

Around him, moving soundlessly through darkened spaces, flight attendants retrieved trays and glasses, adjusted blankets. To his right one of the American escorts studied manila folders under the Cyclopean beam of an overhead reading light. Timetables, addresses, names. They would arrive in Boston in time for breakfast on the ground, at the mayor's private reception, then rest in Anders's hotel until the limousines took them to the president's official residence at Harvard. At seven forty-five they would drive to Memorial Hall, three blocks away, and Professor Martin Spurling would introduce Anders so that the president could present his honorary degree.

Anders stirred and tilted his head against the padded curves of the plane's wall, raising one hand for a moment as if to embrace it. The American beside him made a check mark by Spurling's name and turned the page.

In Cambridge, Martin Spurling tapped his finger on the pad of paper before him and listened to the transatlantic hiss of telephone cables. When the Paris operator finally cut in and asked in rapid French if he wished to try his call again later, he answered curtly in the same language, listened a moment longer to the white surging static of the line, and hung up.

On his pad he had written "Hugo" and two Paris telephone numbers. Above them, earlier in the evening, he had written the central number of the Middlesex County courthouse. In one corner he had begun, then broken off, a sketch of a man's face in profile.

The policeman from California was a doodler, he thought, twitching his mouth in a little grimace of irony. He had watched from his lecture platform as Gilman had traced irregular lines back and forth in the pages of a notebook, unconscious no doubt of what he was doing, a characteristic habit of the intuitive personality; but then Gilman, as he had understood almost at once, was an intuitive man, obsessive, resourceful, dogged. When his wife—his ex-wife, he corrected himself, rising from the desk—when his hysterical ex-wife had called from the courthouse, he knew at once . . .

Spurling lifted the drapery and stared into the night, across Francis Avenue toward the gingerbread outlines of his neighbor's Victorian manse. His father had been a doodler too, Spurling remembered; but hardly resourceful, hardly dogged.

He paced to the door of his study, turned, paced back to the window. On the cabinet of books and mementoes next to it stood duplicates of two photographs in his library office: Verlaine, lifting his chin and smiling quizzically over a cigarette, impossibly handsome, generous; dead, Spurling thought suddenly, these forty years. And his own photograph beside the gasogene car, in the cliffs near the Vézère River. He could remember the day, the very moment the photograph was taken. On the other side of the camera were Verlaine and Brissac, separated by a little distance; with her hand on the shutter lever, mocking, stood Hugo—her back arched like a cat's, her breasts loose against the front of her blouse, scoops of white. In a moment more he would climb into the battered car along with the dozen other men, Brissac would take the wheel, they would wave to Hugo and Verlaine and begin to race away over the winding green roads of the Dordogne, toward the caves of Les Eyzies, singing "La Marseillaise," firing their rifles into the sun. *I loved the fucking war,* Poole said. *I never felt so alive in my life.* Spurling's mouth twisted for a second time in an ironic grimace. What would his undergraduates think to see their eminent professor half naked in a jeep filled with ragtag soldiers, emptying a gun at the sky?

The young man in the photograph had a hard, clear face, impossibly young.

He picked up another sheet of paper from his desk without actually seeing it. Somewhere, in the twenty-fourth book of the *Iliad*, he thought, or in Ovid, a mother is warned of the metamorphoses in store for her handsome young son, the terrible changes that time and war will bring. Better never to have seen the baby, a goddess cautions, than to see him grow up and go to war. He shook his head, feeling his mind struggle and lose the Greek quotation. Five years ago he would have recited it all from memory. The lines from Ovid came more easily.

Quo me servas, annosa senectus? the mother asks. Why linger in old age except to see fresh funerals? *Obmutuit illa dolore.* Grief struck her dumb.

The sheet of paper, he saw, contained the opening paragraph of an article he was to contribute to a scholarly journal. "To speak of Latin as a dead language," he had written, "is a radical error: more than sixty percent of English words trace their origins to the Latin language; their meanings will never come completely clear without a knowledge of their past—words, like persons, have individual histories."

He had broken off without finishing, as he had done with the sketch.

Dead things. Unfinished work. He let the paper drop to the desk, covering Hugo's name. His brilliant golden words were failing him at last, falling from his mind like dying leaves.

The last word on his pad was *confrère*.

29 ▬▬▬▬▬▬▬▬▬▬▬▬▬▬▬▬▬▬▬

Gilman drove fast, alone, across Longfellow Bridge, heading for Cambridge. It was ten o'clock. How much more time did he have? How sober could he stay to ask Victor Turelli questions? The car lurched toward the curb and he lifted his foot from the pedal, slowing, making himself take deep calm breaths.

What were the goddam questions to ask?

At the end of the bridge he turned right onto Commercial Street and followed the river east, holding the speedometer needle exactly on thirty-five. Two blocks past the bridge he turned again and wound up First Street, through a neighborhood of bleak, dilapidated triple-deckers, until he reached the corner of Thorndike and Second.

The first vacant parking slot outside the Middlesex County courthouse had a stenciled notice: "Reserved for District Attorney Harshbarger." Gilman swung the car into it and ran up concrete steps to the entrance.

Inside a set of glass doors he showed his California badge to a uniformed state-police trooper and handed over his gun before he walked through the metal detector. While the trooper telephoned upstairs he stood stamping his feet, blowing into his hands, waiting for the elevator doors to open. On the fifth floor he showed his gun and badge again, this time to a Cambridge police sergeant who sat behind a bulletproof glass window and watched impassively as Gilman unloaded the gun and dropped both it and the cartridges into the locker box beneath the window. When he was finally buzzed into the jail itself, the sergeant wrote his name and the time in an oversized log book and jerked his head toward another Cambridge officer emerging from a side corridor.

"You the guy who called about seeing an inmate?"

His name tag read "Delsey, W. D." and he carried a huge metal ring of keys attached to his belt with a leather strap.

"The one I want to see is Victor Turelli, the kid that Lieutenant Fahey came in with."

"Oh boy, Fahey, the party cop. He's up on the sixth floor, Fahey is." Delsey had narrow shoulders and a long neck, an excruciating slowness in all his motions. "Or the seventh floor, or the eighth. Fahey knows every cop in this county, he comes over it's like a—whaddya call it?—a stately progress. He likes to wander around every floor and visit the peons. He said when you showed up to take you to him first."

They stopped in front of an armor-plated door painted a streaky white, and Delsey carefully selected a key from his ring. When he pulled the door open there was a long, brightly lit corridor, lined on each side with completely empty cells.

"You're the guy from California?"

"San Francisco."

"You got anything like this in California?" Delsey waved one hand at the expanse of corridor, cell bars, shiny green concrete walls.

"We've got people in our cells," Gilman said, controlling his impatience, wanting to break into a run.

"We got fire marshals," Delsey said, scratching the back of his head with one thumb. "This whole building is what? five years old? Top architects, city planners—am I right? They don't leave enough fire exits for the inmates. The rest of the building's got more doors than a rabbit warren."

"Fahey," Gilman said. "Come on."

"We could put out a fire with the goddam pruno we confiscate every day, you know?"

Delsey started slowly down the corridor, peering suspiciously at the empty cells. Pruno was the alcoholic brew that inmates all over the country made from fruit juices fermented in plastic sandwich bags. Gilman tapped the side of his leg impatiently as they passed through an empty cafeteria space, its blue and green chairs stacked neatly on small round tables. Then they stopped in front of another armor-plated door.

"You heard the story about Fahey and the taxi driver?" Delsey asked. Gilman shook his head, glanced at his watch. Donald Kerwin had known Hastings. Why would Hastings protect the kid who had killed Kerwin? What the hell had they worked on in Washington together?

Delsey opened the door onto another empty corridor. Nina could remember nothing else, just the name, just the vague impression that Donald had been angry, angry more than worried.

"Some drunk took a shit in the back of a cab," Delsey said, "and the cabbie yells at Fahey what's he going to do about it, what's the police going to do about the back of his cab? And Fahey looks at him and says, 'If he don't come back and claim it in thirty days it's yours.'"

Delsey was still chuckling when Fahey and another Cambridge cop came out of a glassed-in booth midway down the corridor.

"Sergeant Cochran took the kid upstairs," Fahey said, tilting his head toward the big cop with him.

"He's upstairs in solitary," Cochran said, staring at Gilman. "He raised so much hell I wanted him in solitary. He half bit off a guard's ear, the little shit." Cochran glanced at Fahey. "Kid's supposed to have a lawyer, you ask him questions."

Fahey bounced one of his mentholated cigarettes out of the pack and tumbled it between his lips. "Yeah, yeah," he said, gesturing toward Delsey's keys.

Upstairs, the empty corridor was interrupted a third of the way down by sliding armor-plated doors on each side, leading to blocks of solitary cells, one side for men, one side for women.

Delsey stepped in front of the door on the left and began to rotate his key ring.

"Gilman's from California, Sergeant," he said. He found one key, inserted it, and turned a lock. Then he began a search for a second key.

Over his shoulder Fahey wheezed greenish smoke. "Come on, Delsey, open the goddam door. No wonder the fire marshal wants to close this rathole down."

"California," Cochran said in disgust.

Delsey twisted another key and slid the door halfway open. At the end of the corridor was a stretch of open floor and then a row of ten green metal doors punctuated with small glass windows.

"The county doc came back," a guard said, walking toward them from a desk. "Gave the kid another pop to calm him down."

Fahey led Gilman to door number six. They peered through the window at Victor Turelli, who lay curled on a bunk bed, smaller, saner looking in the gray one-piece jail suit, sleeping with his mouth gently open. Gilman rapped on the door with his fist. Fahey shouted Turelli's name, then simply shook his head and held up a sheet of paper attached to the wall by a strip of tape.

"Gave him five cc's of thorazine half an hour ago," Fahey read. "He can't sit up, let alone talk."

"The kid had two machine pistols in his goddam boathouse," Cochran said behind him. "Nasty little automatics."

Gilman watched a saliva bubble form between Turelli's lips. For Cochran he made a half-curious face, pinching the bridge of his nose.

"Fully automatic?"

He asked because even cops who should know better had fallen into the habit of calling anything more potent than a water pistol an automatic. But true automatics, which fired as long as you held the trigger, were rare. They were also completely, absolutely illegal in the United States, one of the few portable weapons short of a bazooka that the National Rifle Association hadn't championed for the avid sportsman.

"Foreign," Cochran said. "Ballistics had to look them up in *Brassey's*."

Gilman kept his face steady while a thought began.

"One of them," Cochran said, "is called a Stechkin." He pronounced the name with careful disdain. "It's a Russian blowback. The kid had a plastic stock that turns the thing into a horse. The other one's East German; I don't remember the name. They issue them both to Russian paratroops, East German border guards."

Gilman's ears roared. "Did Customs have numbers?" Imported foreign weapons require US Customs license and registrations, a pound and a half of paperwork. No kid could do it. A dozen melodramas spun wildly through his head. He would spirit Turelli away and lock him in the Lenox Hotel till he told the truth. He would storm Martin Spurling's office with East German pistols, capture Hastings, torture him with pruno—every image ended with him looking at his watch, raising his head to see Victor Turelli's unconscious form.

Cochran sniffed delicately. "Not a single number, not on the computer."

"How the fuck do you figure he got hold of them?" Fahey said quietly, looking at Gilman.

The telephone on the guard's desk rang. Delsey pointed with his key ring to the face that had appeared at the window of cell number five, a wide-cheeked, handsome Latino man with black eyes and hair like silk.

"Santo Dominican hit man," Delsey said. "Crazy as a loon, all of them. They kill in, like, squads, they don't care who they kill—they make up their own reasons."

From the small window the inmate stared at the policemen. Then he bared his teeth in a smile. He made a gun with his index finger and thumb, and clicked the trigger at Gilman.

"There's two FBI guys downstairs," the guard said, replacing the telephone. "They're coming up."

30 —————————

"Delsey, lemme borrow your keys a minute," Fahey said.

Delsey wrinkled his brow and hesitated.

"Come on, for crissake. I want to show Gilman here one of the architectural wonders."

Slowly, still frowning, Delsey held out the keys.

Outside, Fahey twirled them in a door, led Gilman down three flights of metal steps, opened another door. At the end of a hallway he unlocked a sliding panel of armor-plated steel, then the sliding bars behind it.

"There's stairs at the other end of the hall," Fahey said. "You walk right out in the lobby."

Gilman nodded. It was the closest he had ever come to blind panic, he thought, and he didn't know why. His mouth and throat were on fire. Brandy whirled like smoke in his head.

"Don't thank me," Fahey said. "Thank the jerkoffs who put this place together."

"You're taking a chance."

"I'll sign you out. If they're really FBI after all, Gilman, they'll find you, you know that."

Gilman squeezed his eyes shut to close down the howl in his

ears. They weren't FBI. Every instinct told him. Every instinct told him to run. Fahey's voice was booming again, out of a fog. Gilman opened his eyes to find the big man studying him, head cocked like a bird, one fat hand still holding the bar frame six inches open. "You had to hand in your piece, I bet," Fahey said. "They don't know you." When Gilman didn't answer, he reached inside his anorak and pulled out his own service revolver. "Here."

Gilman took it automatically.

"Don't shoot anybody I wouldn't shoot," Fahey said and slammed the bars shut.

In the lobby Gilman walked quickly, on eggshells, turning his head left and right for signs of Hastings or Goddard. He had drunk too much; nothing made sense. Up and down the shrill corridors of his mind every intuition was metamorphosing into noise. The state trooper put down his magazine and watched him curiously.

The car was untouched. He lifted the hood, knelt on the frozen pavement to inspect the wheels. When the motor caught on the third try, he fought the impulse to stamp the accelerator to the floor and instead drove soberly, decorously out into Cambridge.

Run where?

He crossed the river at the planetarium and turned left toward the North End. There was a hockey game letting out of Boston Garden and after five minutes of start and stop he pulled free of its traffic onto Commercial Street, looping along black cobblestone streets by deserted wharves, then cut aimlessly back through Government Center, which used to be Scollay Square when he was a boy. Boston sucked him in, he thought, deeper and deeper.

At Beacon Hill—he had no consciousness whatever of crossing the Common—he pulled abruptly into a parking spot on Charles Street and killed the engine. Victor Turelli had used a shotgun to kill Donald Kerwin, a standard twelve gauge Winchester Sportsman, bought three days before in Tahoe City. East German pistols—had he bought them in Paris? Why? How could he smuggle them in? One maybe, not two. Gilman pinched the bridge of his nose. He leaned back and took a huge breath, filling his chest. He pounded the steering wheel once with the heel of his hand. Fahey had done all he could. Pointless to call Vico. Pointless to call Nina again or Cassie.

He was ten years old, staring at a page of numbers on his desk and waiting for the tears to come. If you could choose one question, if you could choose the key question . . .

He looked down to find that his hands had almost twisted the plastic rim of the steering wheel loose. The boy was mad and not mad. He was Martin Spurling's son. Something far bigger than a random holdup had made him kill Donald Kerwin. What had brought Martin Spurling's son and Donald Kerwin together?

On the street a freezing wind was whipping out of the alleys, down the dark hillside from the State House. Panes of glass rocked in the old-fashioned square-cornered streetlamps. Pedestrians hurried by, heads down against the wind. Gilman walked to the corner, turned on his heel, walked back to the car. He crossed in the middle of the street, shoulders hunched. At the back of a quiet tavern, populated by locals bent over newspapers and backgammon sets, he found a pay telephone. The directory had been torn away from the chain below it. He started to dial, then hung up. He could never make his mind remember the number; there was no mystery about that. He dropped in a quarter and dialed 411. When the operator's voice came on, he couldn't hear her distinctly through the whistle of his ears and she spoke again sharply, with Massachusetts surliness.

"Yeah," Gilman said slowly, looking up the length of the bar toward the empty street. "I want to call my father."

Twenty minutes later William Gilman entered the bar and walked directly to his son's table.

"Draft," he told the hovering waitress. He was still in his crisp blue lawyer's suit. Gilman held up two fingers and she bobbed her head respectfully, backing away.

"All right," his father said. "Tell me again."

At the word *confrère* he held up his palm in a signal to wait, reached inside the blue suit for a pen, and began to make notes. He wrote down "Hastings" and "Goddard." When Gilman came to the East German pistols he looked up sharply. "You can't bring in military weapons without a Customs license," he said. "Not from a communist country. They're extremely strict."

"He had them."

His father drew a line on the paper and made a squiggle that, even upside down, looked like a gun. "Cassie's brother worked for the secretary of defense?"

"He quit almost a year ago," Gilman said.

"He had security clearance?"

Gilman shrugged.

"He must have. The Pentagon only uses senior civilian lawyers for—" He broke off the sentence and looked down at his notes. Then clicked the pen in and out and put it away. "I'm going to make a telephone call," he said.

It was ten minutes before he hung up and returned to the table. "Walk with me up the hill," he said, paying the check. "Just to Louisburg Square."

For a moment Gilman bristled at the authoritative tone, Martin Spurling's tone all over again. As he stood he towered over his father, his sharp, hawk-faced father. Why take it? No one had ever said they looked alike either. Then he reached for his coat.

Frederick Welles, his father told him as they walked up Pinckney Street, heads almost bumping to be heard in the wind, Frederick Otis Welles had been an undersecretary of state in Eisenhower's second term; he liked to be addressed as Secretary Welles; he was eighty-two years old. Gilman stiffened and started to point to his watch in protest—it was past eleven o'clock at night—but his father only smiled cryptically and led him up the steps of a port-colored old Federal mansion.

A black maid in a uniform led them into an anteroom and shut the door. They waited in silence while odd, indecipherable creakings passed just outside in the hallway. Gilman paced to one end of the little room, his ears whistling painfully. When the maid returned she simply opened the door to the room across the hall, and a high, thin voice called them over.

"William, my dear old licensed attorney and legal vulture, do come in. This is your son, I can tell—just leave the pot there, Marie—I knew your mother, young man, I must have seen you too at some point, when you were a child. Forgive my not rising, yes."

He was an elfin man, lost in the spaces of an upholstered wingback chair. His head was big, far too large for the diminutive body, nearly bald, and the hands and wrists that poked from an immaculate blazer were dry and white as sticks of kindling. He shook hands with them each, smiling and gesturing almost at once toward Hitchcock chairs grouped around a mahogany butler's tray table and the silver tray of cups and serving bowls that the maid had arranged.

"Lovely woman, your mother," he said to Gilman. "Cancer is a terrible disease." He shook his head. Behind the wingback chair, still within reach, stood an aluminum walker, its bright tubes and black rubber handles in shiny contrast to the subdued elegance of the rest of the room. Gilman counted off the familiar things—expensive books like his father's, family photographs, a small fire in a brick fireplace, mirrors, Wedgwood plates for display. On the padded window seat there was a cushion with the hand-embroidered legend "Old Age Is Not For Sissies."

"And I suppose you're a lawyer too, yes? Always travel in pairs, like snakes," the Secretary chuckled.

"Not quite," Gilman said sardonically, and the old man's head tilted higher, the wet eyes blinked.

"My son is from San Francisco."

"Yes," the Secretary said, still watching Gilman. "Splendid."

"He's a policeman. A homicide policeman."

In the soft light of the room it appeared for an instant as if silver dust had been sprinkled in the cracks of the Secretary's face. He smiled. "I see." The Secretary sipped a tiny mouthful of coffee. *Not a fool,* Gilman suddenly thought, despite the birdlike chatter. "Homicide, yes. May we assume that you are here on business?"

"My brother-in-law worked for the Pentagon," Gilman said, and stopped, feeling his skin begin to flush despite himself. Whatever he had imagined at midnight in the Blue Grill or the Avery Hotel would come out as nonsense in this room, worse than nonsense.

But his father put his coffee cup on the table, leaned forward, and began to explain in concise, lawyerly paragraphs. The Secretary nodded as he spoke. He glanced at Gilman. His wet eyes flickered between father and son.

"I don't like the German guns," he said when Gilman's father had finished.

"No."

"Courier bags?" The Secretary shifted his tiny body in the big chair and stroked the arm cover with dry fingers. "There are rogue elephants in government," he murmured as much to himself as to them. "There always are. Men who like to solve problems by violence. Men who like to manipulate people and events, outside the law. Powerful, anonymous bureaucrats. Unelected, unaccountable. In this administration—"

"It's very late," Gilman said. He wanted to stand up and walk away. His skin was inexplicably cold with sweat. His ears shrieked. He was, he thought with trembling surprise, frightened.

"Old men and lizards," the Secretary said. "We never really sleep. We lie in a bed and listen to the minutes crawl past. I never go to bed before two in the morning. Your father knows that." He turned his head to look at the white birch logs burning on the black grate. "Why should I believe him, William?" he asked bluntly.

Gilman's father made no movement whatsoever in his chair.

"He's my son."

"Victor Turelli is Martin Spurling's son," the Secretary said quietly. Gilman's father said nothing. The Secretary moved his eyes to Gilman and even before he spoke Gilman felt it as a test, an appraisal of his intelligence and something more. "What one thing would you like me to find out, young man?"

"Find out what Donald Kerwin worked on with Hastings." Gilman answered without hesitation. He hated these hard old men, their secret knowledge, their condescension. Dinosaurs. Lizards. Why had he answered so quickly?

The Secretary smiled faintly, as if he read his mind. "Concise. Intense. The fruit never falls far from the tree. When you have both gone I shall make some calls. I may even let you know tonight, William."

It was a signal to rise, but Gilman stayed stubbornly in his seat.

"I also want to find out what Martin Spurling did in the OSS," he said harshly. "I want to know that just for myself."

"In a general way I can tell you," the Secretary said, still smiling faintly, unruffled by his tone. "Or you can read it more easily for yourself in his book, *The Making of a Maquisard*. Your father and I were in the OSS together with him. We both had offices out in Georgetown, in a town house, two doors down the hall from the poet Karl Shapiro, who had come back from duty in the Pacific and was busy compiling an anthology of patriotic verse to cheer the troops. One of Donovan's more implausible ideas."

The Secretary wore a green and yellow bow tie. He lifted a pale hand from his coffee cup and adjusted it, eyes closing in a gesture of reminiscence.

"Extraordinary people," he murmured. "Shapiro. Sterling Hayden the actor was in the OSS; he fought in Yugoslavia for the partisans. Julia Child the television French Chef had her little connection in the Asian theater. Half the faculties of Harvard and Yale. Professor Langer of Harvard. Martin Spurling was a scholarship boy, very brilliant. Most brilliant of the brilliant. He came from a lower-class background, I think; a ne'er-do-well father, mother who died young or ran away. Yes. But he took to Harvard, to the manner born, oh yes. Most clubbable. I briefed him before he went off to Europe, and debriefed him when he came back."

"The war changed him," Gilman said.

"The war changed everyone. Someone like Martin Spurling turned to ice in it. Your father and I had good wars, as they used to say. On the surface, Spurling's war was *very* good, heroic even. Privately, I have always thought it was tragic."

He paused. "Spurling recruited Harvard students for the CIA afterward, of course. Everybody did for a few years. And naturally the CIA liked to take its agents from the Ivy League whenever possible," he added with urbane irony, "just as the OSS had done. Intelligence work appeals to intellectuals. The moral issues are grayer; it's a cerebral and higher combat, a better class of violence. In fact, it's all snobbery, the worst kind of elitism—did you know, William, that every director in the history of the CIA has been an OSS veteran? Half the financial directorships in this country still have OSS connections, all of the great Wall Street law firms. Until a few years ago, when secret agencies began to multiply anarchically, you could have made a case for benign conspiracy, yes? Old boys and secret handshakes. Even today, one has only to pick up the phone."

The Secretary coughed violently into a linen handkerchief and extended his coffee cup with a trembling hand. Gilman's father rose quickly from his chair and took it.

"We've tired you out."

"'All politics are local,'" the Secretary whispered into the handkerchief. "So says our honorable Congressman Thomas P. O'Neill. Actually," he coughed again and looked up to Gilman, now also on his feet, "all politics are familial." The voice had lost its chattering quality, the words came gravely, with an effort, between coughs. "Do you know that I never wanted Martin Spurling to go into the field for the OSS, William? I recommended against it. I thought he lacked loyalty." As Gilman's father began a phrase of protest, the Secretary's hand made a little circle of impatience over the chair arm: "Not political loyalty, of course. Not a crude test of ideology like Joe McCarthy's. I mean that Spurling had no family— he turned his back on his family, turned his back on his father, let his mother vanish. He substituted loyalty to an institution—the army perhaps, or our fair Harvard. I never liked that. I'm too much of a Yankee. I've been in politics all my life. Abstractions sap your humanity. No one should be loyal to abstractions."

"We must let you rest," Gilman's father said, motioning Gilman toward the door.

"Why is loyalty so important?" Gilman said, not moving. In the hiss of his ears his own voice seemed a whisper. In his mind's eye he had stooped to the level of the old man's chair; the cracked Mandarin face was nodding over him.

"Families are random things, friends are." The rest of the body seemed to have sunk back into the chair, empty of bones and flesh, like a doll's body. Only the great head moved, the faint smile returned. "But in a random world they are our givens. We bind ourselves to them. It is meet, right, and our bounden duty. They make randomness into order." He paused and blinked. "Loyalty is repaid by a sense of self."

"Identity," Gilman said.

The old man's voice had dropped again. "At bottom everything is a given in life. Some are strong like your father, like your father's hero Stefan Anders, loyal to other people. Some are weak, some are loyal to self. I don't know why." The voice had trailed off and become almost inaudible. "Loyalty is the price we pay for bridging the gaps between our solitary natures." He closed his eyes and Gilman thought he had finished. He began to turn slowly toward the door. "It is the condition of love," the Secretary said.

In Brookline, Gilman and his father walked single file down the hallway and threaded between the cardboard packing boxes to the kitchen table.

"Will he be able to make the calls tomorrow?" Gilman asked.

"He's undoubtedly making them right now," his father said. "He recovers with amazing speed. The East German guns disturbed him."

Gilman plopped down in one of the two straight-backed chairs and leaned his elbows wearily on the table, closing his eyes, trying to make the questions line up in order again. There was no possibility now of returning to San Francisco on the next flight. Nina could go alone. He was vaguely aware of his father studying him, then walking to the counter and sink by the window and running water.

"He'll still call me tonight, in fact," his father said. He fussed with canisters and a kettle on the stove. "Or this morning, rather. I've known the Secretary for forty years," he added. "As long as I've known you."

When Gilman made no answer he reached in a cupboard for two cups. "You could call Cassie on this telephone now if you wanted. It's still illogically early in California."

Gilman shook his head and felt his father's gaze come up from the stove and study him again. Cassie and Nina; uxorious men. Who the hell had told Fahey they were getting divorced? He rubbed his eyes and looked around at the familiar proportions of the room. Why weren't they? In their worst fights about world politics, about violence, about cops' cynicism and accommodation, in their worst fights he had never really seen himself divorcing her. What he saw, he thought, what he saw was wall after wall of photographs of Cassie, moving gracefully from youth to middle age. Photographs of the two of them moving together, stepping in time. He saw her as she had been the night the girls called, as she had sat on the edge of their bed, holding the phone toward him. You were loyal to family.

His father placed a cup on the table in front of him.

"If I remember, you take your coffee black, don't you?" his father said.

31 ━━━━━━━━━━━━━

"That old blowhard in Boston must think you're the cat's pajamas, fella." Frank Hannah's face wore a sour, put-upon expression. "You know how many asses he crunched for you last night?"

"He told me you were the man who could answer my questions," Gilman said, trying to keep the edge out of his voice. "You're the man in Washington that Donald Kerwin worked for last." Hannah grunted and stayed where he was, blocking the way. Gilman thought he had never disliked someone so much on sight.

"That's who I am, all right," Hannah said finally. He was a trim, wide-shouldered man in his early forties. He had dressed in Saturday morning casual—checked shirt, Norfolk jacket, cavalry twill trousers—but everything was neat, pressed, and crisp, and the impression he left was less casual than military. Over gold-rimmed granny glasses his hairline made two sharp inverted Vs, repeating the downward tug of his frown. He had the biggest hands Gilman had ever seen, and after a moment he used one of them for a quick, perfunctory shake, then to gesture toward the open door of his office.

A typical businessman's office, Gilman recorded automatically as they crossed the empty reception area, in a typical businessman's all-purpose building. You went a block north off Connecticut Avenue, through a big charmless lobby of streaky brown marble, past the florist shop and the Dart Drug to the elevator rank, then straight up to the sixth floor, where on a weekday a secretary would greet you and sit you down to wait for one of the movers and shakers to emerge. "Zenith Capital Enterprises," said the discreet gold letters on the wall above the switchboard. "Limited Partners."

"He must have called twenty people," Hannah grumbled over his shoulder. "And each one of them called twenty more. My damn phone at home's still ringing." He waved a huge hand toward the open door of his office. "And another old OSS goat up there's been making calls too, both of them."

"My father," Gilman said.

"Is that right?" Hannah was unimpressed. He closed the door securely. "All in the goddam family. So you had to fly down from Boston this morning just to see me, Gilman, is that the story? Whatever this is couldn't wait till Monday?"

"The Secretary thought," Gilman said. He was choosing his words with special care, cautiously. "The Secretary felt there was a certain urgency."

Not true. The Secretary had felt that next week would do fine, Gilman thought. It was me who was exploding minute by minute in impatience. Gilman's father in fact had made the last few calls to Harvard classmates in Washington, cementing the appointment. Gilman himself had borrowed a too-small overcoat and rushed in a cab to Logan Airport, only to be delayed for more than an hour as they circled National and finally landed in snow flurries at faraway Dulles. Hannah's office, he saw, had wooden-framed, double-glazed windows, dark walnut paneling, and built-in bookcases lined with books and folders. There were thickly upholstered leather chairs near the windows and a desk that belonged in a men's club in London. The wall just behind Hannah's desk was covered by detailed, expensive maps of the world, maps of Europe.

Gilman watched as Hannah crossed to the other side of the desk. Beyond his chair a small color television set, tuned to a college football game, sat on a typewriter stand, its screen tilted up like the face of an inquisitive pet. Hannah leaned to his right, snapped it off, and sat down behind the desk, all business.

"All right," he said. "Let's get to work. I want you to know that ordinarily I wouldn't see *anybody* on a Saturday afternoon when Penn is playing Penn State." He fumbled with a rack of pipes and grunted to indicate that Gilman could take the club chair opposite him.

"Ordinarily, in fact," he said, "I wouldn't talk to a nongovernment person about Don Kerwin's work at all. I told you that on the phone."

Gilman sat down, tapping his fingers on the chair in impatience. What was it he disliked so much? Hannah's sarcasm and abrasiveness rolled off his back; in self-defense any cop learned early on to be impassive, thick-skinned. The eyes? The eyes were not demented and obsessive like Victor Turelli's, but they disturbed Gilman: pale blue eyes, strangely flat behind the glasses. The eyes are the windows of the soul, Gilman's mother used to say. He hadn't thought of one of her sayings in years.

"Now first off, that had better not be a tape recorder of any kind," Hannah warned, leveling a pipe stem at Gilman's ears. "Not that I'm going to tell you one syllable of classified information. I don't care how many tottering old generals call up and bluster."

"It's called a tinnitus masker," Gilman said. He jerked the wires he had tried to repair on the flight down. "It treats a disease of the inner ear. It's not a recorder."

Hannah grunted skeptically. "All right. You want to know about Don Kerwin's last project here; I'm supposed to cooperate within reason." He pressed tobacco into the bowl of a stubby pipe and tamped it with a massive thumb the size of a hammer head. His face had set in a scowl, but he talked with gathering energy.

"All right. I left the DOD about a year ago myself. I came over here to make some bucks before the big tuition crunch and before the liberals put the economy down the tubes." He waved the pipe stem at the office furnishings. "But at one point I used to have something to do with what the Pentagon calls the division of archives. It's not big as the Pentagon goes; it doesn't do anything glamorous. Most of the work consists of keeping historical records up-to-date for the services and cooperating with civilian scholars who happen to be writing military history. That includes keeping the records of the

OSS—the Office of Strategic Services—one of the great bullshit names in the history of government: 'Office of Spies and Sabotage' would have been more like it, or just 'Research and Dirty Tricks.' Now the OSS records are *still* restricted material, right this minute, and that's because in 1947 the OSS became the CIA, and so there's classified documents in the archives that you can't just hand over to any old graduate student doing a thesis on General Wild Bill Donovan, say. That's also because from time to time, believe it or not, we still have an active OSS case."

Hannah paused to flick a metal lighter horizontally over his pipe and puff, scowling. An arrogant man, Gilman thought, like Spurling. But Hannah lacked Spurling's ice-cold distance, glacial and silent. Hannah was pleased with himself, Spurling wasn't. Hannah liked to impress you, liked to talk.

Let him talk.

"For instance," Hannah said, "sometimes you had OSS agents dropping into France or Yugoslavia with huge sums of cash in their pockets, meant to be used by the partisan groups for food, bribes, whatever, but completely untraceable, unaccountable to anybody. You don't run an audit on a bunch of maquisards. Once in a while archives has to do a security clearance on somebody who's supposed to have parachuted in, buried the money under a tree, and come back after the war to dig it up. And once in a while it's true."

"Confrères," Gilman said impatiently. "Donald Kerwin was working on a group of Frenchmen called *confrères.*"

Hannah looked up from his pipe and studied Gilman with unfriendly eyes. The Secretary had called a federal judge and the executive publisher of *The Washington Post,* Gilman's father had said. The Secretary believed that a certain part of Washington moved only when a spotlight approached.

"Another kind of OSS case," he said, taking his time. He paused, puffed on the pipe until smoke rose in slender, weblike filaments. "Another kind of case that we check has to do with political assassinations."

Gilman leaned forward in the chair, his ears suddenly roaring so loudly and crazily that for all practical purposes he found himself reading Hannah's lips.

"Most partisan groups had execution squads set up early on," Hannah said, "especially the ones in France and Holland. In the war there were usually three reasons for execution." He held up one hand and ticked off the numbers on big, pale fingers. "One, they killed collaborators and traitors. This was very private stuff, somebody who had betrayed a resistant for money or blackmail, disloyalty, or sometimes it was just revenge in a private quarrel—you don't get too much due process when two guys ride up to your house in the middle of the night and drag you off to the local quarry for a bullet in the back of the head.

"Two, terrorism. What the French Resistance really introduced to the modern world, lucky us, was the concept of state-sponsored guerrilla warfare, terrorism by assassination, even if the state happened to be just a shadow government in exile like de Gaulle's. The Resistance would kill a Vichy mayor or a German officer in some kind of ambush, the Germans would kill twenty or thirty French prisoners in reprisal, and the next day the Resistance would start the whole thing over again. Toward the end everybody was shooting everybody else; by early 1944 you could really call it a civil war."

"The OSS ran execution squads?" Gilman said. The first rule of cross-examination is never ask a question if you don't already know the answer. But in his mind another answer was forming, a shape seen once in the distance, seen in the darkness, still maddeningly out of focus.

Hannah had the bureaucrat's reluctance to answer direct questions. He stood up from the swivel chair behind the desk, paced six or seven steps, and ran a palm through his thinning hair, ignoring Gilman.

"As a lot of people know," he finally said over his shoulder, "after the war not all of the execution squads disbanded." He stooped to peer out the window at the snow beginning to stick for the second time this month.

"In fact," he said, still peering, "in the two years after V-E Day the assassinations of collaborators, accused traitors, and just plain enemies went on pretty much as it had all during the Occupation, maybe even bloodier. There were the political factions jockeying for power—the communists, the trade unions, the monarchists, the socialists, the cis-alpine lesbian-vampires of Gaul, you name it. There were guys after revenge, the way there always are after a war. There were guys who wanted to 'readjust' their war records by eliminating witnesses and fellow collaborators. Of course, this was an all-French show, but you can look it up in any history book, anybody will tell you—postwar France was a goddam bloodbath."

"Donald Kerwin's project," Gilman reminded him. Hannah was wandering; Hannah was laying down a smokescreen.

"Yeah." Hannah turned and braced himself against the double-glazed window. His hands at the end of his slender wrists looked as big as axeheads. "I want a beer. You want one?"

Gilman stood and followed him to a small refrigerator in the corner, built into the shelves beside a teleprinter. Hannah took out two cans of Miller's and gave him one.

"Don Kerwin came on loan from the secretary of defense's office six months before he left the Pentagon to go to California." Hannah closed the refrigerator and stood up. "We asked for him because he was fluent in French. Plus he'd traveled a fair amount in Europe, he knew his way around; he was an experienced senior attorney, he knew how to keep his mouth shut. What he did for us amounted to a simple, routine clearance investigation of a French businessman who had former OSS connections."

Hannah jerked the tab on the beer can, cursing at the snake's head of foam that rose up, hissing. Between hasty sips he stared at Gilman with a face verging again on belligerence.

"How does a Frenchman have OSS connections?" Gilman said. "You're talking about the American army."

"He was in a maquis unit under the command of an American."

"What's his name?"

"I can't tell you another goddam thing about the investigation, Gilman. Classified until further notice."

"The name of the American?"

"No."

"The maquis unit?"

"No."

Gilman swallowed beer and walked a few steps along the bookshelves, lightheaded, carried in his exhaustion like a swimmer on the top of a wave. There were thick volumes of financial reference books, tax-code reports, *Who's Who,* a line of orange-backed letter folders starting in 1978. Gilman touched one with a finger. The next shelf up held personal books. A Michener novel about Afghanistan, travel guides to Poland, Germany, Austria, the *Almanac of American Politics.* The archivist had no books on history, no books in French.

"Did Donald Kerwin finish his investigation?"

"I can't say. I left the Pentagon too, remember."

Gilman turned from the bookshelves and looked at the desk. Military neat, as expected. A photo cube with family pictures. A pen set. A tooled leather blotter. A spotless gray IBM PC. There were three telephones lined up precisely on the edge; the middle one had a red flashing LED device clipped to it that Gilman had seen only in police catalogues. He raised his head slowly to take in the office again. Ten years ago he had come to Washington on a homicide case and in the most unlikely way been escorted to a movie theater on Capitol Hill and then upstairs over the theater to the FBI's most secret fingerprint lab. Every cabbie on the Hill seemed to know it.

"You said there were three reasons for assassination."

On the other side of the room Hannah grunted and watched him speculatively, waving the lighter again over the bowl of his pipe.

"You've got a stubborn mind, Gilman." He snapped the lighter shut and drank in billows of smoke. "Yeah. There's a third kind of assassination in the archives, not nearly as common as just terminating somebody you didn't like, but it happened sometimes. It was real."

Gilman replaced the photo cube he had been handling and advanced two steps toward Hannah. A real person. He felt his bones moving loosely inside their tubes of flesh, smelled the dank, familiar smell of his dirty collar, his skin. Nina's skin, the bedclothes at the Park Plaza Hotel. He was a real person advancing into someone else's dream. Under a new angle of light, Hannah's brow was flecked with liver spots, like the belly of a fish.

"It's harder to explain," Hannah said. "Example. Marcos of the Philippines has been one of the rougher dictators around for the last decade or so. By now he's only got one real opposition leader to worry about, and that's a guy named Benigno Aquino, an extremely popular, charismatic guy who happens to be in self-imposed exile in this country. Anybody challenges Marcos, even Aquino, even in a fixed election, everybody knows the reprisals are going to be terrible, one way or the other."

He expelled smoke and moved his eyes away from Gilman, toward the wall of books.

"If you really wanted to get rid of Marcos," he said, "you might try to arrange for Aquino to come home."

Gilman waited.

"And if Aquino came home and were killed—" Hannah said. His voice reached Gilman faintly, through a grid of rising noise. "If he were killed and people thought Marcos did it, reprisals or no reprisals, all hell would bust loose. You could get even money whether it would be nationwide riots or new elections, honest elections. Either way the people would probably rise up in a democratic mass to avenge their hero. For a little while."

Gilman put down the beer can, trembling. Hannah was circling the desk, retreating toward his chair.

"The theory is," Hannah said, "sometimes the most charismatic leaders are the most expendable."

Gilman closed his eyes. The impossible memory forming in his mind slipped away again, dodged into shadows, behind a screen of sound. Donald Kerwin was dead. The shot that had killed him was still ringing in Gilman's ears. All the guns of the war he had never fought were still ringing in his ears.

Gilman opened his eyes and sat bolt upright, fists suddenly gripping hard the armrests of the chair, heart pounding. It was no accident, none of it. Donald Kerwin did everything for a reason. Spurling's book, Colonel Verlaine—in the 7-Eleven Kerwin had started to tell him a story about the Resistance. *The past is alive, criss-crossing the present.* The face Gilman saw floating before him was Martin Spurling's, young and old, splitting apart like a dividing cell, splitting again into the face of his mad son Victor.

"Who were the *confrères*?" he asked thickly.

"It's a French word that means 'colleague,' Gilman, that's all I know." Hannah was cocky now, a wise guy. He drank his beer standing behind his desk, feet planted wide apart, head tilted back. "How about letting me get home to my football game, sport?"

"Who's Hastings?"

Hannah's face changed slowly from cocky to thoughtful. He put the beer can on the fancy blotter and sat down.

"A man named Hastings came to see Donald Kerwin about that project," Gilman said. "Two weeks before Kerwin died. Two phony FBI agents named Hastings and Goddard have been trying to intimidate me for three days."

"Never heard of them."

"You didn't actually work for the Pentagon archives, did you?"

Hannah fingered his gold-rimmed glasses and said nothing.

"And you haven't stopped working for the government over here, have you," Gilman said. It was a statement, not a question. There were rogue elephants in government, the Secretary had said; there were multiplying secret agencies, faceless bureaucracies. Donald Kerwin had hated them. A venture capitalist wouldn't need a wire sweeper, no matter how rough the business world was. Wouldn't need an office with better insulation than a tank, wouldn't have started up a year ago with a letter file that began in 1978. "Who the hell's Hastings?"

"You know, Gilman, now that I listen you don't talk much like a lawyer." Hannah's voice was hard, sarcastic. The pale blue eyes seemed flatter than ever.

"Who told you I was a lawyer?" Gilman said, "I'm a policeman. I'm a homicide cop from San Francisco."

Hannah swiveled half an inch in each direction. The chair made painful squeaking sounds. Flecks of ash from the pipe lifted with his breath and floated lazily down onto the checks of his shirt.

"You're not telling me this is some kind of official visit?" he said softly.

"I'm on leave," Gilman said. He yanked again at the wires of the tinnitus masker. "Disability leave. This is personal."

Hannah nodded and casually pulled open one drawer of the desk, and Gilman was moving even before he saw the glint of the metal. Hannah's hand came up with the gun just as he jumped. The television crashed to one side, the three phones cascaded jangling toward the floor. Gilman bounced him in a bear hug off the wall, the maps. The gun flew loose and Hannah dove, but Gilman was nearer, heavier, and they went down together, tumbling. He felt Hannah's big hands gouging for his crotch. The pistol was foreign-made, the kind Hannah could get with no trouble. Gilman smashed at his head with the barrel, ripping the scalp, and warm blood sprang out in rings. Under his knees Hannah arched his back and lunged at Gilman's eyes and he caught both hands at the wrist.

"The American was Martin Spurling, wasn't he?"

Hannah bucked and rolled, knocking books off the shelves. His hands were incredibly strong.

"You're in deep shit, Gilman!"

"Wasn't he?"

Hannah struggled to stand, and Gilman, still on his knees, rammed the barrel into the fleshy hollow just below his left ear. "Who was the Frenchman?"

"Bidac, Brissac, something like that." Hannah's breath came in pants, his hands were red with blood from his scalp. Gilman nodded and jerked the barrel higher. Brissac was a name in Spurling's book.

"Spurling was in an execution squad in the Resistance, right? That was his secret? Killing civilians? Killing traitors?"

Hannah panted and said nothing. His pale flat eyes were fixed on their distorted reflection in the polished wood of the door.

"And Donald Kerwin found out?"

"You won't make it to the street alive, Gilman."

"And Victor Turelli found out too. Who told him? Who followed him to Paris?"

Hannah tensed his shoulders as if to move. Anger rose boiling in Gilman's throat. His finger, slick with blood, started to squeeze the curved trigger, pulling the hammer back with a click and lifting a cartridge into the breech. His ears thundered. His whole body shook.

"You set up the crazy kid to kill, just like his father."

Hannah's face was motionless, crowned with blood. His eyes never for an instant left the distorted reflection of pistol, hand, ear.

"Kill who?" Gilman asked in a whisper.

And his mind turned like a door. There were reasons for assassination, Hannah had said. Revenge, politics. A charismatic leader. Cassie's world, Cassie's nightmare.

Victor Turelli had taped five pictures to the wall in the Avery Hotel.

Every one was of Stefan Anders.

32 ▬▬▬▬▬▬▬▬▬▬

"You'll never stop it, Gilman. The kid will use the gun we give him; the Poles will think the Russians did it."

"Shut up."

"The fucking Russians will have to march in to stop the riots—it's going to be Hungary all over again, we'll see to that. The fucking Russians are going to look so bad in the Third World they won't recover for twenty years. You'll never stop it."

Gilman rummaged furiously in the desk. Another pistol, Smith & Wesson, made in America; ammunition in three small cardboard boxes. Under the Washington-Maryland telephone book was a blue-jacketed federal directory. In a locked drawer were lists of names on unmarked stationary, a pamphlet of phone numbers labeled "NSC CONSULTANTS—NOT FOR CIRCULATION."

Gilman jammed the lists in his pocket and looked down at Hannah sprawled and rocking on the carpet, trussed with phone cord as tight as he could make it, his belt, a cord snapped from the base of a lamp. When Gilman left he would use the corduroy strap from the Norfolk jacket as a gag. Somebody would find Hannah Monday morning at the latest.

When he left for where?

"You're dead, Gilman."

"You're not CIA," Gilman rasped. Left to do what? His neck was bruised and tender from blows he couldn't remember, Hannah's huge hands. It was impossible to think. His head spun and his ears howled. "The government doesn't do this," he said stupidly.

"It's a big fucking government," Hannah sneered from the floor. He stopped rolling and tried vainly to get up. "Be glad somebody knows how to use it."

Call Secretary Welles? The FBI? Who the hell would believe him?

Stefan Anders would be in Boston just one day and go home. Hannah must know what had already happened in Boston. Nobody could touch Anders now; the Poles wouldn't riot, the Russians march. Why was Hannah so cool?

Gilman swayed and closed his eyes in nausea, seeing Cassie, seeing Martin Spurling. When he opened them again he pulled the only working telephone across the desk and dialed a number from his notebook. Almost at once a voice at the other end said, "Middlesex County Jail."

"Give me Sergeant Cochran." Be a hero.

"Cochran went off watch at two, you just missed him," the voice said. "I'm Sergeant Muscalino."

"This is Inspector Gilman, San Francisco homicide—I was there last night with Lieutenant Fahey and Sergeant Cochran, seeing a prisoner. You'll have it in the log."

There was a long pause. In the background Massachusetts voices clattered, clacked like wooden shoes.

"OK. I got it."

"Can you arrange for me to see the kid you're holding in solitary? Can I see him late tonight, early tomorrow? Victor Turelli?" He looked up from the telephone to see Hannah sneering again, about to laugh.

"You could do it, Inspector, if you brought the kid's lawyer too. But you're too late for this office anyway. There's a federal gun charge now. About an hour ago he got a special custody release; they handed him over to somebody else."

Hannah rolled on his side, thumping the floor. The static on the line seemed to flame for an instant, like the head of a match.

"You still there, Inspector?" said the voice on the phone. "The kid's gone. We released him to two FBI agents named Hastings and Goddard."

33 ▰▰▰▰▰▰▰▰▰▰▰▰

At six o'clock exactly, three black stretch limousines swung north off Massachusetts Avenue in Cambridge and roared a block and a half the wrong way up Quincy Street.

Gilman leaned forward, concentrating furiously, until his forehead pressed against the metal hood shading the tiny television screen. On either side of him, teenage boys were watching identical black-and-white sets attached by brackets to the arms of their chairs, oblivious to the noise of National Airport. Farther down their row a bored janitor was sweeping green sawdust into a pile and craning to catch a glimpse of one of the screens. Gilman glanced up at the departures board, wrapped one hand around the coin slot where he had put his two quarters, and tried to block out the overhead lights.

In swirling snow the limousines were now rolling past dull black outlines: the Harvard Freshman Union, the announcer said impressively; the Harvard Faculty Club, a classroom building designed by the French architect Le Corbusier. As the cars slowed and began to turn left into the opening gates of the president's official residence, the waiting crowd surged forward over police barricades, their voices going up in an enormous cheer. Placards rose and fell, fanning the snow. In the headlights of the first car faces and banners burst into brilliant white focus—"SOLIDARITY FOREVER!" "NOBEL PRIZE FOR ANDERS!"

Nearest the iron gates, behind police sawhorses, Polish-American demonstrators chanted while a small motley counter-group with Russian flags and communist signs began to heckle. A young man carrying the Polish flag fought his way free of the police and dashed ten yards up the driveway before burly plainclothesmen wrestled him out again. Flashbulbs popped like strings of firecrackers as the camera followed, illuminating faces staccato, pressed between the iron bars of the gates.

When Stefan Anders stepped from the first limousine into the glare of the television lights, another great cry of approval went up. He turned, blinking in the snow, toward the next limousine and the emerging figure of the secretary of state, who had flown up two hours ago simply to greet him, the announcer murmured. On the porch of the big Georgian house, stamping their feet occasionally in the wet snow, both men faced the cameras for a moment or two of meaningless conversation. Behind the cameras dozens of reporters kept up a chorus of shouted questions.

"Your comment on the death of Brezhnev?" one called out, and the secretary of state shook his head with impersonal amiability.

"Will there be war over Poland? The Russians—"

"Stefan, Stefan, are you afraid for your safety here?"

Anders was smiling gravely, holding his hands over his head like a boxer. A black woman in a fur coat was tilting a conical microphone toward his mouth. Secret Service agents were peeling away from the porch and limousines, squinting into the shadows, and the front door was opening to reveal the president of Harvard, tall, dark suited, but without overcoat, stepping outside and waving in an expert gesture of welcome. Behind him on the porch, first among the guests of honor, Martin Spurling extended his hand.

Gilman raced for the phone.

"Last call for Eastern."

Gilman pounded one fist into the wall and glared at the man in the next booth, who jumped away from his telephone in surprise.

"Secretary Welles is not able to take your call," the maid repeated patiently. "The doctor's been here all afternoon." Through the plexiglass hood of the booth, Gilman saw the line of boarding passengers shrink to five, three. The ticket agent held the third passenger while he spread out her ticket on his desk and scanned the screen of a computer.

"I'll tell him you called again," the maid said and hung up gently.

Gilman grimaced. The woman had left the ticket counter and started for the rampway, and the line had shrunk to two.

What was he supposed to do? His father didn't answer. He'd called the Secret Service and gotten a machine. He'd called the FBI in Boston and gotten a human machine who took down his name and address and thanked him politely for the warning.

It was none of his business. A ticket agent on another desk had begun to square the stubs in his hands and glance around the waiting room. Geopolitics, geo-cynicism. He was in deep shit enough, Hannah was right. He had no business being a martyr, no will for it, call for it—you're the old man, his father had shouted. Cassie's hero—he could take a flight right here from National, stop once in Salt Lake City, be home before dawn.

His ears whistled in pain, making him sway again with nausea and dizziness. The nearer of the two ticket agents was speaking rapidly into a microphone at the desk. Through the black windows of the lounge Gilman could see the last passengers taking their seats on the plane; the caterwaul of the jet engines penetrated the cinderblock walls and drowned the sound of his ears.

She fell in love with my sense of justice, Gilman thought; she said so. I am old, father William. Inexpressible sadness welled into his throat. When you were middle-aged and knew how the world went, the Combat Zone was as close as you got to heroes. Who do you love? When he was a kid he had fallen in love and marched against war. The day that John Kennedy died he had wept for hours in his room. The ticket agent had reached for the door handle to the rampway and released it when Gilman yelled.

As he ran a vision of Martin Spurling came suddenly into his mind, like fire bursting into a darkened room.

*   *   *

"And you," Stefan Anders said in thickly accented English. "It is my honor as well to meet you, Professor Spurling!"

Around them undergraduates, awkward in unaccustomed suits and dresses, crowded closer; rows and rows of men and women in evening clothes stood just behind them, drinks in hand, beaming. From the end of the bar table a photographer's flash captured the handshake, the two gray heads bowing toward each other, the smiles of recognition and admiration.

"I am deeply serious," Anders said, still gripping Spurling's hand with both of his own. "I have heard of some of your books of literary criticism. By those who know I'm told you have the mind of a poet. But more moving to me—" he raised his left hand to Spurling's shoulder, holding him. The president of Harvard, pushing through the crush, hovered with a glass of champagne for Anders, listening. "More moving still," Anders said, "is your account of the life of the famous Colonel Verlaine."

"In *The Making of a Maquisard,*" the president murmured.

"Exactly!" In a room glittering with jewelry and rich dress, Anders wore a plain black suit, baggy and heavy woven, a blue cotton shirt buttoned at the collar, no tie. His intensity seemed to batter Spurling, whose upper back arched in frozen retreat as Anders continued to grip hard his shoulder and hand.

"Exactly. *The Making of a Maquisard.* A classic book. My son read it first, in a French translation, and made me read it later in Polish, and I credit it with the inspiration for the marches he led."

"No, no." Spurling was pulling away, shaking his head in a gesture of modest disavowal.

"They say in the end a son always takes his politics from his father." Anders released Spurling's hand at last and showed bad, yellowing teeth. "But we reversed."

"Your son died for his country," someone said loudly behind Spurling.

Anders nodded in vigorous agreement. "If only you could have saved him," he told Spurling, whose face for an instant registered complete bewilderment: save Anders's son? He looked up in pained surprise. "If Colonel Verlaine had lived," Anders explained, "he would have changed French history, yes? French literature? Even French politics after the war?"

Spurling moved sideways, spreading his arms, as if to invite the others into the circle of their conversation.

But Anders smiled again and pressed closer.

"He meant everything to you, I think?" he insisted. "Colonel Verlaine? At such a point in your life—in the war—you were so young—how could he not be your hero? A poet and soldier who would give his art, his very life, for freedom?"

Spurling lowered his eyes toward his own untouched glass of champagne. "In that, my dear sir," he said formally, in the lecturer's voice that held his students enthralled, yet at a distance. His face was a white mask of pain. "In that, if I may say so, you remind me very much of Colonel Verlaine yourself."

He raised his champagne glass as a toast. The students around them broke into little exclamations of agreement. Someone applauded for a moment, and others joined in. Anders turned his face to them in unsmiling seriousness.

"Your life has also been dedicated to freedom, just as Colonel Verlaine's was," Spurling added grandiloquently.

"My son showed the way," Anders said simply. Another flash from the cameras recorded the two men side by side, Spurling erect and smiling, Anders shorter, heavy browed, the same age as Spurling but thanks to his prosaic clothes and deeply lined face seeming at that moment the elder of the two.

"Fathers and sons," Anders said, "are opposite and continuous, like the east and west edges of a flat map."

The plane banked, droning. Gilman inhaled the smells of plastic upholstery and stale, recirculated air; smelled his own body, like a great shaggy coat of bone and flesh. His jacket flapped loose; his shoulder holster bit into his underarm. Police officers were permitted to board domestic flights carrying their own weapons. He had shown his badge and gun at the metal detector in National Airport. He would be too late to fire it.

The wing dipped into a galaxy of lights and came up again, shining. Gilman twisted in the narrow seat and sat forward abruptly, imagining Stefan Anders as he had seen him on television, as Cassie saw him, striding across a stage an hour away, raising his hands in triumph to his audience.

Victor Turelli.

Martin Spurling.

Goddard, Hastings—who knew how many others?

Spokes converging on a center, fuses converging on a bomb. How come a streetwise kid hits a 7-Eleven, Fahey had asked, just when you two walk in the door?

Gilman sat back again, shaking his head, and twisted in the other direction. Something was still not quite right, not clear. He had seen Turelli, watched him move, heard him speak—whatever else he was, by his own lights, by his own system, the boy was rational. What had he gained by the death of Donald Kerwin? Turelli's father had served on French execution squads forty years ago—who would care now? They all did it in the Resistance; it was an open secret. Was Harvard going to fire him in disgrace if they knew? Would other professors denounce him? Scorn him?

The great source of tragedy—for the second time that day a saying of his mother's sprang into his mind. The great source of human tragedy, she had told him more than once near the end, lying in the huge white bed, is that children can never love parents as much as parents love children. Was that true?

Gilman's mind changed pace and slowed. He closed his eyes, hearing his raspy breath, his body. Feelings never burn out, he had thought walking up the steps to his father's house. Feelings were like stars. Every cop knows, every preacher knows, every lawyer, every poet: there is always an earlier crime.

Who had gained by the death of Colonel Verlaine?

The stewardesses were collecting cups and returning seats to their upright position. Goddard and Hastings wouldn't be alone. There would be others working with them, rogue elephants like Hannah, men who put ends before means. Sacrifice a hero, bring the Russians to their knees. A moral victory, an upright position. Fahey had said it in the Combat Zone; sometimes you have to use the other guy. Geopolitics, war—the ethics of it slid out of his grasp, eluded him. They would have people waiting at the airport. How do you get by them to Cambridge?

In Boston, the captain announced cheerfully, it was twenty-nine degrees and snowing. Gilman saw Stefan Anders falling from his high podium, exploding in blood.

The first one Gilman spotted was dressed like an IBM executive.

As Gilman came hurrying into view on the sloping rampway, towering over the passengers ahead of him, from the other side of the terminal the man turned his white-collared neck, fingered his tie, and lifted a radio to his mouth. At the same moment Gilman saw the two uniformed policemen flanking the check-in counter. Without a pause he cut around the nearest passenger, stooped under a guide rope and disappeared behind a concrete pillar.

One patrolman continued to stare into the exiting crowd. The other shifted his right hand automatically to his holster and stepped in the direction Gilman had taken. Across the big hall of the shuttle terminal, the white-shirted man was running now toward the rampway. Gilman straightened again twenty yards from the pillar, emerging next at an auto dealer's display of a Chevrolet Camaro that slowly revolved under a circle of lights and on top of a carpeted pedestal. To his left was the conveyor belt that carried luggage to the planes for shuttle passengers, a swift black stream of leather and canvas that ran twenty yards between two separate computer stations, then dove through a horn-shaped opening to the runway level. For an instant Gilman calculated the chances of fitting his own big body onto the belt and through the vertical plastic strips of the horn. At the front of the Camaro, looking the other way, the uniformed policeman squinted and unsnapped his holster.

"Here!"

Gilman's father was at the taillights of the car, walking briskly through the milling passengers, a distinguished figure in fur-collar overcoat, snow-brushed hat, waving one hand at Gilman, then catching his arm and propelling him toward the exit. From one of the doors to the ticket counters Hastings appeared and signaled frantically.

"I've met every plane since three o'clock," his father began. "When I didn't hear from you, I knew you needed my help. The FBI—"

"Where's your car?"

"At the curb—I circled and used the five-minute slip. Listen—"

But Gilman was stumbling through a revolving door and leading him out. Ten feet beyond the overhang, wind white with snow pounced, shook their coats open, and staggered them back a step. Hastings was scrambling on the other side of the plate glass window, heading toward the door.

"It's the Mercedes?"

Gilman's father was slipping on the pavement as they ran, one hand fumbling for keys and thrusting them toward him. An instant before Hastings burst through shouting, Gilman had flung the driver's door open and his father was tumbling behind him, into the back.

"The FBI," he tried again, but Gilman had already started the engine and was swinging into the path of a braking bus, spinning the wheel wildly and launching them out of the terminal.

"Do you know where Sanders Theatre at Harvard is? Where Stefan Anders is speaking?"

His father was on his right, in the back seat, gripping the strap and nodding.

Gilman cut across three lanes and up the wrong way on a service road to the parking garage. A shuttle van flicked its lights and veered sideways, blowing its horn. He drove over three ribs of open pipe trenches marked by sawhorses and blinking lights, hit the main road again and accelerated past the Airport Hilton.

"What the hell are you doing!" his father shouted.

"In Washington—" as quickly as he could, in snatches as he steered and passed, Gilman told what he knew—Hannah, Anders, Victor Turelli.

"Unbelievable," his father said, but his pale white face showed shock, utter belief. "They said they were FBI, two men. They came to the house in Brookline. They wanted to unpack all the boxes and search your old room."

"You didn't let them."

"I threw them out!" At the MBTA station Gilman turned left onto the East Boston Expressway and headed for the Sumner Tunnel, ignoring the rising whine of sirens somewhere in the airport behind them. "It would be war," his father said. "The East German gun—the Russians would march into Warsaw, the Polish unions would riot—how many other times have they done this?" He shook his head violently. "I don't believe in conspiracies, I *don't*."

Gilman was slowing as traffic bunched for the tunnel entrance. "Sadat," his father said behind him. "Your mind keeps going back—the Kennedys. King. The Pope and the Russians."

Gilman rolled down the window, and flung a handful of coins into the snow-covered tollbucket. "Anders speaks at eight," he said, stamping the accelerator again.

"And Sanders Theatre's the perfect place," his father said. The car was lurching forward, shuddering. "There'll be television cameras, crowds of people—it's the back end of Memorial Hall, a huge, huge building."

Memorial Hall, Gilman thought—a Victorian monstrosity a city block square. They used it for dances, examinations, he'd seen it a hundred times. He maneuvered around a panel truck. How the hell would he ever find Victor Turelli in Memorial Hall? Who else would ever believe him? With a blast of the horn they plunged into the tunnel.

At the halfway point, near a glassed-in guard booth, the red taillights ahead of them began to bounce and wink, flashing rapidly on in sequence, and Gilman tapped his brakes, tapped again harder, and skidded to a halt. He yanked his cuff back to see his watch.

Seven thirty-four.

His father rolled down his window and peered ahead. "A stall. Or a car spun out changing lanes."

Gilman cursed and drummed the steering wheel with his fingers. Exhaust fumes hit his chest like a boot.

"Walk," his father said. "Get a cab in the North End and take it to Cambridge. I'll call the FBI."

Gilman threw the Mercedes into reverse, slammed into the bumper behind him, and angled the hood into the next lane, pounding his horn. For a split second he dropped his head to escape the noise. The Mercedes hit another bumper, tore a fender. Horns and engines all around him bombarded his ears, echoing insanely. Gilman gunned the engine, braked. Someone behind them screamed in anger and the guard in the booth opened his door and shouted. The Mercedes jerked forward, past an open hood, and they were suddenly riding toward the bone-white mouth of the exit.

Gilman wrenched his watch to the light as they passed Haymarket Station.

Seven forty-one.

In the driveway of the president of Harvard's house, Stefan Anders shook his head forcefully and stepped back from the black limousine.

One of the Secret Service agents trotted around the front of the car, gesturing a gloved hand toward its open door, while the crowd of students on the other side of the iron gates, picking him out from the others, began to chant Anders's name.

"For just two blocks," he told Spurling, who bent closer to hear, "a terrible waste to ride in a car. From childhood I love the snow, I love the cold."

More Secret Service agents surrounded them, guiding firmly toward the car. "We're running late, sir," the nearest one said, a bland-faced man in an overcoat, smelling of cologne. He wore the red and white lapel pin of a Secret Service commander.

"Security reasons," Goddard shouted through cupped hands from the other side of the car, over the noise. "We can't let you walk." Inside the limousine the driver reached for a radio mike.

Anders sighed, waved both hands solemnly toward the students, and as they broke into cheers he ducked behind Spurling and into the car.

At Nashua Street, the Mercedes skidded badly on the snow, ran up the curb and clattered down again sideways, fishtailing. His father barked something from the back. Leverett Circle came out of the snow. The road lifted toward the Charles River Dam. To their left the bright outlines of the Museum of Science and the dome of the planetarium appeared, flickering. Then the snow descended in clouds and they were gone.

Gilman glanced once to his left as they clattered over the bridge, passing the other traffic. The snow was blowing horizontally now, so that the car, the lights, the city, all seemed to be spinning, suspended and spinning over the wide dark band of the river below. The whole goddam city was buried in snow, he thought, buried in history, suffocating. How many other times had they done it? Who knew? His mind was filled with Spurling, nothing but Spurling, obsessed with Spurling's pain and arrogance, Spurling's disloyalty. Boston blew toward him again, its weathered brown face lowering to the windows.

"Seven fifty-five," his father said. "We'll never make it."

At Cambridge Street he pounded Gilman's shoulder and pointed left, and the car skidded again as the tires failed to grip.

"Goddammit, Spurling!" Gilman cried. He downshifted hard and swerved around a lumbering bus. Snow rose in cyclone-shaped spouts from the gutters. His father snapped another instruction and the car lurched left once more, through a veil of white.

With one hand on the bucking wheel, Gilman fumbled for his pistol. In such a storm Turelli would be harder than ever to see, to stop. He was a fool; he was a fool to try. The triple deckers of East Cambridge slid past the windows, over the windshield, breaking apart into fragments of black and white. The wipers pushed them away, up and away, falling. In his mind Stefan Anders was already rising, Victor Turelli was already raising his pistol.

Cambridge Hospital.

An ambulance churning toward them through the snow, flashing its lights.

Holy Ghost Hospital.

In two minutes more, under a snow-crested sign for Quincy Street, Gilman yanked the big Mercedes to the curb, bouncing over it and onto the sidewalk. Before the wheels had stopped turning he was already pushing the door open, against the wind.

In front of him a two-story brick building, dimly lit, to the left the gaping mouth of another traffic tunnel, lined with sawhorses and strings of flashing amber lights, apparently still under construction, meant to dive under the Yard and come up in Harvard Square.

"Memorial Hall!" his father shouted, pointing. He had followed Gilman into the snow and was gesturing broadly with his right hand. "Sanders Theatre's down at the end, by all the lights!"

Gilman ran three steps, slipping over patches of snow. Water splashed into his shoes, wind lifted the ends of his coat and buffeted him sideways. Where his father had pointed he could see an enormous crowd of people pushing toward doors. Searchlights waved huge white fingers crossing in the sky. Students were chanting Anders's name; television trucks lined the entrance. Turelli would still have a student ID. Faculty would know him.

Gilman dodged into the street. Did Spurling know too? Or guess? An orange snowplow bore down on him out of the darkness, its high-pitched horn sounding a steady pip, its signal lights revolving, red, then white. Gilman slipped on ice again, felt his trousers tear at the knee. Students were forming lines and passing through doors at one end. Farther up the building there was another entrance, and in the blowing snow he could just see the three black limousines pulling up, the cameramen, reporters, and microphones. A phalanx of policemen in greatcoats held back the crowd. Secret Service agents surrounded the cars. Gilman stumbled out of the snowplow's path and headed toward them.

More than a monstrosity—it was an aircraft hangar, a cathedral. His ears boomed like guns. The crowd burst into applause. He had forgotten how gigantic Memorial Hall really was—a hundred yards long at least, five stories high, a square, broken-off tower at one end. Through the snow his eye registered tesselated patterns of stone and brick, stained-glass windows, a vast black sloping roof lined with crazy battlements and gables.

"Spurling!"

The crowd drowned his voice, but the nearest policeman was turning toward him. From the other side of the unfinished tunnel, chimes in a tower began to sound and the wind rose in an answering wail. Out of hearing, out of reach, Stefan Anders and Spurling were walking quickly up a short flight of stairs and through a wooden double door held open by cops.

"Spurling!"

As the first cop grabbed him, Gilman was pulling out his badge to show.

When he struggled out of the cop's big gloves a moment later, the wooden door was halfway closed. At the threshold other hands held him. Snow blew over their backs, into the light. For three seconds the scene before him hung fire, motionless and clear as if it were a photograph he had studied, a painting he had learned by heart—the wide hallway jammed with television cameras, the microphones and spotlights, snakes and tentacles of wire, carved wooden steps to the right leading to a platform and a door, a sign for Sanders Theatre. Fields of white faces everywhere, turned toward him, turned toward Stefan Anders—white-crested hats and caps, flashbulbs caught in the instant of explosion, everything poised for a final heartbeat, a deep last breath interrupted and held.

And then from the left-hand corner of the hallway a louder flash, a sound like the cracking of bone on rock.

The Cambridge policeman beside Anders staggered backward two steps and pivoted slowly toward the door, his face spurting blood.

The part of Gilman that recorded, that counted and remembered, heard the automatic stutter out a dozen more shots and saw Anders sinking to his knees, right hand clasped to left arm, disappearing behind a shield of bodies. A crewcut man in a raincoat was toppling forward. A second cop was clutching his brow. At the back of the cop's head a hole appeared, bloody and torn, bulging with rubbery gray matter, as if an invisible fist had punched through his skull.

At the far end of the hallway Victor Turelli fired one more time, wildly, into a starburst of lights.

For a minute or more Gilman lost sight of everything completely. The crowd rolled over him like a wave, driving him out of the cop's arms and into a cloakroom wall. Spurling's tall figure was slicing past on the right, hawk's profile, white shirt striped with blood; Turelli was diving behind a closing door.

By the time Gilman broke to the middle of the hallway they had both vanished. A voice behind him sounded like Fahey, but Gilman shook it away, lowered his head, and pushed, a shaggy bull charging. Students beginning to rise from the floor, pale, distorted faces on stalks, parted in rows and screamed again and again as he drove toward the closed door.

There were two more doors beyond it.

The door to the outside was chained shut and padlocked. The door to the theater was blocked by a girl in a sheepskin coat, crying. At Gilman's question she pointed in the direction of a narrow stairway built into a corner and turned to run.

Gilman felt his gun slide somehow into his hand. The stairs were stone and narrow, badly lit by spaced, low-wattage bulbs, a workman's stairway to the roof. He began to climb them three at a time, ricocheting on his shoulders from wall to wall, gasping. His breath roared up his throat like a torch. His ears thundered in pain at every step.

"Spurling!"

There were sounds ahead, out of sight, around the curving steps.

"I know *why,* Spurling!"

Gilman's wet shoes missed a step and he went sprawling forward, still holding on to the gun. His legs were too old, too thin. As he struggled to his feet, the gun weaved in his hand, an outstretched shadow undulating up the wall. The voices above him rose and vanished. Three landings, four—at the top of the stairs, without a pause, he rammed his left shoulder against the fire door and spun backward into the storm.

As always, Verlaine awoke early. For a long minute he lay motionless in the bed, listening to Hugo's breathing beside him. When he finally stood and looked down, she was just stirring in her sleep. The thin blanket had pulled away from her breasts, exposing them to the faint streaks of light that entered the window from the east. She moved again, and he glimpsed the dark patch of hair between her thighs before she reached one hand sleepily down to retrieve the blanket.

On any other morning, he thought. On any other morning he would have returned to the bed, straddled her, filled his hands with her. Consoled his being with her, as the quaint English phrase had it.

But since midnight the BBC *messages personnels* had warned with increasing urgency that the Das Reich division was readying its trucks and tanks for movement. Every Resistance network in the Dordogne was poised, hanging fire.

He dressed quickly and walked to the adjoining alcove, where the breakfast that he had ordered was waiting as usual. Part of a baguette, black coffee laced with cognac, a piece of fruit from the blue and white terra-cotta bowl on the little table. Spartan and decadent at the same time, he told the mirror, with an expression of weary irony. No matter how long he slept now, no matter how much he ate, he still resembled, he thought, a corpse sitting up in a coffin.

When Hugo appeared, dressed in trousers and a peasant's blue working blouse, he had smoked two cigarettes and lit a third, and covered the table with maps. He took without comment the note she handed him and watched while she sat down to her own breakfast. Only then did he unfold the paper and see that it was from Spurling.

An appointment was requested, as soon after dawn as possible, no later than seven. He would be waiting in a cave they both knew some three kilometers north of the farmhouse, in the valley of the Vézère. "Of greatest importance," Spurling had written in his excellent French. "Concerning the movements of the Das Reich division. *Tell no one.*"

Verlaine refolded the note and slowly placed it in the breast pocket of his suit jacket. It would have been pointless to ask how Hugo came to deliver it, he told himself with a sad enigmatic smile.

He would like her to come with him to see Spurling, he said, putting it in the form of a question. After a long pause she shook her head in the negative. Verlaine nodded and stood up.

Five minutes later he was walking northeast along a woodland path, parallel to the river, in the hot, silent dawn. The rest of the maquisards, seventy or eighty by now, would soon be gathering around the farmhouse for another day of waiting, and another and another—he had issued the strictest possible orders: there were to be no maquisard raids, no Resistance actions of any kind, until the Das Reich had passed harmlessly through the Dordogne, on its way north to Normandy. Anything else would provoke the most terrible reprisals yet against the defenseless civilians.

And if despite his orders Brissac meant to attack by himself, or attack with a handful of rebels, to slow the Das Reich— He rubbed his face with the palm of his hand, weary, perpetually exhausted. In his mind now he carried on constant imaginary dialogues with France, with history—great, indistinct, watery hallucinations, floating across his consciousness wherever he looked. If Brissac rebelled, France would bring words to his mouth once more. He was a conduit from the past to the future, his only task now was to prevent the Germans and the Americans from setting ablaze and destroying the little garden of destiny for which he alone was responsible. He would stop Brissac, he promised the voices in his mind. He would stop them all, before the first tanks arrived or reprisals began, with one last speech to the people, death-bed words from an eloquent, still-living corpse. Verlaine moved cautiously down a forking path, into a glade of pines. And after the war his maquis would be remembered for its heroic forebearance in crisis, its patriotic self-discipline when the lives of the people were at stake, its loyalty.

The truth evolves, he thought. He had watched Spurling's eyes narrow at the idea. A boy with no heart yet for ambiguities. Let it all be certain, his eyes pleaded. A boy at bottom selfish and frightened. For a time he had suspected him too of rebellion, but apparently he had gone on his own instead, in the night, to scout the Das Reich; so Hugo said. So his note implied.

If it had been Brissac he would not have come. Brissac was not to be trusted any longer. But Spurling was still so young, so malleable, so blindly infatuated with the war, with winning the war. And with Hugo. Did they think he had lost all powers of observation, the two of them? Had he faded so far and so fast? Ten minutes of walking and his legs trembled, his heart pounded. Let the Das Reich pass, let the war pass away from the Dordogne, and he would yield everything that youth required.

He crossed a gully and began to climb, and his mind relaxed. Limestone cliffs were the landscape he had grown up with, loved best. He had heard that Auden had written a poem in praise of limestone; and though he had never read it, Verlaine could guess what it was that Auden praised. No other stone was so protean, so metamorphic, so open to time. There was nothing in it like the cool, dead impregnability of granite or marble, or the prissy, chipped fragility of slate. Limestone opened itself to life, as wise men do. It shaped itself imperceptibly, day by day, like a human face. He touched his own face with one pale hand and stopped to light a new cigarette. Like truth, it evolved.

After the war he would write a book about the prehistoric cave paintings of his native region and his favorite theme of universal metamorphosis. After the war, after the war—his mind lost its momentary energy and sank back into the bleak, paralyzing melancholy that each new morning had brought for months. He would never survive the war. Behind him forest birds chattered. Distractedly he glanced at his watch and thought that, as always, he was early. He brushed aside the hawthorn bushes growing on the cliffside, holding them back with one stiff arm, and descended into the cold comfort of a limestone cave.

"Spurling!"

Twenty yards along the roof Spurling stopped and turned back toward Gilman in amazement.

"You!"

The open door banged shut in the wind, and Spurling's face seemed to leap closer, sharp and clear against the darkness. Gilman took a tentative step along the gutter ledge. His left hand braced on the point of a Victorian gable, wet with snow, cold as metal. His right hand raised the gun to Spurling, rose past him to the spot a few yards farther on where Victor Turelli could be seen hands raised and clutching brick, as if he were about to scramble up the side of the tower.

Verlaine stood and allowed his smile to fade. Snow swirled. In his hand Spurling held a gun, but the darkness made it impossible to see his finger moving on the trigger.

"I know everything now!" Gilman shouted.

Behind him Hastings's voice was calling his name. At the far end of the roof flashlight beams swung up and down, criss-crossing in the dazzling snow.

"In the war," Gilman cried. *Spurling came closer, step by step, aiming the gun, blocking the entrance.* The wind dove and carried away whatever he was saying.

"In the war," Gilman cried again. "Do you hear me? Do you hear me?" They were ten yards apart. Spurling's right shoe, coated with snow, rested on a railing between two gables. Victor had lowered his arms and crept close behind his father.

"You killed Verlaine in the war!" Gilman cried. His ears shrieked with the wind. The whole vast building swayed under their feet. Cambridge, Harvard, Boston were spread out below, shifting in the wind, a world going in and out of focus, departing. Sirens and lights were converging from every direction on the square of black and white ground beneath them.

Spurling raised his pistol higher.

"You murdered Verlaine," Gilman shouted, "and blamed it on the Germans!"

For another ten seconds he hardly realized that his ears had suddenly gone clear, the long unending howl of pain inside his head had gone blank and clear, open. Even the wind of the storm paused for a moment, drew back and up.

And the first shots hit Verlaine full in the chest,

"For the war!" Victor cried, two feet behind his father, staggering,

thumping red mushrooms of blood out of his heart, his lungs, the pit of his stomach,

"To bring out the people! To win the goddam war!"

and sending him tumbling sideways and down, off the ledge of the limestone cliff, falling away toward the valley below, into the gray-eyed and unchanging future.

It was miraculous how everything had gone clear, Gilman thought. He heard Victor begin to shout again—

"They made him do it—he was only a boy—they *made* him."

"Who?"

"The army did—the OSS!"

Spurling was twisting to look at his son, his face was a shroud, his eyes were a dead man's eyes, and Victor was stretching one hand toward him.

"The old man in Paris told me—those were his orders! They both had those orders!"

Gilman staggered in a burst of wind and tried to keep the gun steady. Snow raced and flew down the slopes of the roof and the broken-off tower. Spurling had betrayed Verlaine and killed him, and fed on his life for forty years.

"If he didn't do it, then Brissac would!"

"And you shot Don Kerwin to keep your father's secret."

"He'd never survive if anyone knew—look at him!" Victor cried.

"And Stefan Anders!"

"They *made* me do it too—to save my father." Blood ran down Victor's shoulder, streamed from the point in his side where he clasped his hand. And children can never love parents. "In the war he was a hero!" The boy had murdered Don Kerwin, Gilman thought, wounded Stefan Anders, killed two Cambridge policemen. Whatever disgrace came down on his father, the boy would never live to see the outside of a jail.

Behind him voices were shouting. "Gilman!"

At the stairway door, where shadows massed and darted, Hastings was gesturing wildly, other men were pulling him down and away.

Spurling lowered the gun he had taken from Victor and turned his face toward the edge of the tower. The wind filled great sails of snow, billowing, drifting closer. His shoulders were caked with whiteness, white epaulets. Snow clung to his hair and arms. Slowly, visibly, he willed his other foot onto the railing.

"*No!*"

The wind was rising off the Atlantic now, the air was white with snow. Snow was general all over New England, falling softly, softly falling. Gilman's mind was overflowing with faces. The sky beyond the roof was a bursting cloud. Spurling stood with both feet between the gables, looking down at the white, unsteady earth. Victor was three feet away, staring. Spurling reached his hand toward him, as a father might greet a son, and without releasing him stepped slowly backward and jumped.

Acknowledgments

For indispensable help I thank Kate Byrd, David Byrd, Diana Dulaney, and Detective-Lieutenant Thomas E. Spartichino of the Massachusetts State Police. Virginia Barber has been Patience herself. Nessa Rapoport is a wonderful writer, editor, and most especially friend.